THE
ACCOMPLICE

THE
ACCOMPLICE

DARRYL
PONICSAN

HARPER & ROW
PUBLISHERS
New York, Evanston
San Francisco, London

FIRST EDITION

Designed by Janice Stern

Library of Congress Cataloging in Publication Data

Ponicsan, Darryl.
  The accomplice.

  I. Title.
PZ4.P797Ac   [PS3566.06]   813'.5'4   74–5802
ISBN 0–06–013379–1

To Katie

BOOK 1

1

Noon, nearing the end of a long, steady summer of county fairs, and Beef Buddusky squats and peers into the mystery of the stalled carousel. The crescent wrench in his shaky hand slips off the nut and he skins his knuckles. He puts them in his mouth. The children on their unmoving mounts are ready to be cruel. One of the boys yells, "Stupid!"

Without rising, Beef turns to say, "My mother didn't raise no stupid kids. She *drownded* 'em." He turns back to the gears and mumbles to himself, "And that was the day I learned to swim."

He pulls the pint of Kessler from the hip pocket of his greasy white coveralls and takes a long drink, hoping to quiet last night's calliope, still in his ears, hoping to stop his stomach from following the ponies, up and down, up and down, round and round and round, *"In the good old summertime, in the good old summertime . . ."*

Beef straightens up and looks at the frozen herd; the cowboys stare at him with contempt. "C'mon, mister, get it going, will you."

He is a passable hand at a number of trades: he can lay a leach line, he can roof a house, he can even fry an egg if he has to. But he can't work for a living, not with everybody hassling him every minute of the day.

"Get it goin' yourself, shitass," he says, and he gives the works his heel, throwing the crescent wrench to the ground. He steps up to the platform and slaps a wooden rump. "So long, old paint."

Before he can step off, the thing starts up! He lurches and anchors himself, one hand on a tail, the other on a nose.

But his mind is made up. This job has run its distance. He steps off the merry-go-round, his foot skims across the ground, and he lands on his back, raising around him a cloud of dust.

Look at him lying there, stunned and blinking at the sun. Know that he is no longer a lumbering, oafish, ignorant follower of county fairs. Ah, but often he wishes he were.

2

Beef reenlisted in the ragtag army of young men who muster along the highway's edge, dipping in and out of semi's and half-tons and plain and fancy automobiles on their one-man missions to end despondency and rootlessness.

Harold Buddusky, where it says *Print Clearly*, Harry to his father, but "Beef" since he was fifteen. On the tit until he was three, on a nipple bottle of milk or beer until he was five. Almost thirty, but still locked into a stage of adolescence, frequently betrayed by a glowing red pimple on his forehead, and an inability to articulate what he feels inside. Once a high school football player with a conspicuous talent for running over other high school football players, now grunting under the lard of his own dissipation.

A southward Dodge picked him up in Fort Morgan, Colorado. The driver had just buried his brother and was returning home to Pueblo. Beef did not like the sound of the place.

"I got no brothers," he said, to make conversation, ". . . that I know of."

"Where you from?"

"Scranton." Liked the sound of it too.

"Huh?"

"Scranton, in Pennsylvania."

"Oh. You're a long way from home."

There was an ex-wife back there, or somewhere, hopelessly attracted to sailors. There was a little boy named Nelson whom he missed desperately and about whom he made up plaintive country songs and sang them in his heart, or aloud when he drank too much or when he was standing alone on the empty highway and feeling about as wasted as dog piss on a telephone pole.

He is a veteran, but his service record would bristle the hairs on a Legionnaire's neck; and he once served a thin slice of time behind Old Crossbars, but he never hurt anyone, not deliberately.

Ohio State had given him an excellent deal after high school, but one semester there proved to Ohio State that Beef Buddusky, even with the combined tutoring of an entire fraternity of athletes, would never average out at C. He stayed around campus for a semester anyway. There was nothing better to do, and he liked being around students. He liked to overhear them talking. They often spoke of very serious topics: war, religion, truth, man— things he didn't like being left out of.

"You headed back there?" asked the driver of the Dodge. "To Scranton?"

"I gotta put some money together first."

There was a time he had $6500 together, the net result of a night every man who's ever warmed a set of dice between his sweaty palms has known in dreams. Six-five-oh-oh, in currency, and even then he knew that a man can hope to have a night like that only once in a lifetime. Fact is, a man *can't* hope to have a night like that, not even once in a lifetime. A man has got to look at his sixty-five hundred in the green and say, *"Moj anajomy, we're gonna stick together, we're gonna go somewhere,"* but it was the money that went somewhere, gone, gone on a short series of long-legged, big-assed ladies who think a whole world of Beef Buddusky.

The thing to remember, though, is that he never hurt anyone, not deliberately. He never ran away from a fight (he *said* he never ran away from a fight), but he never hurt anyone deliberately. (He never *did* hurt anyone deliberately.)

It was 3 A.M. when they came into Colorado Springs. They stopped for a red light.

"How far you say you were goin'?" asked Beef.

"Pueblo," said the driver.

"There's a town between here and there, ain't?"

The odd colloquialism threw the driver. He did not know an answer was expected.

"Ain't?" said Beef.

"Not unless you count Fountain or Pinon, but there's nothing there for a boy like you."

"Hell, I'll get off here."

Beef opened the door and got out. He leaned back into the car. "Too bad about your brother. Thanks for the lift."

He walked down Cimarron Street toward the town, looking for a mission or the Salvation Army. He paused at a well-lit drugstore window. He pulled himself away, but returned again to gaze through the window. Someday I'll go home and all of this wandering will be over and I won't be looking in the Rexall window, wondering why in the hell I want that big bright bowie knife, sharpened on both edges. Where would I get $29.95 anyway?

He found the Salvation Army, but it was closed. He went around the back to the alley and slept on some empty cardboard boxes. The night was chilly. In a dream he relived his earliest memory. "Papa, I'm ready," calls the three-year-old Harry from the toilet. His father, suspenders over his bare torso and pleasantly smelling of rye, routinely comes to him and gets the paper and gently pulls Harry toward him. Beef remembers leaning forward and putting his head against the coarse cloth of his father's trousers. How he loved that man!

In the morning he was hungry and his throat sore from the cold damp night. The dream on his mind, he called home collect, turning and raising his head so that his neck could draw some heat from the morning sun.

"Mama? It's Harold, Mama. I'm in Colorado."

"You sure get around, don't you?"

"Can I come home for a while?"

"Sure," said his mother flatly.

"I'll need the fare."

"Get yourself a little job in Colorado, Harold. Shape yourself up."

"I just finished a job. It petered out."

"Get another one."

"I could use a vacation."

"I don't need nobody to take care of. It's all I can do to take care of my ownself. You go off on your own now. Like your old boy."

The old boy, gone since Beef was seventeen. He had been a coal miner. On Saturday mornings he had been a barber, and the kids came from all over the neighborhood, their quarters in their fists, and lined up in the yard, waiting their turn on the kitchen chair. People loved him without reason, for his face told them he would die an untimely, unkindly, unnatural death, and probably he did. Didn't everyone say he would? The problem was that, if he did, he did not die at home. One day he was gone, only his lunch bucket left as legacy to a frightened son.

Beef has his bad teeth. The only gold he owns is in his molars. What's more, he finds himself laughing cautiously, like his father, at things he knows are not funny. If the rest holds true he will finally vanish. Perhaps he already has.

"I'll take care of you," Beef promised his mother.

"I'll take care of myself."

He knew she would too. She needed no one. Beef was the one who cried when his father left. She immediately found work and made plans to live without him. When Beef himself left, she wished him well. She even gave him some money. Her strength, however, was her own, and others must find theirs or do without.

"Just for a while, Mama? This is no good, the way I'm doin'."

Begging her made him feel small, like a child.

"You gotta be a man. You gotta grow up." She knew what he felt but had no time for it.

"I got about thirty cents."

"Well, that's a dime more 'n me."

Beef stroked his thrice-broken nose.

"Okay, Mama, I won't keep you on the line. Are you feelin' pretty good?"

"I'm all right."

"Okay, then, I'll be in touch. I don't know where the hell I'm gonna be next. Like a yo-yo."

"Be a good boy. Stay out of trouble."

Beef hung up and rested his forehead against the phone, still holding the receiver with both hands, wanting to be home, *home*, to sit on the front porch and follow the patterns of smoke from the nearby stacks. To lie on the glider on his mother's porch, nestled between the anthracite strippings, drinking Moxie and watching the high school girls walk by on their way to and from school. He wanted to see again the rattling coal trucks, dripping water from the breaker, on their way to customers. He wanted to sit amid the familiar comforting odors of home. He wanted to go down to the cellar, blow the dust off his father's scattered tools, and finish the job abandoned so many years before. The place would need better lighting and a few more wall receptacles. He'd have to call in an electrician for that. The rest he could probably handle himself. It would be necessary to camouflage the furnace, maybe with a fake beaver-board wall. At one end he could build a bar, and if he could find an old refrigerator he could convert it to a beer tapper and have draft beer at home. He would have to lay some fancy linoleum over the concrete floor. It would not take much to complete the room.

The Salvation Army had opened and Beef went inside and stood at a kind of sloppy attention before the counter, almost inclined to bring hand to brow smartly and say, "Reporting for duty, missus." He eyed the coffee mess doggedly until the lady gave him a cupful. He swallowed and felt it sear through his chest. "I'm high and dry in town without any money, and I sure would like to do some work for a Christian employer."

She consulted some cards and said, "There's a lady wants her windows washed, dollar and a half an hour."

"I'd ruther do yard work," said Beef, responding to a sensation in his palms.

"Do you do a good job of washing windows?" asked the lady. She had no yard work.

"I'm a window-washing maniac," said Beef without enthusiasm.

She gave him the name and address of the lady who wanted her windows washed. It was a walk of some twenty blocks, toward plunging his hands into water and hearing the squeak of wet glass when it's wiped. He was warm by the time he reached the apartment and sorry to have walked so far, because to wash the windows of this apartment unit would not earn him $1.50, even if he stretched the job. A dollar and a half would not cover what he could do to bread, pepperoni, and milk, his favorite meal on the road. And then what? Already he felt tired and without substance. He rang the bell.

The woman who answered was small, her head did not reach Beef's shoulders. She smiled at him, a coy, studied smile. She was in that curious stage of her forties where beauty hung in the balance, where it might mature and stay until the end, or slip and vanish forever. Perhaps it would not go well for her; a hardness had taken hold around her eyes, and, under Beef's gaze, she moved her hand to her throat, where the skin had grown coarse, like alligator hide. There was, however, something about her smile that sang to him softly, something from the cover of a schoolboy's tablet of foolscap. *Mona Lisa?*

"The Salvation Army sent me, missus."

"Onward Christian soldiers," she replied, still smiling. She had the voice of a seventeen-year-old, an unnatural, slightly annoying bit of acting. Yet he liked it. He laughed politely.

She stepped back, opened the door wider, and Beef walked inside. Another woman was seated at the coffee table, a cup and saucer in front of her. She was an old woman, a very old woman, whose bamboo cane lay across her legs.

The apartment was overly tidy and tight with heavy furnishings, everything to make Beef self-conscious of the dust and sand he carried on his back and the smell of his body that could usually be ignored on the road.

"This is my friend, Mrs. Lister," said the woman. "And I'm Mrs. Wynn, but you call me Ginny. Better call her," indicating her friend, "Mrs. Lister, if you want an answer out of her."

11

Beef stood silent. He expected to have no reason to call either of them anything.

"What's your name, Bomba?" she asked, giggling at her ancient friend.

"They call me Beef."

"I should say so," she said seductively. She put her hands around his bicep, covering the tattoo there.

"I'm here to wash the windows," he said, to establish his duties definitively. He had no objection to sleeping with a woman like her, provided they meet in a bar when they are both too drunk to care.

"You low on money?" she asked him.

"I'm flat. Hitched in last night from Nebraska."

"A traveling man, huh?" She seemed happy about that. "I've been around too, Bomba, just like you."

"Better 'n me, I hope. Why you callin' me Bomba?"

"Don't let present circumstances fool you. I've come up the hard way."

"Yes, ma'am."

Beef never met anyone who had come up any other way.

"I didn't always have a nice place like this. When I was a kid we lived in a shack on the flats, Kansas. That's the only thing you could call it, a shack. I wonder the wind didn't blow it away. We nailed old tobacco cans against the holes in the walls. Lived like that till I was fourteen and starting to develop nice."

"Is that right?" said Beef, as he had to so many other life stories that were of no interest to him.

"Bomba, you're with friends here, do you know that?"

"No, ma'am, I didn't know that."

"You look like you could stand some breakfast."

"I could always stand some breakfast, I don't care if it's ten o'clock at night," said Beef Buddusky.

She laughed at his wit and sat him at the table in the dining alcove. Mrs. Lister, the old lady who did not speak, hobbled to join them, fiddling with her fingers as though counting calluses.

Ginny took a ham from the refrigerator. Beef's eyes followed the magnificent piece of meat.

"A fella can overcome his birth, though, if he keeps his ear to the ground," she said as she cut the ham and tossed the thick slices into the frying pan. "You don't see any tobacco cans nailed to the walls here, do you?"

Involuntarily, Beef turned around and looked at all the walls. The apartment was nothing special, but what she said was true. He could not locate tobacco can one. "No, ma'am, I don't," he said.

"Damned right, you don't." She stabbed the ham pieces with her fork. "This is our own furniture, you know."

"Good, good," he said.

She put the ham aside and opened two eggs into the frying pan. She looked again at Beef, smiled sweetly, and cracked open a third egg.

"I can handle it," Beef assured her.

Mrs. Lister sat across the table from him and watched nothing.

"A fella," said Ginny, "has to size up the situation and . . . you thought I was going to say make the most of it, didn't you?"

Beef hadn't even heard her. He was listening to the eggs sputtering in grease. "Yes, ma'am, I did at that."

"Well, that's where you missed the boat. You've got to size up the situation and *change* it."

"I'm gonna remember that."

"I wish you would."

She took the full breakfast plate and placed it before him. He

13

looked down at it in wonder, and from somewhere four pieces of toast appeared. He took one of them and pushed it into the iris of the egg. He fell to eating, the plate trapped within the corral of his hefty forearms.

The two ladies sat and watched him.

"Huh, Mrs. Lister?" said Mrs. Wynn, nudging her. "Huh? Old Bomba can whack away the groceries, huh?"

Old women, it seemed to Beef, always got a thrill out of watching young men eat well. He could not understand it, but such a phenomenon was in his favor. It was as solid a basis for friendship and mutual admiration as any other. What a breakfast! Ain't this livin'!

"More, Bomba?" offered Mrs. Wynn when he had finished his second plateful.

He had four more slices of toast and jam. "Now I'm ready for the windows," he said.

"Well, as you can see, they're sure ready for you," she said. "I'm a very good housewife, but for the life of me I can't wash windows. Everybody has his little quirk, the one thing he can't do." Suddenly she was nervous. "Do you have anything you can't do?" She waited a second for his answer, then spoke quickly, as if she did not want to hear it. "Some women can't iron, some can't vacuum. Me, I can't wash windows, can't bring myself to do it."

"I'm your man, then. Don't bother me at all."

She looked at him long and closely. "I believe you may be," she said, relaxing again.

He slapped his hands on his knees, indicating his readiness.

"But dirty as those windows are," she said, "I think you're one up on them."

Beef lowered his head in humiliation. "Not many comforts on the road," he said.

"Up!" she shouted and scared Beef to his feet. She took his elbow with both hands and led him across the room. "You march right into this bathroom and have yourself a long, hot tub."

"Hold on, now, missus," objected Beef, but the thought of relaxing in hot water overtook his initial embarrassment.

"Go on, go on." She pushed him into the bathroom. "You hand your clothes out here and I'll send them with Mrs. Lister to the laundromat."

"That's okay, you don't have to go to any trouble on my account," he said through the closed door. He did not want the ladies to see the holes in his dingy underwear.

"Hand them out," she insisted.

"Won't have you goin' to any trouble," said Beef.

"Guess I'll have to come in and get them," she said. "Here I come, ready or not."

Beef quickly handed out his clothes. She sure gets her way, he thought.

He turned on the hot water. He heard them mumbling and heard the door shut. He lowered himself slowly into the comforting water. He leaned back and shut his eyes. Wonderful!

Soon he was dozing. The sound of the calliope, all the way from the fair in Nebraska, drifted into his head, but as quickly faded away again. Forever, he hoped.

"Ready for your back?" came her voice from the other side of the door.

He came out of his reverie. "Huh?" he asked.

"Ready to have your back scrubbed?"

"No, my back is just fine," he answered. "Don't need any scrubbing on my back."

She opened the door and walked in. He quickly covered his organ with the washcloth.

"Smart as God's supposed to be," she said, "you'd think He'd give us something to scrub our backs with." She took a sponge from the side of the tub and knelt behind him. "Course, could be He meant for us to scrub each other's."

She soaped his back. "Doesn't that feel good?"

Beef had to agree it did. She rubbed for a moment longer, then asked, "You know about lye?"

"Lye? What about it?"

"Well, it's pretty powerful stuff, isn't it?"

"I guess it is," said Beef.

"What would happen if there was a dead body in your bathtub, let's say, and you covered it up with lye?"

Beef grew apprehensive. He did not know this woman and her friend, they did not know him; but he was thousands of miles from home, in a place where no one knew him, except for others like him, who knew from instinct.

"Why do you want to know a thing like that?" he asked her.

"Just curiosity. Wouldn't the lye dissolve the body and float it right down the drain? Wouldn't that be the perfect way to get rid of a body?"

"Jesus."

"And it's getting rid of the body that always trips them up," she said.

"Oh, I get it. You're a cops-and-robbers enthusiastic."

"I should say so." She rinsed his back with a sponge and finally massaged him sensually with her two hands.

"You're all tensed up in your neck," she said, grabbing hard the muscles from his shoulders to his neck.

"Missus, all I want to do is earn me a few bucks. Then I'll be on my way."

"Don't you worry about that. There's more than a few bucks around here." It sounded like a promise. Beef let her massage his shoulders.

"It would smell up the whole place," he said.

"What would?"

"The body. In the bathtub."

"I suppose it would," she said. "Do you have a mother?" she asked.

He scratched his ear and looked at the dirty water in the tub.

"Yes, missus," he said.

"Does she kind of watch out for you?"

Old women ask such crazy questions, he thought. You wonder what goes on in their heads.

"No, she pretty much lets me go my own way," he said, making it sound like a virtue.

"Are you happy, then, Bomba?"

"What do you mean?"

"Well, are you glad the way your life turned out? Can you look back and be satisfied that you made all the right decisions?"

"I want to meet the man who says that. I can't say that, lookin' at me."

"So you probably would be happier today if your mother was there to protect you from yourself, to keep you from foolish mistakes."

"I guess . . . I guess I would, if you put it that way."

He made his belch keep quiet as it slipped away under his hand.

How could she know his mother was uncaring; how could she know he yearned for the protection of a parent? He was glad she asked no more questions. He shut his eyes and drifted with the rubbing on his back.

3

Beef was sitting on the sofa in a bathrobe Ginny had lent him when Mrs. Lister returned from the laundromat with his clean clothes in a paper bag. The robe was too small for him. The seams were under stress.

She refilled his coffee cup.

"You like the coffee?" she asked him.

"Sure," said Beef.

"Good to the last drop."

Mrs. Lister handed him the bag and self-consciously he excused himself and went into the bedroom. The clothes were warm, fresh from the dryer. Among them he found a plastic package containing a brand-new pair of briefs, Fruit of the Loom. He shook his head and laughed silently. She doesn't miss a trick, he thought. Already he liked her.

He took off the bathrobe and opened the closet door to hang it up. The closet was neatly arranged with a woman's clothing hanging on the left, a man's hanging on the right. He took out one of the sports coats to look at it. It was too small for him. On the inside of the door were two hooks. On one hung Ginny's robe; nothing was on the other. Beef put the robe there.

Near the closet was her dressing table and mirror. There were several porcelain angels on the table, amid powder, make-up, and perfume in disarray. He moved away from it to dress, past the single bed in the room, to the opposite wall. On this side was a plain square chest of drawers with a leather jewelry caddy on top. Everything was square and straight and neat, and reflected a man who needed order.

Dressed, he went back into the living room. "Thanks," he said, and laughed shyly.

She pretended to be surprised to see him. "Who's this fine-looking young man?" She shook his hand very briskly. "How do you do? Would you like to be the vice-president of my company? Marry my daughter? Vacation on my yacht?"

"Aw, c'mon," he said.

"Have a Fig Newton." She handed him the bowl.

He ate the Fig Newtons and wandered across the room, where he had noticed several thick scrapbooks on a bookshelf. He touched one, half afraid they represented a dead child.

"Go ahead," she said, "you can look at it."

He saw Mrs. Lister observing him curiously. Would she never speak? He put down the Fig Newtons and pulled a scrapbook off the shelf. He opened it on a page where a heavy metal disk was anchored. The American Legion Award Medal: *For God and Country, in recognition of his courage, leadership, honor, service, and scholarship.*

"They don't go giving those things away to monkeys, you know," said Ginny.

"Yours?"

Ginny laughed. "Are you kidding? I dropped out in the eighth grade. It's my son's."

Beef voiced his intuition. "Not dead, I hope."

"If he were dead I would be dead."

Beef closed the scrapbook and returned it. "You're probably very proud of him."

"He's always had a way with his classes," she said. "I used to give him a dollar for every A he got. Sometimes those dollars were hard to find too. I still try to reward him with something when he brings home an A, which is most of the time, I can tell you."

"He's still in school?"

"He takes night courses at C.C."

"Sounds like an ambitious kid."

Ginny rocked her flat palm in the air to indicate the wavering of her son's drive. "The potential is there, but left to himself he'd throw it all away on a scheming little bitch."

"Yeah? Who?"

"Where do I start?" she said. She sat on the arm of an easy chair. "Where do I start?"

"It's up to you," said Beef. He looked at Mrs. Lister for a suggestion. She was preoccupied with no more than the years behind her.

"It's not easy," she said, "to tell someone that you tried to kill yourself once."

"You did that?" asked Beef. He did not think she was the type. She seemed to like a good time.

"I'm not ashamed to say so."

Mrs. Lister shook her head grimly, her sleepy face almost falling to the handle of the cane she held in front of her.

"A person's got to be either really brave or really a coward to do somethin' like that," said Beef, putting into one observation all he knew about suicide.

Mrs. Wynn contemplated for a moment and concluded, from an insider's point of view, "I can tell you, it takes a lot of courage to do such a thing."

"What made you do it?" asked Beef. "I could never do it, not even if I wanted to, which I don't."

"It starts with the little things," she said, "and the next thing you know . . ."

"You mean you really wanted to . . ." He too had often wanted to commit that mortal sin. But he would never confess to it.

"Yes, rather than live without Gordie, I would die."

"Gordie?"

"My boy. He wanted to move out."

Now Beef knew that the robe he had worn belonged to her son.

"He wanted us each to find an efficiency apartment and live separately. He would call me every day, he said. Ha!"

It seemed a reasonable desire to Beef. The boy probably wanted a place to bring some girls and horse around. Mothers are fine for cooking and keeping house but they sure as hell can scare away the pussy.

"He probably only wanted his own place so he could call his friends over to raise hell," he told her.

She looked at him in a most peculiar way. "My son does not raise hell."

"Ah," said Beef, "I'm sorry. I didn't know that. Tell me, how old a fella is he?"

"He's twenty-four."

Beef wondered what he did instead of raising hell. "But he wanted to move out, huh? What'd you say?"

"Quite frankly, Bomba, I couldn't say anything. I had to lie down on the sofa. I have this recurring malady, a mystery to the doctors. My blood gets light, and my breath gets short, and I don't know what all. I just have to lie down and shut my eyes. And he has the brass to say I always and only get sick whenever he talks about another living arrangement."

"Do you?"

"I don't know *when* I get sick," she snapped at him. "I get sick."

"Only reason I asked, is if you do maybe it's all in your head."

"There's a world of people around eager to tell me what's going on in my head; I can't open up the *Reader's Digest* without somebody telling me what's going on in my head, and now comes a window washer from the Salvation Army to join the throng. Je*sus!*"

"Only tryin' to help."

"I know I was sick. I knew I'd be dead in three days if I were left alone. I can't live alone. I can't, I can't."

"Well, maybe you could get married or something," said Beef.

"You're an intelligent boy, you know that?"

Beef was embarrassed. It was a compliment he had never before heard, and one he could not possibly take seriously.

"Without knowing anything about the situation, you were able to put your finger right on the problem between us. I had recently got married."

"You're startin' to lose me now," said Beef.

"But he had had it annulled."

"Whoa, you're really losin' me now."

" 'I'm *glad* he got the annulment,' Gordie tells me. 'Sam Leonard was *my* age,' he says. 'So what?' says I. My answer to someone upset about a woman marrying a younger man is, 'So what?' "

"I've seen marriages like that work out real nice," said Beef.

"He accused me of offering that young man money to marry

23

me, a great deal of money. How outrageous! Where would I get any money, I asked him."

"What'd he say to that?"

"Well, he said something very mean."

"What?" asked Beef. He felt entitled. He had listened this far.

"He brought up an unpleasant memory."

"Oh." Beef was content to drop it and leave her unpleasant memories to herself. He ate another Fig Newton.

"He reminded me of the time I bought a cattle ranch for three hundred thousand dollars when I didn't have but thirty-two dollars in the bank."

That might well be an unpleasant memory, thought Beef.

"He didn't have to remind me of that, I won't ever forget. Someday I'll *have* that ranch or another like it. I'll call it Rancho del Buen Amigo. It'll have a grand high arch to pass under, and will we have cattle! Soundest investment in the world, Bomba. People have got to eat. We'll have horses, naturally, and we'll keep some chickens, for Mrs. Lister to feed. But the main business we'll be in will be cattle. The Rancho del Buen Amigo."

For a few more seconds she followed the dream of it.

Beef took a bowlegged turn around the sofa and said, "Ma'am, I reckon you'll be a-needin' a good foreman." He laughed nervously. She did not join him.

"After that," she said, "I got off the sofa and went into the bedroom. The sofa opens up for his bed. All I can remember is taking a handful of pills and lying down on the bed to expire. If that's the way he was going to be, he could make it on his own. I had stayed beyond my welcome. I would not be missed, neither would I be mourned."

"How come you didn't . . . you know?"

"Are you afraid to say it? I'm not. *Die*. I didn't die because he came into the bedroom. He had his choice then, of his own free will. There was nobody there but him and me, and I was unconscious. He could have gone for a milk shake and come back an orphan. But he did the right thing, as he always does, finally. He's a good boy, at the bottom of it all, and he loves his mother. I know that. I often have doubts, sure, but I know . . . I know."

"They pumped out the old gut, huh?"

"Oh, they had me figured for a goner. She's a dead one, indeed, they thought. They were all ready to pluck out my eyes and kidneys and liver and give 'em all to some beaners on welfare."

"But you pulled through."

"It would be nice to say we lived happily ever after."

"Uh-oh, trouble."

"The worst."

"He moved to another place anyway."

"Nothing so ordinary. While I am lying in the hospital within touching distance of no tomorrow, where do you suppose he is?"

"At your side?"

"Not on your life. He's being interviewed."

"The papers?"

"Now, do you suppose anyone in Colorado Springs would be interested in reading the circumstances of my demise?"

Beef wouldn't know about that. "Well, who's interviewing him, then?"

Whoever it was, Ginny's expression indicated she had little use for the individual.

"Apparently the first thing they do when you try to kill yourself is get a woman to interview your son, to talk to him intimately while he's most vulnerable." Her voice became that of the baby coquette. " 'Tell me, Mr. Wynn, has your mother ever attempted anything like this before? Oh, I see. Well, can you describe her

25

state of mind, Gordie, prior to the unfortunate event? Poor baby, can I do anything for you, honey? Here, put your head against my breast.' "

It seemed like odd treatment to Beef. He had never heard of the practice.

"Oh, they call them psychiatric social workers, but if you ask me it's a glorified title for a hot-pants bitch. I'm dying and he's making goo-goo eyes at a psychiatric *social* worker."

"A stiff joint's got no conscience."

"Bomba!"

"Sorry, missus, my mouth ain't fit for polite company."

"It might help for you to try to picture the scene. Believe me, I have."

"Rotten of me."

"I know her type. Seen 'em all my life. While the poor fella is at his weakest, emotionally speaking, they wage their campaign. She's older than him, three years older, and she's a . . . a . . ." In the present context the word was so foul Ginny was having difficulty saying it. ". . . she's a beaner."

"Mexican?" asked Beef.

She nodded. "She smokes marijuana and she runs around with nigger boys . . ."

"Now, now, now, you're storying," said Mrs. Lister, her first words in Beef's presence. He was startled at the sound, like the dry and frail yielding to the wind.

"Don't now-now-now me, lady. I didn't raise a son to be manipulated by some south-of-the-border slut."

"What's her name?" he asked.

"Maria, naturally," said Ginny contemptuously.

"What's she look like?"

"She's lovely," said Mrs. Lister.

"Oh, shut up." Ginny poured another cup of coffee for Beef.

"You can't deny that, Ginny," said Mrs. Lister.

"It helps to be lovely, that's my experience," said Beef, dunking a Fig Newton into his coffee.

"I wonder how lovely she'd be with a good splash of acid in the puss."

"Some hoodlums once threw acid at a newspaper columnist," explained Mrs. Lister. "It blinded him."

Beef gritted his teeth just in imagining it. "Well, missus," he said, "maybe it's one of those mild flirtations we all go through."

"Would that it were, Bomba, would that it were."

"Hell, I wish I had a nickel each for *my* mild flirtations."

"We saw her with him, Mrs. Lister and I," said Ginny. Mrs. Lister nodded. "On a night he was supposed to be working. We saw the car in the parking lot of the Chef's Inn, and we just went in to see for ourselves."

"She was very pretty to look at," said Mrs. Lister. "Her hair was so black and shiny."

"She sat with him so brazen, as though she owned him."

"They were holding hands across the table," said Mrs. Lister.

"In a public place, and me supposed to be convalescing at home after almost dying."

"Maybe it wasn't what it looked like," said Beef. "Did you go up and talk to them?"

"Not on your life. We went right back outside and let the air out of two of the tires. A man caught me, but I told him to go to hell, I was only letting the air out of the tires on *my* half of the car."

"Why don't you call her up and tell her where you stand?" suggested Beef.

Ginny turned to her old friend and raised her voice. "Mrs.

Lister, Bomba the Jungle Boy says I should give Maria a ring on the telephone."

Mrs. Lister giggled behind her claw-like hands.

"Well, it seemed like a sensible thing to me," said Beef.

"Boy, I've been calling her night and day for these many days. I wake her up three or four times a week to talk to her. She changes her number, but I find it again. Child's play. I tell her when everyone else is sleeping what I think of beaner bitches who take dope."

"Bet she enjoys hearin' that," said Beef.

"She usually hangs up on Ginny," answered Mrs. Lister.

"She's a nervy bitch, I give her credit for that, but she will not have my son. If there's to be a winner in this contest, it'll be me. I promise you."

"You got my vote," said Beef.

"I don't quit. I'll never quit till I'm six feet under."

"I'm here to wish you good luck," he said. "May the best man win. Think it's gettin' time for me to do the windows, huh?"

She looked at the clock.

"My goodness, boy, I've been keeping you from lunch with all my troubles. How 'bout I make you a Dagwood? A meal in itself. Here, Mrs. Lister, you come help me."

Beef followed them into the kitchen and sat at the table and watched them. Mrs. Lister opened the refrigerator and poised before it. Beef worried that she might fall into it. She handed Ginny the mustard and mayonnaise, the turkey and ham, the salami and cheese, the condiments. As quickly as she handed them, Ginny arranged them on a huge roll.

If this ain't the damnedest thing, thought Beef. Come to earn a buck and stay to eat like a rajah. Looks like I'm hired out today as a sympathetic ear. Nice work if you can get it.

They served him a sandwich fit to be photographed for the Sunday supplement. Next to it was placed a cold quart of milk and a glass. He was in business.

Mrs. Lister watched him finish his first bite, then said, "Tell him about the flowers, Ginny."

He listened to Ginny Wynn as he ate his sandwich.

Gordie had been in bed with the flu. Ginny and Mrs. Lister, who were devotedly nursing him, had intercepted the box of flowers when it was delivered to the apartment. Ginny opened the box and read the note, which said, *"Will tell you a secret, but first get well, my darling. Come by as soon as you're able. All my love, Maria."*

Ginny clenched her fists and stood before the dozen red roses and trembled in anger. Even Mrs. Lister, who had thought she had seen Ginny at her angriest, was frightened and moved several feet away, afraid that she might explode.

Ginny inhaled deeply and managed to calm herself. She picked up the card again. She even sniffed at the flowers to prove she was once more in control.

"Secret, huh? What secret?"

She called the florist and wheedled out of him Maria's new address and phone number.

"Tell him the rest," said Mrs. Lister. "Come on, Ginny, tell him the rest. You're leaving out the best part of it."

"There was no more," said Ginny, laughing. "That's all there was to it. I still haven't found out what the secret was."

"Oh, c'mon, Ginny. Tell him what you did then."

"Don't hold out on old Bomba," said Beef, really enjoying himself at last.

"It was nothing. I'm surprised at you, Mrs. Lister," she said, giggling like a girl.

Mrs. Lister said, "She snapped at me, 'Get out on the balcony and see if anyone's around.' I went out and there was no one on the balcony or in the court below. Ginny took the flowers out of the box, these dozen lovely red roses, the long ones, smelled so nice, and she took them out to the balcony and she . . . she . . ."

Mrs. Lister was giggling now too, along with Ginny, covering her mouth with her hands. Even Beef began to laugh, with a mouth full of sandwich. He tried to remember the last time he had honestly laughed aloud, but he could not.

"She *peed* on them!" yelled Mrs. Lister finally, and the two women laughed the salami right out of Beef's mouth. He covered his mouth and signaled them to stop before he sprayed the walls.

"All Mrs. Lister could say was, 'Oh, my. Oh, my.' Until I got my broom and swept it all over the side of the balcony. Remember, Mrs. Lister, 'Oh, my. Oh, my.'"

They laughed again. Beef was choking and slapping the table with his palms. Ginny hit him on the back repeatedly until she dislodged the food in his throat. "Sometimes I don't know why I do the things I do," she laughed.

"She got a can of deodorizer," said Mrs. Lister, "and sprayed the whole balcony! Oh, my . . . oh, my."

Beef singled out the moment and said to himself, look at me, I'm laughing. See, I am happy. Impulsively, Ginny threw her arms around him from behind and kissed his cheek.

4

Beef Buddusky's sympathies were divided. He too had had in-law problems and was convinced that he and his wife would be together today except for her meddling mother, who had always wanted her daughter to marry a GI and get an allotment. On the other hand, this lady gave him a pair of underpants and was feeding him well and probably wouldn't let him go away empty-handed. His loyalties were cheaply bought, consistent with hand-to-mouth living.

"What I'd do," he volunteered, "is get old Gordie interested in another broad, or maybe get her interested in another guy." He smiled. "I just happen to be available."

"You married, Bomba?" she asked.

"I'm divorced, about as divorced as you can get," he said.

"Think you're apt to take the plunge again?"

"Not hardly, dear missus. I ain't cut out for it. Footloose and fancy-free, that's me."

"Don't shut the door, Bomba. I've been married . . . well, let's say more than once. You'd get married again if the deal was right, wouldn't you?"

"Huh?"

"If it was a good proposition."

"When's it ever a good proposition?" asked Beef.

"Well, try this one on for size. Fifty thousand dollars."

He had a standard against which to measure it, his lost $6500. Damn, *no* one could honky-tonk away $50,000.

"What's the story with this fifty thousand, missus?" he asked, knowing there was no way for a window washer sent by the Salvation Army to be worth $50,000 to anyone. But Beef was a man who held on to a few fantasies. After all, he did have $6500 once, which proved that a fantasy *can* come true.

"Well, I have this lady friend whose husband passed on, and in his will he said she couldn't receive his money, maybe half a million dollars, unless she got married again. Her husband was a funny guy, didn't want his wife running around after his death. All you would have to do is marry this woman and she'll give you fifty thousand dollars. After she gets her inheritance you get an annulment and stroll away with your big bag full of money. Nothing wrong with that, huh?"

Beef would marry and be a devoted husband to a one-legged orangutan for fifty grand, but he knew that no woman with that much jack has to go shopping at the thrift shop for a husband. Still, he had his fantasies.

"I'd be pleased to meet this lady friend of yours and like talk it over."

"That can certainly be arranged. She's an older woman, Bomba. Would that make a difference to you?"

"No, missus, I sure don't think it would."

"Who knows, you may be a rich man before this is all over."

Before what is all over? This strange day?

They did not discuss the proposition further, but Ginny continued to talk through the afternoon about her fears for her wayward son. She certainly had no objection to his knowing a girl, she told them. One would expect a boy of his age to know several girls, perhaps well enough to take one to a movie even. But romantic involvement was dangerous. It was dangerous to his career, to his studies, to his finances, to his . . . health? To his mother, to be sure, because the very first thing to be discussed would be, "What are we going to do with your mother after we're married? I won't have her poking around *my* china or bunching up *my* doilies." And after some research Gordon would approach her with, "Ginny Mom, I've found the most wonderful little home in Boulder called Leisure Life, where you'll meet lots of people your own age and have worlds of organized recreation. You'll love it there, Mommy, and the princess and I will drive up every Sunday and take you out to dinner at a fancy restaurant. Won't that be keen!" No, acquaintances are fine, but loves are out of the question. There will be plenty of time for love and marriage, later.

Beef stretched out on the floor and shut his eyes.

"You listening, Bomba?"

"Yes, ma'am, just resting my eyes."

She talked on of her son's involvement with the psychiatric social worker. Beef rested, almost euphoric. He pressed his palms against the thick pile carpeting. Having had a big meal, he was in the best of all places to be: flat out on the living room floor. He had done this, just so, every Sunday afternoon of his youth. How it all came back to him! He loosened the laces of his brogues and pushed them off with his toes.

He let her ramble on, catnapping, awakening to say, "Is that right? Yeah?" and falling off again to soft and easy darkness.

He awoke with a start when he heard the door next to him open and felt the air rush in from outside. A cop stepped into the room.

Panic immobilized Beef. What if the talk about lye on dead bodies and acid in the face . . .? What had he got himself into?

The cop closed the door behind him and took off his cap. A newspaper was folded under his arm. He looked down at Beef and his face took on a pained, frustrated expression. Mrs. Lister turned her head and looked away from him, afraid of his presence. He stepped around Beef's inert form and kissed Ginny on the cheek.

"Hi, lover," said Ginny.

Beef began to feel his body come back to life.

"Hello, Mother," said the cop. "Who the hell is this?"

Beef took a deep, comforting breath. Apart from the uniform, Gordon's appearance surprised him. He had in mind something more to his idea of a mama's boy, a little guy with thick glasses and curly black hair, and pudgy fingers. Gordon was tall, nearly six feet. His complexion was fair and he wore his blond hair in a crew cut, still not out of fashion with cops, Mormons, and gym teachers. He reminded Beef of many of the fraternity men he used to see dashing about the Ohio State campus on endless important errands. Would such a man stay subject to a mother's wishes? Above all, a policeman?

"This is Bomba the Jungle Boy," said Ginny. "He's been washing our windows."

Gordon did not bother to inspect his work. "Did you pay him?"

"Give him five dollars, will you, honey? He's been such grand company for poor Mrs. Lister and me, cooped up here all day."

Gordon handed down to Beef a five-dollar bill, which he accepted as a windfall he could credit to the law of averages. His stretch of poor luck had been overlong. He got up off the floor and put the bill in his pocket. "Thanks, guy," he said. Something seemed so odd about taking money from a cop.

"So long, Bomba," said Gordon, as if to say the sooner the better.

"Oh, sit down and stay for dinner."

"*Mother!*"

"Don't be such a snob, Gordie. Everyone has to eat."

"Has she mentioned the fifty thousand dollars yet?" Gordon asked Beef.

"Now, Gordon, you zipper your lip."

So John Law's in on the proposition too, Beef said to himself.

"The abuse I take from this boy," said Ginny to Beef. "Any other mother wouldn't put up with it. But what am I going to do, I love the lousy guy."

Gordon smiled wryly; Beef laughed cautiously. The cop took off his holster and hung it in the hall closet with his cap. Beef saw the tool of his trade swing to stillness before the door was shut on it.

"I'm going to shower and change before dinner," said Gordon.

"Do you have a class tonight?"

"Monday, Wednesday, and Friday, Mom."

"Wonderful! We can all have an evening together at home."

"I thought I might go over to the range and get some shooting in."

"Surely," said Ginny coolly, turning away from him and going to the kitchen.

"Okay, what's bugging you, Mom?"

"Mrs. Lister, Gordie won't be with us tonight. He has something he'd rather do."

Mrs. Lister nodded. Granted, if permission were hers to grant.

"Well now, Mother, it's not as if you'd be left alone. You always have Mrs. Lister, and now you have . . ." Gordon waved a hand in Beef's direction.

"Look," said Beef. "You folks do what you want. Don't pay no attention to me."

"I haven't said a word," said Ginny to her son. "You've been out every night this week and you must have noticed that I haven't said a word."

"Yes, Mother, I have noticed," he said on his way to the bedroom. "I mean, how could I not notice?" He went into the bedroom and shut the door behind him.

"You see, Bomba?" said Ginny. "You *see!*"

"Well, missus," said Beef, scratching his jaw, "I'm not really sure that I do."

They soon sat down to dinner, which began with a glass of prune juice. Beef downed his in one gulp, with no regrets. Mrs. Lister took her glass in both hands and brought it to her lips like a prize. Gordon would not touch it.

"You saw the way Bomba drank his," said Ginny. "You don't suppose he got that big being finicky, do you?"

"Cut it out," said Gordon.

"Was it so awful?" she asked Beef.

"Tasted pretty good," he said.

"There," she said to her son.

"Mom, did it ever occur to you that I don't like prune juice? Wouldn't that be reason enough for me not to drink it? I mean, what if you put some octopus in front of me? Couldn't you understand me not eating it, just because I had no taste for it?"

"Who's talking about octopus? We're talking about something good for you. Just drink it down. You're holding up dinner."

All three around the table looked at him and waited for him to do the simple thing and get on with the meal.

He took the glass in his hand and said, "All right, I'll drink it."

"Wonderful!" said Ginny.

" 'Atta boy," said Beef.

"If you'll do something for me," he added.

"Have I ever denied you anything?"

"Promise me you won't ever bring my lunch down to the station again."

For one glass of prune juice, he was asking a great deal, more, evidently, than Ginny was willing to commit.

"Don't drink it, then," she said. "It would serve you right."

"I appreciate your going through all the trouble, but you have to stop it. Everybody acts funny around me."

"You know what your problem is? You're a paranoid."

"The chief, the desk sergeant . . ."

"I read an article about it. You imagine everybody's making fun of you."

"I used to know people like that," said Beef.

"Of course they're making fun of me," said Gordon. "What do you expect them to do when they see my mother coming down to the station to blow my nose for me?"

"Come to think of it," said Beef, "these people I knew, they really were made fun of."

"I haven't blown your nose," said Ginny, "since you were . . . I don't know, ten or eleven."

"It's the same difference," said Gordon. "Nobody ever brings a sack lunch. We always stop somewhere in the black-and-white."

"Yes, and what do you eat? Hamburgers, fries, Coca-Cola?"

"Yeah, usually."

"No wonder you're constipated."

Gordon grabbed his prune juice and drank it with an angry vengeance.

"From one extreme to the other," his mother observed, for the benefit of Beef and Mrs. Lister.

The dinner itself was tongue, boiled with potatoes and parsnips. A fair compliment to the cook would be to say it was tasteless.

Gordon, more relaxed now, leaned back in his chair. "During the shortages of the Second World War, a man went into the neighborhood grocery store and said, 'Give me two pounds of tenderloin.' " Here Gordon smiled, a bit nervously. Beef looked up from his plate. An anecdote or a joke was in progress. " 'Two pounds of tenderloin!' said the shocked grocer. 'Don't you know there's a war on? All I've got is tongue and eggs today.' 'Tongue!' said the disgusted customer. 'Do you expect me to eat something that came out of a cow's mouth? I'll have a dozen eggs!' "

Gordon chuckled and blotted his mouth with his napkin, looking around the table at the three stone faces waiting for a punch line.

"Don't you see . . ." he said.

"Is the idea . . ." began Beef.

"Oh, Christ, forget it," said Gordon.

"It wasn't a very amusing story, Gordie," said his mother. "His sense of humor," she explained to Beef, "was never his strong suit. But I don't believe, for a policeman, it's all that necessary. If he likes really amusing stories, he should read 'Life in These United States,' and they're all true too, in the *Reader's Digest.*"

"I do so have a sense of humor," said Gordon peevishly. He pointed at Beef. "This one has an IQ of about 82, and Mrs. Lister doesn't hear a word I say." (Not even this one.) "And you only hear what you want to. But I know lots of funny stories." He added pointedly, "At least *some* people think so."

The point struck home.

"I always thought you wanted to be a cop," said Ginny, "I never realized you had this burning desire to be a comedian, to amuse *some* people. Well, you'll learn that life is not a comedy. Your father was a comedian."

Beef happened to be looking at Gordon. It appeared he had taken a punch. His eyes widened in shock, not so much for the pain of it, but for its speed and force.

Beef wanted to draw attention away from Gordon. "I got a riddle," he said. "If you're going down the highway sideways at forty miles per hour and your canoe springs a leak, how many pancakes does it take to shingle a cathouse, true or false?"

Gordon cast an icy glance back at Beef and said very calmly, "It's been a long time since I've seen the overhand grip on a fork."

Embarrassed, Beef tried to put his fork into his hand in the proper fashion. It fell into his plate. He pulled it out with two fingers and licked the food off its handle.

Gordon shielded his eyes with his hand and shook his head. "Mother, give your boyfriend a shovel."

"Aw, I know when I ain't wanted," said Beef. He got up to leave, rolling his shoulders self-consciously.

"Sit down, Bomba, and ignore him," ordered Ginny. "He's just being bratty."

Beef sat down to another helping. If he were Ginny, he'd want that kid married and out of the house as soon as possible.

After dinner, out of hearing of his mother, Gordon said to Beef, "There isn't any fifty thousand dollars. There never was."

"It all goes in one ear and out the other."

"Where do you live?"

"I'm on the road."

"You got a record?"

"Long ago and in another state."

"Mind your ass while you're in the Springs," warned the cop.

"I ain't gonna be here long."

"Good idea."

While Ginny and Mrs. Lister set about washing the dinner dishes and cleaning the kitchen, Gordon set up a small portable typewriter and several books on the coffee table.

"I thought you were going to the range tonight," said Ginny.

"I remembered a paper I have to finish for my sociology class."

"Yeah?" said Beef. "What's it about?" He had a curiosity about all things academic.

Gordon ignored his question and put two sheets and a carbon into the typewriter.

"I used to go to college once," said Beef.

Gordon looked at him in disbelief.

"I really did." He turned to the kitchen. "I did. I was gonna be something, I don't know what. Was gonna get a degree in something and all. Ah, well."

"Gordon doesn't know what he wants to be yet," said his mother. "He's leaning toward the sociology, psychology area." Gordon began to type, referring to his notes and textbooks. "Which for my money is worth about a dime a dozen. But I guess it could pay off if he stays with the department. There's no real hope for advancement in law enforcement unless you have a degree. Otherwise you could spend your whole life as just another flatfoot."

"Let's not bite the hand that feeds us," said Gordon.

"For Gordie to remain where he is, what a terrible waste, when he has the stuff to amount to something."

"What about happiness?" said Gordon.

"But as long as he keeps working hard and exercises patience, he'll make the grade."

Beef wondered why she kept talking about him rather than to him.

"In about ten years," said Gordon. "That's how long I figure it will take me, if I'm lucky."

"He'll be an old man of thirty-four," said Ginny.

"Most men thirty-four have kids in school."

"Most men thirty-four should never have got married in the first place. They threw away all their options, all their hopes, all their real chances, and for what?"

"For what every man wants, I think."

"What?" asked Ginny.

"You know."

"I'd love to know. I've been used, abused, and confused by a variety of men without ever learning what they want. I don't think they know themselves."

"They want to be the heads of their own families."

"I can understand that," said Beef.

"You're the head of this family," said Ginny, at last speaking directly to her son. "Who pays the bills, who makes all the important decisions?"

"Yes, yes," said Gordon. "Look, I really have to finish this."

"God, what he makes me sound like," said Ginny, perhaps to Mrs. Lister.

Beef had inconspicuously moved behind Gordon, who now caught him looking over his shoulder. "Get away from me!" he snapped.

"Hey, Ginny," said Beef, "I think I'd better shove off."

"Stick around for coffee and dessert," she said.

"Well, sounds good, but to tell you the truth I get the feeling Gordie don't like me."

"Nonsense. Gordie, you like Bomba the Jungle Boy, don't you?"

"No."

"See," said Beef, "that was the feeling I got. I'd better shove off."

"It's me he doesn't like," said Ginny. "A recent development."

"Go, if you want to," said Gordon to Beef. "If you stay, just stop snooping."

"It's not like I was copying or anything, I was only curious."

Beef sat on the other side of the room, opposite to Gordon, watching him write. Whenever Gordon looked up at him, Beef averted his eyes and pretended to be deep in the examination of some other detail of the apartment or his own fingers or knees.

After the ladies had cleaned up the kitchen and dining table, Ginny called out, "Front and center, front and center!"

The Scrabble board was set up on the table. Mrs. Lister sat and fingered the tiles with shaking hands, turning them around and around, seemingly unable to find the business side of them.

"I'll just sort of sit and watch, if you don't mind," said Beef. "Wouldn't mind nibblin' on another Hostess Twinkie."

He loved the game but was a notoriously absurd speller.

"Nonsense," said Ginny. "Of course you'll play."

Reluctantly, Beef took a place at the table, knowing that soon someone would imply or state outright that he was of inferior intelligence, a judgment he always thought was based on faulty criteria.

"Gordie?"

Beef knew immediately that Gordon actually wanted to join them. Given the least chance to do something more social, even if it's Scrabble, a certain type of student will ditch his studies for the time being, after the usual perfunctory protestations.

"I don't know how you expect me to 'amount to something' if you never give me the chance to get my work done."

"All work and no play, et cetera, et cetera . . ."

Unlike most Scrabble players, they had agreed to accept foreign words, archaic words, proper nouns, slang, abbreviations, any word that was in the dictionary.

"We used to have an egg timer," said Mrs. Lister, "to tell us how long we could take at our turns, but Ginny threw it up against the wall and smashed it."

"Now you can have as much time as you need, within reason," said Ginny Wynn.

"Who says what's within reason?" asked Beef Buddusky.

"I do," said Ginny. No one questioned her right to do so.

Gordon won the first match by arranging the word CHIGOE, which Mrs. Wynn challenged. Gordon took the battered *Webster's New Collegiate Dictionary* that was at his elbow and looked up the word.

"Just as I thought, the deadly tropical chigoe, a hell of a flea."

"I don't mind losing if someone happens to be better than me," said Ginny, "but when someone uses chigoe and through dumb blind luck it happens to be a word, why, then I become a sore loser."

"Good winner, though, aren't you?" said Gordon as they overturned the tiles, mixed them up, and drew seven each for the next game. He seemed to take a great deal of pleasure in the victory over his mother.

"Most people are good losers because they're used to it," said Ginny. "I'm not that way."

"It's only a game," said Beef. "All that counts is you have fun playin' it."

"That shows how much you have to learn, Bomba," she said.

43

"And I'm sure you mean to teach him," said Gordon.

"You haven't done so badly by my advice."

"Just once, though, I'd like to do something, to have something all my own."

"I would never object to anything you did to better yourself."

"Some things are not meant to advance you. Some things are just natural."

"In the toilet are things natural."

"Crissake, Mother, crissake."

During this exchange, Beef laid ALOT on the board, a mistake he had made all through grammar school, high school, college, and forever. Gordon noticed it and said, "I don't believe it." He gave the tiles back to Beef and informed him he had just lost his turn.

"We're absolutely broke," Ginny said to Beef and Mrs. Lister. "I don't think we have five dollars in the bank. And he wants a girlfriend."

Gordon shifted uncomfortably. "I get paid Friday. We've always spent every cent we made. If I made ten thousand a month I'm sure we'd spend it to the last penny."

"Lots of folks are like that," offered Beef.

"Is that right?" said Gordon sarcastically.

"I just wish we had a good buffer instead of always being down to the lousy dime," said Ginny. "Wait till my ship comes in from *Reader's Digest.* What bothers me is they give you three choices and I can't make up my mind. At first I thought the hundred a month for life was just the ticket. Every month of your life, there it would be, above and beyond your other income, to do with as you please. But then I found out you can take two thousand a month for a year. What a year that would be, Gordie! Mexico City, Hawaii, Europe, can't you see it! But then the year would be over and we'd be back where we started. There's another choice, though. A twenty-four thousand lump sum. I'm not so sure that if we took the twenty-four grand we couldn't put a good down payment on a cattle ranch and finesse it to a heck of a lot more than a paltry hundred a month."

"Well, let's go out and buy the ranch now," said Gordon. "Why wait?"

"Gordon," she said plaintively.

"I insist on thrift this time. I don't want to go a penny higher than two hundred thousand dollars."

"You won't ever let me forget it, will you?"

Gordon said nothing for a moment. "I'm sorry, Mom. We've both said enough."

She reached across the table and touched his hand.

They concentrated on the game, Beef usually gnawing at his cuticles and missing his turn for taking too long or trying to do impossible things like COFF. Mrs. Lister hobbled along and kept alive with RAT and THE and plurals.

Gordon played KNEE. Ginny laughed.

"That's really the way they spell it, Ginny," said Beef.

"I know it is, silly. I was laughing at something I remembered. When Gordie was just a baby, about three years old, he scraped his knee . . ."

"Oh, *Mother!*" pleaded Gordon.

She waved away his objection and continued telling her story. "He came crying to me and I put some Mercurochrome on it. What I did was draw a funny face on his knee with the Mercurochrome so that when he bent his knee the face would move."

"Mother, I'm sure they don't need to hear baby stories."

"That's real cute," said Beef.

"So then he wanted me to do the other knee, but I told him

that I wouldn't do it because he hadn't scraped that knee. Well, the little bugger went right out and deliberately fell on his good knee so I would have to draw a funny face on that one too."

"The little devil," said Beef, and he and Ginny laughed together.

"Fine," said Gordon, "now can we get on with the game?"

"Should I tell them what happened when I painted the second funny face?" said Ginny coyly to Gordon.

"Oh, Mother, please . . ."

"His little peanut stood straight up!" she cried.

"Crissake, I was three years old," said Gordon.

"It starts early," said Beef. "Ends too early too, is my guess."

Ginny roared and slapped his shoulder. Beef felt so satisfied to be as entertaining as he obviously was, he tried for a topper. "Guess it's fair to say you made his peanut brittle."

Ginny laughed until she coughed. Mrs. Lister, oblivious, pleaded with her seven tiles to reveal their secret. Gordon was not amused.

"Honey," he said at last to Ginny, "I'd like to know, if you can tell me truthfully, the answer to a question."

"Shoot."

"Why do you enjoy embarrassing me?"

"Am I embarrassing you?" she asked, injured.

"You know damned well."

"Because I happen to have wonderful memories of your early years?"

"Instead of picking away at each other like this, why don't we face the real problem head on and come to a workable compromise?"

The suggestion was innovative. Ginny preferred her own methods.

"I haven't a notion what you're talking about."

"You've been harassing Maria on the telephone, in the middle of the night."

"Well, I may have called her once or twice. It's a free country."

"Why don't you leave her alone, Ginny Mom, she hasn't done anything to you."

"It's what she's doing to you I can't stand."

"I hear she's a beautiful girl," said Beef.

"In a cheap kind of way," said Ginny.

"You can't deny she's pretty," said Mrs. Lister, out of her reverie.

"I'd like to see her sometime," said Beef. "She's all I heard about since I come to town here."

"She wears falsies," said Ginny.

"No, she doesn't," said Gordon with some authority.

"She runs around with niggers and smokes marijuana with them."

"Now, Ginny Mom, that's a lie and you know it."

"What if I prove it to you?"

"Can you?" asked Mrs. Lister.

"You could prove conclusively that . . . that Eisenhower was a cook in the Japanese Navy. I know you could, but that doesn't make it true. You're always proving things that aren't true. You're a genius at it, and if it makes you happy, why, then go right ahead, just don't expect me to believe you."

"Why would I expect you to believe anything I say? You never have."

"I have, that's been my problem."

"Like all men you prefer to believe what comes out of the mouth on a pretty face. It was a trait of your father's I prayed would pass you by. I was in labor pains and he had his middle finger up some . . ."

"Honey, let's can all that. Not with . . ." Gordon gestured to Beef and Mrs. Lister.

"I didn't hear a thing," said Beef.

"*I* was enjoying a game of Scrabble. If you didn't want to discuss it, you shouldn't have brought it up."

"I *want* to discuss it. I want to discuss it in a reasonable way."

"Okay, here I go," said Ginny. "I will be reasonable. You want to fool around with this beaner? Go ahead, that's what she's there for, but I will fight to the final bell your marrying her."

"You do expect me to get married someday, don't you, Mom?"

"Not as a cop, I don't. Policemen should never get married, don't you ever watch TV?"

"Practically every guy on the force is married."

"If every guy on the force cut his throat tomorrow, would you have to cut yours too?"

"You don't even give yourself a chance to let it work out. You won't meet her. You don't even know the girl, and you carry on like this."

"I know more than you think. What about her parents?"

"They're dead."

"Oh, an orphan," said Beef.

"I happen to know that," said Ginny.

"How?"

"Never mind how, I do. What I would like to know is how they died."

"I can enlighten you. They got old, they got sick, they died."

"It all sounds very mysterious to me. A woman comes into town. She has no people here, no one knows her, and she starts asking a lot of questions, prying into people's personal affairs . . ."

"That's her job, Mom."

"Did you know she was married once before, to one of her own kind?"

That was known to him. What amazed him was that his mother knew it too.

"Mother, how in the world did you find that out?"

"I have my ways. You can do so much better than used goods."

"Who'd she marry?" asked Beef.

"She was married when she was eighteen," said Gordon. "It didn't work out. They were both too young."

"Well, why did she marry so young?" asked Ginny.

"*You* can ask that?"

"Things were different then. I bet she *had* to get married."

"No, she didn't but what if she did? Those things happen, don't they? Can you hold something like that against anyone, in this day and age?"

"I most certainly can, when such a woman means to ensnare my son. Where's her child?"

"She has no child."

"I'll tell you where it is. With her mother, who never died, but was deported to Mexico, where she deals in dope."

"I can see as usual I'm getting nowhere," said Gordon sadly. He rearranged his tiles.

"I can be as reasonable as anyone else," Ginny declared to no one in particular.

"Is that true, about her mother?" asked Beef.

Gordon put his elbow on the table and pointed his finger into Beef's face. "*You* are not to talk about her, you understand?"

"Take it easy, I don't even know her."

"And you never will."

"Okay, okay. But is it?"

"*No*, you big dummy! Now, play, dammit."

The conversation then centered around the game in progress. By the time they were down to their last set of tiles, Ginny had an edge of three points over Gordon and was well ahead of the others. The board seemed to have no possibilities for a play, with the one strong exception of the lower left corner, where a triple word score was possible if Gordon could come up with a four-letter word that had N as its second letter. He pondered it as long as she would allow him and when she insisted he play or pass he discovered SNOT and triumphantly played the word.

"There it is," he said. "Double letter, two, three, four, five. Triple word makes it fifteen. Tough luck, gal."

"Not so fast," said Ginny.

"SNOT: mucous membrane."

"It's pretty slangy."

"*Woi Yesus*," said Beef, "I'll buy SNOT any day of the week. No arg'in' there."

"I bet it's not in the dictionary," said Ginny.

"Every six-year-old knows snot," said Gordon.

"It's got to be in the dictionary."

"Well, are you challenging or not?"

"I challenge," she said, and looked for the word in the dictionary, the others leaning toward her to see for themselves, watching her forefinger glide below the space where the word should have been. "Sorry, lover, you lose," she said.

"I be damned," said Beef, amazed that he knew something the dictionary did not.

"Let me look again," said Gordon.

"Read it and weep," she said, handing him the dictionary.

He searched for the word, but could not find it. He calmly put down the dictionary and said, "Maria was not pregnant."

"Well, maybe she was and maybe she wasn't."

"But she is now."

The coffee cup she was extending to Mrs. Lister fell out of her hand.

"Why did you call the ambulance!" she screamed at her son. "You want me dead, why didn't you let me die in peace?"

"I resent that, Ginny Mom," said Gordon.

"Ginny Mom, it ain't the end of the world," said Beef. "It happened to me, so I know."

"It's just the thing she feared most," Mrs. Lister whispered to Beef.

Like a member of the family, Beef said, "Well, if you want my advice . . ." and like a member of the family he was cut off by Ginny Wynn.

"You'll never marry that scheming little bitch!"

"Mother, I am above the age of consent."

"Oh, stick that shit up your nose!" She picked up the board covered with tiles and carried it to the kitchen sink, where she slid the tiles into the garbage disposal and flipped the switch. Tiles burst upward like so many bubbles in a glass of champagne. Beef could not keep from laughing.

Gordon rushed to the sink and turned off the disposal. "I just hope you didn't break it," he said, rolling up his sleeve. He dug into the disposal and began removing handfuls of broken tiles. "You know the landlord will make us pay for it."

"She is a cheap beaner, she is a cheap beaner . . ." chanted Ginny.

Beef could not stop laughing.

"Good night, Bomba," said Ginny curtly. "Good night, Mrs. Lister." Then she turned back to Gordon and continued her catalog of Maria's vices, the most damaging of which Ginny imagined was her unremitting passion for black lovers, one of whom she credited with knocking her up.

Beef helped Mrs. Lister walk to the door, unable to stifle his laughter. Ginny called after him, "Stay at the Folding Hotel. I'll be in touch."

The last thing he heard before closing the door was Gordon's cry of pain. Evidently he had cut his finger on one of the blades of the disposal.

5

He knew he should get back on the road again, to Oklahoma maybe, and out of old Mother's problems; but he had been fed so well and had spent the day inside a home, sitting down with folks to eat and play and argue. An element of pride returned to him, a whisper of an earlier security, thought lost forever when his father disappeared and he was set out against the world, as though to find him. He had the curious sense of belonging once again to a family, peculiar as it was, and he was falling into its embrace. His face was still warm where she had kissed him in a spontaneous burst of affection he could never remember receiving from his own mother.

He walked along Nevada Avenue, quiet except for a score of people leaving the last show at a movie theater. Beef paused to look at the posters and to wonder where the disbanded members of the audience would go now and what they would do when they got there.

He passed into the seedy end of Nevada, where there was still song, however sad, beckoning from curtained doorways between closed pawnshops and greasy lunch counters, pool halls, and vacant stores.

He chose a place for no particular reason, moved aside the curtain, and went inside. It was called the Ponderosa Pines, but because of the lack of any exterior or interior theme it could have been called the Sheltering Palms with equal justification. A few cowboys sat at one end of the bar, arguing the virtues and short-comings of the various General Motors models; a lone old rummy held down the other end of the bar with both his numb elbows; Beef took a seat in the middle. He ordered a Coors from the barmaid and asked her, "What's a fella do around here?"

"Everyone he can," she said without interest.

One of the cowboys called her "May," and Beef pointed out that it was the month of his birth, maybe they had something in common.

"M-A-*E*," she spelled; they had nothing in common but the melancholy mode of their lives.

They rolled dice for the music, she won, Beef slid a quarter across the bar. She took it and came around the bar to the jukebox. Beef liked large asses well enough, but he relished the dainty kind he could, if permitted, grasp with one hand, like Mae's. Her hair was blond, peroxide, an inch or two longer than the black Dynel wig she presently wore over it. Her skin was not healthy, from too much smoke and darkness. She did not look happy. But what a nice behind in off-white jeans.

On her way from the jukebox to behind the bar, she was caught at the arm by the old rummy in a fumbling expression of affection. She whipped her arm away so hard he spun off his stool and fell to the floor. She never even looked to see if he had broken anything. The rummy eventually got to his knees and crawled back on his perch. "Goddamn, Mae." Some barmaid.

"She swallows it whole," a fellow barfly would later tell Beef.

What? (Understanding something sexual in that.) "Life, she swallows it whole."

"I need a place to stay," Beef told her.

His full stomach made him feel confident and he was equal to taking long shots.

"The Folding Hotel," she recommended. "Right around the corner."

"That's the same place Ginny said."

"Well, Ginny was right," said Mae.

"Don't like the sound of it."

"There are hotels for flying and hotels for folding."

She is a deep person, thought Beef.

"I got wings a mile long," he boasted, undaunted, as deep as she.

She looked at him with something like pity; Beef thought it was her own doughy sadness.

"Bet you a beer I can make you laugh," he said.

Her look warned him not to deal with her humorlessness, but she said, "Go ahead."

Beef Buddusky had mastered a wide variety of tricks involving food: he could drive a straw without bending it through a raw potato, he could remove the peel of an apple in one continuous curl, he could make three wieners give you the directions to Biloxi. He could do a whole show around the wonderful egg, infinite in its natural secrets. Every trick had this in common: at some point in it the examples would wind up in Beef's stomach.

"You got a raw egg?" he asked Mae.

She took one out of the refrigerator and gave it to him.

"Pencil?"

She handed him a pencil.

Under cover, he poked a tiny hole in the egg and sucked out its contents. He blew into the hole and sealed it with a bit of wet coaster. He dropped the egg to the bar and sure enough it bounced back into his hand unbroken.

"That'll be a dime for the egg and a quarter for the beer you owe me," said Mae.

It's been a good day anyway, he thought. He paid her, and said, "See you around."

"Sure."

"The name's Beef."

She looked him over. Who the hell cared what his name was?

A small sign hung over the sidewalk on Nevada Avenue; the actual entrance, a single door, was around the corner on Colorado, as though trying to keep itself a secret. It was actually called the Flouding Hotel. The other name must be a local joke, thought Beef. He lay on his bed and put his hands behind his head. In the john at the end of the hall someone was being terribly sick, too much so for concerns over his own privacy and others' sensitivities. Beef pushed the retching sound out of his fantasy of Mae above him, astraddle, and he arching his back so high he swept her knees off the bed. She held onto the hair of his chest and challenged him in passionate screams to drive her through the ceiling if he could. In his fantasy he could.

He would stay in Colorado Springs, at least until something pushed him out of the place, as something had always pushed him out of one place or another.

6

Beef Buddusky's vocational demands were very simple. He wanted a job at which he could work two days and honky-tonk five.

Ginny Wynn had called, as promised, and sent him on two job interviews with assurance that in mentioning her name the interview would be over and the job his. Neither boss had ever heard of her, but Beef did not want to insult her with this information when she called to send him on a third interview, this time to a pool maintenance firm. She was unknown to this boss too, who looked at Beef with mild amusement and said, "What can you do, kid?"

Thirty years old and they were still calling him kid. In answer, Beef went to a nearby pool heater, lifted the huge thing easily, and carried it to the other side of the room.

The boss smiled and said, "Well, can you paint a house?"

Beef looked at him for a moment. "Shingle it too," he said. The old fart.

"Can you wash a truck?"

"Wax it too."

"Can you suck a tit?"

"Pussy too," said Beef, capping the litany and making the old fart laugh as loud as he longed to make Mae laugh.

"You're hired! Come by my house tonight, my old lady'll be ready for you!" cried the boss, wiping his eyes.

That is how Beef became a swimming pool maintenance man, a line of work he had never done before, but one to which he would adjust quickly.

He celebrated with dinner alone in an Italian restaurant. At a table close by, three couples clicked their glasses together in a toast. As they drank, Beef picked up his own glass, accidentally clicking it against the saltshaker. The couples all looked at him as though in his solitude he were mocking their happiness. The hell with 'em, thought Beef, but he felt himself shrink to nothing. After dinner, he went to Ginny's place and watched television with her and Mrs. Lister.

In the days that followed, he saw Ginny and Mrs. Lister often, and when his schedule allowed it had lunch with them at the Purple Cow or Howard's or the Colorado Lunch. Ginny always picked up the tab. By no means did he drum himself out of the fraternity of boozers on lower Nevada Avenue, and he continued trying to make Mae laugh, sometimes raising a crooked half grin, which, if it told anything, Beef was unable to decipher. Most of his evenings, however, were spent sitting in either Ginny's or Mrs. Lister's apartment, doing the job on their iceboxes, or walking in the evenings to find and hide Gordon's car. She wanted the car hidden so that Gordon would associate inconvenience with wanting to see Maria.

Beef had told her the first time in the police department parking lot, "Missus, I want to confess to you that I have got in trouble once for driving other people's cars."

"This is half *my* car. But I don't know how to drive, dammit.

Never had the patience to learn."

Two policemen going into the station waved at them and one called cheerily, "Hello, Mrs. Wynn!"

Beef turned his face away from them. Ginny returned their wave and shouted, "Hi, honeybunch!"

The first few times he hid the car, he called Gordon to tell him where it was, but Gordon was so cold, unappreciative, and downright unfriendly that Beef stopped telling him. He wanted to be friends with Gordon. He began to think of him as a bright younger brother whose future (and therein the hopes of the family) was in peril, a typical family problem affecting all members.

He liked his job. It was good to work in the air, and he liked the smell of chlorine and the way the sun worked out its routine on the blue water of the pools he serviced. One morning he was skimming a pool, picking up the dead insects floating on it, when the owner's daughter came out in her bikini and stood next to him. She was perhaps seventeen, no older. "When will it be ready?" she asked, looking at the water. Beef could actually smell her, a heady aroma of fresh, clean skin. "Won't be long," he said, trying not to stare at her. Slightly pigeon-toed, she ran back to the house, probably to call her friends. Beef inhaled deeply, capturing the last trace of her odor. I'd like, someday, he thought, to make love to a seventeen-year-old named Maria. I'd like to lie with her and have her tell me she adores me, to be in her and hear her moan, "Fuck me, Beef, fuck me." He shook the insects out of his wire mesh and dipped it back into the pool.

He bought a pair of used trunks for fifty cents at the Goodwill Thrift Shop and after servicing each pool he cannonballed into it, just to stir around the chlorine, he said. The owners usually kept a supply of Coors beer, the champagne of Mexican gardeners and Anglo day workers, and were loose with it on a hot day. The Mexicans laughed at Beef's large marble-white body, tan only on the face and the arms, like any other short-sleeved laborer.

Soon Beef tanned evenly and began to look a bit like the athlete he once was.

Woi Yesus, he told himself, this life here is agreeing with you. You're comin' near settlin' down.

7

Meat loaf was Ginny's most complicated dish. It had lodged within it four whole hard-boiled eggs, like impacted wisdom teeth. She served it with instant mashed potatoes, canned gravy, and a pre-tossed salad the supermarket sold in cellophane bags. Yet once she had tried to buy a restaurant with her imaginary $50,000. The dinner was so dreadful that even she wouldn't touch it, which did not stop Beef from having seconds.

"Sometimes it turns out pretty good," said Ginny, astounded by Beef's appetite.

"Long as it fills the stomach and makes . . . well, long as it fills the stomach. That's what my mother used to say."

"We'll have to invite her to dinner sometime."

"No chance of that," said Beef, wiping his plate with a crust of bread.

"Well, we might as well invite somebody. Lately there's been an empty plate around here."

"He probably had to work late again," said Mrs. Lister, softening up a piece of garlic bread in her coffee.

"That's what they always say."

"You want to save what's left for him and keep it in the oven?" asked Beef.

"No, eat, go ahead, he wouldn't want it anyway."

Beef transferred the heel of meat loaf to his plate, spread a thick layer of mustard on it, and continued eating.

"Where the hell is he?" asked Ginny.

He was with Maria in a hotel room in Manitou Springs, trying to open an iced bottle of champagne that had been there for their arrival. Didn't that prove there was no doubt about his going through with it? Even so, now that it was done he was almost too nervous to pour. They clinked their glasses together and Maria offered a toast: "To the three of us."

Gordon did not drink. "That your idea of a joke?" he said.

"Darling, to you, me, and the baby."

"God, Maria, I'm sorry. I thought you meant my mother."

They had had a few bad moments on the way to the courthouse, when Maria learned that he had not told his mother they were to be married. She did not want to feel she was sneaking off to her own wedding. They were not sneaking, Gordon told her, they were adults. "Wouldn't it be nice to think so?" said Maria. She wanted to delay the wedding for a day, but was afraid to offer that postponement to Gordon, for fear she might lose him forever. She looked at the small bouquet he gave her to hold during the ceremony and said, "Are you sure you want to go through with this?"

"I *want* to get married. I love you."

It was only the second time he had ever told her.

There was another bad moment, quite a bad moment, when they arrived at the judge's chambers. Judge Montgomery knew Gordon as a frequent witness in his court and seemed to like him.

After meeting Maria and commenting upon what a lucky fella Gordon was and what a handsome couple they were, the judge said to Gordon, "I spoke to the clerk. He will not include your names when he gives his list to the local press."

"I don't understand," said Maria, but she did too well.

Judge Montgomery looked from her to Gordon. "Well, it was my understanding that you wanted the wedding kept confidential."

Gordon turned to her. "I have to do it my own way, honey. I don't want her winding up in the hospital again."

It was, she knew, her last moment to seize. There were too many things wrong with a day that should be perfect. But Gordon took her arm and she moved with him uneasily into the event she had once longed for.

Now, in the bridal suite, the evening attained some small festive air, but even that soon began to unravel. They finished the bottle of champagne and ordered another from room service.

"I hope it will be a boy," she said. "Don't you?"

"Do you know what I felt when you told me you were in trouble?" he asked.

"Not trapped?"

"No, not trapped. Proud. I felt pride."

She loved him for his pride.

"It's a wonderful thing to be able to do, when you examine it," he said. It would make him like the other men on the force. They would not exclude him now.

"If it's a boy, I hope he becomes a doctor," she said.

"We'll let him become what he wants. If he wants to be a cowboy, we'll let him."

"But wouldn't it be grand to have a doctor in the family? I'd like him to go to school in the East."

"Maria, he's not even born yet and you're mapping out his life for him."

"No, I'm not, I'm just dreaming for him."

"That's how it begins," he said.

"I just want him to amount to something," she said. "Why are you looking at me like that?"

The bellboy arrived with the new bottle of champagne. He opened it for them and filled their glasses. Gordon raised his glass and said, "By God, I hope it's a girl."

Soon they were pleasantly intoxicated. They liked each other that way. Gordon, never very demonstrative, became affectionate under the influence; and she, generally conventional, became more daring. He undressed her to her stockings and then undressed himself. He stopped her from removing the stockings. She was disturbed by male fantasies but agreed to oblige this innocent one. He caressed each nipple in turn with his tongue and then with a mouthful of champagne bathed them. They were exquisitely proportioned but small breasts, and as he pressed his face between them he wished they were large, large enough to hide him. Her skin was olive, flawless and incredibly smooth. He lapped her shoulders, breasts, and belly. "I want you in me," she whispered, but he crouched over her on his knees, one hand cupped around her breast, his mouth over the nipple. He guided her hand and told her to stroke him. She grew more and more uncomfortable. He directed her to a point just under the glans, the "acorn" he called it, and asked her to concentrate on that small spot. She wanted to please him; she had never heard him moan with such sweet pain, but as his intensity grew hers diminished and she felt too much like an instrument. Couldn't the touch of her fingertips be matched by a million other women? He told her to use only her little finger and not to stray from that spot below the acorn, and she did as she was told, and the aching that asked for him in her passed.

Mrs. Lister was nodding off to sleep in the recliner, singing drowsy bits of songs, waiting with Beef and Ginny for Gordon to come home.

Beef sat in the dimly lit living room gazing at the gift he had given Ginny, which sat on her television set. It was a lamp that heated wax, sending globs of it floating through a liquid solution. He loved it and could watch it without boredom. It had been behind the bar of the Ponderosa Pines, but Beef had made a deal for it. He wanted Ginny to have it, for all her kindnesses.

She sat beside him on the sofa, snuggled to his side. He put his arm around her shoulders and together they watched the hot wax rise and fall.

"Big old snuggle bear, aren't you?" she said.

"It's nice like this, ain't?"

"I know it hasn't been that long, but seems like you've always been here, Bomba."

"Don't it?"

She was as peaceful as he had ever seen her. Usually she was riding her nerves, unable to relax.

"Have you given any thought to the fifty-thousand-dollar proposition I told you about?"

"No, I sure haven't."

She sighed. "Maybe in the long run that's best."

"I kinda figured that out for myself."

"It's hard not to hate yourself sometimes."

"It's often I can't stand my own company," said Beef.

"Wish I was twenty years younger."

"I used to wish I was an old man," he said, "and have it all over with. I have lots of strange wishes, dependin' on the mood I'm in."

"You know what I did when I was fourteen?" she asked.

"I sure don't."

"You want to take a guess?"

Beef tried to think of the really notable things a girl of fourteen could do. "You got married," he said.

"Right! You ever hear of such a thing?"

"Oh, yes, Ginny Mom."

"Wanted to get out of the crummy house. A man twenty years older than me. But I'm not ashamed of it. All my brothers and sisters left home early too, trying to better ourselves, and today I'm the only one has a pot to peel potatoes in."

"You done all right for yourself, lady."

"He left me, that man, got tired of me and went, and for a time I was on my ownie. I sure didn't like that, I'm a person can't tolerate being alone, and then along came Gordon's father. You won't believe it, knowing Gordie, but his father was a slack-jaw weakling. I think I married him 'cause I felt sorry for him. He'd follow anything that'd call his name."

"I always felt sorry for that type of individual," said Beef. "It ain't an easy life."

"By the time I had Gordie, I couldn't stand the man. But, God, I was dependent on him. There I was, a young mother with no skills to speak of. Made me hate him more, and of course he took off too. I saw the necessity of another husband and quick, so I was already hating my third husband before I ever met him. Poor guy, he didn't stand a chance. I guess from the time Gordie was born it was pretty much him and me. My brothers and sisters gave birth to waitresses and baby-sitters, soldiers and taxicab drivers . . ."

Her voice choked up. Beef wondered what his own mother had to say about him: that he was thirty and still lost, bouncing from one town to another, all across the country, telling lies to himself and joining in the lies of others like him, no prospects for the future, no benefits from the past.

"Ain't nothing in the world the equal of a mother's love for her child," said Beef.

"I'll forsake everything for Gordie, and he knows it. I love you, boy, but I'd sell you down the river in the blink of an eye for my son."

"I'd expect you to."

"But what can you do against pretty young women?"

"Not much. The world be*longs* to pretty young women."

"Not all of it, Bomba, not *my* piece of it."

Mrs. Lister had fallen fast asleep. The kitchen clock could be heard ticking. Beef felt a wonderful sense of relaxation and oneness with himself.

"It's almost midnight," she said. Then, bitterly, "Where can he be?"

A few minutes after midnight, Ginny took her customary Seconals and asked Beef to see Mrs. Lister to her own apartment. From there he hurried to the Ponderosa Pines for his fill before last call.

At the Ponderosa Pines that night of the clandestine wedding Beef sat at one end of the bar and followed Mae's lethargic moves with a longing almost tangible. He watched her put the glasses over the wash brush and jerk them slowly up and down, creating a suction. Beef got an erection. She knew he was watching, she knew what he was feeling, she knew men, if nothing else. She began to tantalize him purposely, taking a kosher dill out of the gallon jug and sucking the end of it sensually before biting through. It's a curse to be a man and ugly as a bus depot, thought Beef.

A cowboy at the other end of the bar sang along with the jukebox. *"I ain't gonna take a thing I didn't bring. I'm leavin' with my saddle, you can stay here with your ring . . ."*

"I sure get tired of all this gunsmoke and horseshit," said Mae directly to Beef.

"I can't get you out of my head. I dream about you," said Beef. He had been honest with himself all evening.

She almost smiled, biting down hard on the kosher dill.

"If I knew how to lie and cheat my way into your pants, why, I'd do it, Mae. I got it real bad."

She looked at the clock and announced, "Last call for alcohol." Beef ordered two. He finished the first by the time the last barfly left and Mae locked the door behind him.

"You want me to drink up and go?" asked Beef.

"Take your time." She turned out every light, leaving on only the beer signs. In the darkened room, the blue streams became deeper; the hunter almost alive, the geese higher, the bright rising and falling spots more brilliant and hypnotic.

She stood at the end of the bar, at his right elbow, and helped herself to a swig of his beer. He took a swig after her, flattening his tongue where her lips had been. She leaned on the bar and laid her hand on his leg. She took another swig of beer, she patiently fussed with his zipper, he sucked in his belly to help. His penis sprang out like a paper snake out of a tin can. He stood up and moved her through the square of moonlight from the skylight to the darkness of the corridor that led to the rear entrance. She hiked up her skirt, he pulled off her pants and let his trousers drop to his ankles. He lifted her a foot from the floor and pinned her to the wall. Her legs came around him and squeezed like a good memory. He put his beery mouth over hers.

To make this good thing last longer he studied the unfinished wall behind her, the smallest fibers of it. He tried to think of the technical word for this cheap construction material, the same his father and he had once put up in their cellar, trying to make it into more than a cellar. "A rumpus room" they had in mind, an unclear plan for middle-class leisure.

Mae stuck her tongue into his ear and cried urgently, "Give honey, you big goddamn grasshopper, you! Give honey!"

What *was* the name of that material? They beat the wall with her behind. *Boom! Boom! Boom!* The whole of the Ponderosa Pines seemed to shake.

"Give honey!" she pleaded.

Beef rose to his toes, an instant away from that sweet release, still focusing on the wall in front of him. What *was* that stuff? He remembered as they crashed through it.

"Beaver board!" he screamed as he came, and he fell like an oak.

Crashing through the wall, Mae clinging to him in a scissors grip, he was amazed at how long it took them to reach the floor. He had time to picture his father's hammer on the floor of their unfinished "rumpus room," covered with a layer of dust.

Finally they landed and lay panting on the ladies' room floor, pieces of the wall around them, a broken mirror under them. Beef slid the pieces of mirror away. They caught and reflected some moonlight. Beef looked around at where he and Mae were lying and said, "Well, when you gotta go, you gotta go."

At last Mae laughed, all the way from Oklahoma somewhere, showing her snaggletooth and saying, "You're a real hard come, ain't you?"

8

Later, on his bed at the Folding Hotel, Beef crossed his hands over his hairy stomach and said aloud, "I sure love that little broad."

She became part of the comfort and confidence and warmth and passion that had befallen him since arriving at the Springs, all made possible because he wisely would not go on down the road to a place called Pueblo. For the first time in a few years he felt proud of himself and pleased with himself. He was close to putting a lot of bad times behind him. He wanted to tell Ginny and Mrs. Lister. He wondered if telling her about Mae could possibly make her angry.

How could it, he reasoned on his way to her place. He was not her son, after all. He was free to involve himself with anyone he pleased. Still, he could easily withhold the subject of Mae and Ginny would probably never be the wiser, unless she should happen to see them together somewhere, and then he might have some explaining to do. Ginny was a friend, though, and Beef felt very much in her debt and considered her privileged to his confidences, since she had shared so many of her own with him. Who knows, she and Mae might hit it off and Mae could join their little family. Beef would like that.

He found her and Mrs. Lister sitting, each with a shoe box full of snapshots of Gordie on her lap, each with a pair of scissors with which they laboriously cut the pictures into tiny pieces. He reached into the box on Mrs. Lister's lap and helped himself to a handful of the pictures. Some of them included a youthful Ginny Wynn. He was struck by how beautiful she had been. She had had a long, smooth, elegant neck.

"Once a picture's gone," he said, "it's gone forever."

"It will satisfy me," she answered distantly.

Beef concluded that Gordon must have done something terrible to deserve this symbolic torture. Married, he thought, he must have married the girl. Would he at last have a look at Maria, now that Gordon had married her? He wanted to see her, to see what it was she had that kindled such a rage in Ginny.

Beef looked at a picture of Gordon as a toddler holding Ginny's hand. His other arm was raised, holding someone else's hand. The rest of the picture, all but that self-existing hand holding Gordon's, had already been neatly trimmed away before ever being put to rest in the shoe box. His father, Beef believed. The picture filled him with sadness. Both of them had been cut away from their fathers, falling to mothers who failed them.

He tossed the pictures back into Mrs. Lister's shoe box. "Any milk in the reefer?" he asked.

Ginny did not acknowledge. He went to the refrigerator and took out a quart of milk. Mrs. Lister called, "There's pepperoni." Ginny always tried to keep a supply especially for him. He cut six inches off the pepperoni and chewed away at it as he walked back into the living room. He drank the milk from the bottle.

He sat on the floor in front of Ginny and said, "Ginny Mom,

you ain't gonna believe what's happened to me. I think I . . ."

"Bomba, Bomba," said Ginny, "my boy's gone off and got married on me. He'll quit his classes now, watch."

"Well, it was bound to happen," said Beef begrudgingly. He wanted to get his own news out first, before he lost heart.

"Can I stand by and allow it?"

"I don't see you can do much else."

"I had a feeling, a mother's feeling, that told me."

"Woman's intuition," said Beef.

"It's not a picnic to be a mother nowadays, not with the type of girls they have running free, coming in from other countries. God bless me. Bomba, I have this peculiar feeling he did it just to show off. They start by trying to bite off your tit for you."

"And after all those phone calls," said Mrs. Lister. "You'd think she'd be too scared."

"It's the Latin blood," said Ginny. She turned to Beef. "I called her office, and one of the clerks there told me. That's the announcement for the mother of the groom." She started to cry. "A Mexican!"

Beef laid the stick of pepperoni across the mouth of the milk bottle and took her shaking body into his arms.

"There, there," he cooed. "It'll all come out in the wash."

"Ginny got her new phone number and address out of the clerk," giggled Mrs. Lister. "Told her she was a friend of hers from Mexico and wanted to buy silverware for her wedding present. Told her she already knew Maria's pattern." That bit of invention appealed to Mrs. Lister's sense of humor.

"What're you gonna need with her phone number, address?" asked Beef.

"I'll think of something," she said, working out of his embrace. He saw her place the scissors directly between Gordon's legs and slice quickly but deliberately. She put one side on top of the other and cut off the two halves of his head.

Gordon did not come home for dinner and this, she told them, was expected. She had visions of him dining with the slut in some expensive restaurant. She could see the people around them, watching and saying, "Look at the new girl with Officer Wynn. Where is his mother?"

His mother was literally not in the picture. But pictures can be altered so easily, with a scissors.

They walked to the Purple Cow Drive-In Restaurant for dinner. They ate there often, a lumbering oaf and two little old ladies, incongruous to the setting, a mottled neon haven for small-town hustlers and nymphos, dragsters and bikers, teen-age rocks and their chicks, snooker shooters and pan players. The place was known as a good bet for a job in order to strike for parole. Winos drying out became fry cooks there. Women just passing through town went there and became waitresses or carhops until something else got shaking. The shortest tenure of record belonged to a strawberry blonde named June, who after forty-five minutes on the job was seen getting into a dechromed and lowered '49 Merc with Texas plates, never to be seen again.

Ginny held four envelopes of sugar in her hand and tore off the tops as though they were one and poured the sugar into her coffee as though it were one envelope instead of four. She stirred the coffee, sipped it, and made a face. "They probably never clean the pot," she said. She looked into her cloudy coffee for a moment, then raised her head erect, laid both palms flat on the table, and said, "Bomba, how would you like to earn three thousand dollars?"

"I got no objection."

"Are you willing to listen?"

"Like a bartender on a slow afternoon. I do that good."

"That girl wouldn't let my son alone."

"Ginny Mom, I never knew a man yet couldn't let a woman know he don't want her around anymore. There's bound to be a little yelling and maybe a beer bottle up alongside somebody's head, but, hell . . ."

"I want you to get rid of her."

"Really?" said Mrs. Lister.

"Like I say, let old Gordie stand back a few steps and tell her to pack up her gear and *icdo domu spac.* But if he had a mind to do that, he wouldn't of married her."

"I want you to kill her."

"You shouldn't even kid around about stuff like that," said Beef, looking nervously around him to see if anyone had heard. "If I thought you was serious, I'd slide right out of this booth and you'd never see me again. You been good to me, missus, a mother prit' near, but I ain't gonna total no girl I don't even know and wind up strapped in some goddamn gas chamber."

"I got pills and acid and all to do it. You can use Gordie's car."

"We're in a public place, Ginny, watch what the hell you're sayin'!"

"Three thousand when the deed is done."

"I didn't hear a word of it. As far as I'm concerned I come here to chop wood but you're cookin' on gas."

He slid out of the booth and left the Purple Cow.

Ginny paid the bill and the two ladies hurried down the street after him. When they finally caught up with him, Mrs. Lister grabbed his arm for support. She was panting like a finished parade.

"No it was and no it is," said Beef to Ginny.

"Slow down, for God's sake," she said.

"I'm a fun-lovin' sort, Ginny Mom. I believe we're put here to enjoy ourselves."

"Somehow, Bomba, you don't strike me as the life of the party."

"I've had some unhappiness, but, goddamn, I never hurt nobody."

"All right, all right, forget I mentioned it. God forbid you should burst a blood vessel or something."

"If you can't have fun outa life, what's it for?"

"You're too late with that question."

"I respect your problem, but you gotta respect my way of thinkin'."

"All right, forget it. It never happened."

"You were only kiddin', huh?" asked Beef. "Tryin' to get a rise outa old Bomba, huh?"

"Only kidding, yes," she said. Her mind was already on something else.

"That'll be the day," said Mrs. Lister, in a voice the others could not hear.

Back in Ginny's apartment, he tried to calm her, unsuccessfully. Nothing could put her at her peace. Like a hyperactive child, she could not sit still. Her hands were constantly slapping, picking, shaking. He was unable to tell her about Mae.

He turned on the eleven o'clock news, but no one could watch it.

"Look," said Ginny.

Neither Beef nor Mrs. Lister knew where to look.

"Look, there's another way out of this," she said.

"Another way out of what?" asked Beef.

"We might be able to settle this without killing that bitch."

"Now you're talkin'," said Beef. "You can move most people

out of the way without killin' 'em.''

"What do you want to do?" asked Mrs. Lister conspiratorially. "I'll help."

"I know I can count on you, dearie. But will you help us, Bomba?"

"Depends."

"I've been going about this the wrong way."

"I can't help agreein' to that," said Beef.

"Our only problem," said Ginny, "is bringing Gordie back to his senses. This girl has him bewitched. He doesn't love her. All I have to do is show him that."

"How're you going to do that, Ginny?" asked Mrs. Lister.

"I'm going to take him back to Denver. We could return to those early struggling years."

"But you always told me those years were hard and awful," said Mrs. Lister.

"It will give him a chance to come back to his senses," said Ginny, ignoring her.

"Maybe in the long run that's best," said Beef. Secretly, he was delighted with the idea of Ginny and Gordie going to Denver. It would give him a vacation from them.

"Will you help us?" she asked Beef.

"Be glad to. What can I do for you?"

"My plan," said Ginny, leaning closer and dropping her voice, "is you and Mrs. Lister hide in the closet. When Gordie comes home I'll knock him out with sleeping pills. Then we can tie him up, throw a blanket over him, and Bomba can drive us all to Denver."

"Ginny," said Beef patiently, "that's called kidnapping, and they treat you unkind when they catch you doing it."

"There's got to be a victim," Ginny argued.

"Well, I guess old Gordie would fill that bill."

"What are you talking about? We'd be returning to our old haunts. He'd be coming back to his senses. That's not kidnapping in my book."

"It ain't your book they go by," said Beef.

"Besides, he's my *kid.*"

"Kid, hell, he's an officer of the law!"

"I'll do whatever *I* can, Ginny," said Mrs. Lister.

"A woman in her eighties will help me, and you stand by like an overgrown good-for-nothing."

"Why don't you just *ask* him to go with you?"

"If you were married yesterday and I asked you to go to Denver with me tonight, would you go willingly?"

No answer was an answer.

"You're sure Gordie won't throw us all in Old Crossbars?" asked Beef.

"He's my *son,*" she said, laying her hand on his arm.

"You want to do it tonight? That quick?"

"Why not?"

"It's the damnedest thing I ever heard of."

"What do you want *me* to do, Ginny?" asked Mrs. Lister.

"Well?" Ginny asked Beef.

"I'd sure rather help you straighten out Gordie than all this other noise you been bringing up, but I got to be at work in the mornin' and so does he."

"Oh, *please,* Bomba, you are the silliest thing."

"Yes, *please,* Bomba," affirmed old Mrs. Lister.

"Truth is," said Beef, "I'm expected somewheres tonight."

"I beg your pardon?" said Ginny, unable to accept the idea of Beef's having any previous engagements.

"Somebody's waiting for me," he explained.

"A girl?" asked Ginny, with almost total disbelief.

"Well, I . . . that's what I was gonna tell you when I came over here today, but you never gave me a chance."

"Is she a nice girl?" asked Mrs. Lister.

"Some folks might not think so, but I say yes, she's a nice girl. Got a cute snaggletooth I really kinda like."

He broke into a proud grin, and waited for Ginny to smile too. She did not.

"Well, Bomba, it sure didn't take you long," said Ginny. "Already you have a girlfriend."

"I don't know that it's all that serious, but a lot of the thanks goes to you. You made me feel . . . I don't know."

"I'm very happy you have a girl."

"You are?" he asked, strangely disappointed. He expected a bit of the jealousy over Gordie's involvement to transfer to his own.

"You deserve some young female companionship. You're a fine boy."

"You sure are something, Ginny Mom. I never know what you're gonna say next. I'm lookin' forward to having you meet her. Her name is . . . Mae." It was, apparently, the most romantic of names.

"Tell me, Bomba, did you meet her at a church social?" asked Ginny.

He laughed. "You know me better 'n that."

"Oh, then she must be a secretary down at that place you work. Is that where you met her?"

He grew uncomfortable. "No, not there."

"Well, where? You weren't visiting a dying relative in the hospital, were you? Mae isn't a psychiatric social worker, by any chance, is she?"

"No."

"Prying her nose into everybody's affairs?"

"She ain't a psychiatric social worker," he said, his discomfort becoming anxiety.

"Well, who are her parents?" she asked.

"Not sure as she has any."

"How old is she?"

"Probably my age."

The next question, whatever it would be, would bring humiliation and guilt, he knew.

"Bomba," she said, with all reasonableness, "you tell me you have a girlfriend, you tell me you want me to meet her, but you don't seem to know much about her. Or else you're ashamed of her."

"I ain't nothin' of the kind. I met her in a bar."

"Ah, all right, now we're getting somewhere. She had stopped for cocktails with a few of the girls."

"She *works* there," said Beef defensively.

"She's a barmaid," said Ginny, unmistakable judgment in her voice.

"That's an honest living, Ginny Mom."

"Let me ask you one more question and we'll let it go at that."

"Shoot," said Beef, glad to bring it to an end.

"Is this a love of the spirit or have you already done your humping in some dirty dark corner?" Her eyes were electric, the corners of her mouth tightened.

"Ginny!" said Mrs. Lister.

"That's a private matter," said Beef.

"Well, do me a favor. Don't bring your whore up to my place."

Beef stood for a few seconds, coaxing his anger to the surface. When it arrived, he kicked the hassock, sending it rolling across the room. Mrs. Lister scrambled after it to set it aright. He spun around to face a stunned Ginny. "I ain't no goddamn Gordie boy!" he shouted. "*I,*" jabbing his chest with his thumb, "do what the hell I please. *Nobody's* gonna tell me what girl to do what with, and you better get that straight, lady. You want me to help you kidnap Gordie and then you have the nerve to insult my girl and belittle me. You think I'm gonna help somebody like that? Up a pig's ass!"

Mrs. Lister covered her ears with her hands.

"Go, then!" shouted Ginny in return. "Go to your little live wire. I'm sure if she doesn't see you every day she'll forget all about you. Go to her!"

"Don't worry," said Beef boastfully, "she ain't gonna forget *me.*"

"Get out of here if you're so worried about her. Mrs. Lister and I will do it ourselves. We don't need you, you don't have the brains God gave a rag doll. Go back to the Salvation Army where you came from."

Ginny sat on the sofa and cried piteously into her hands.

"Now look what you did," said Mrs. Lister to Beef.

He stood there breathing heavily, unable to kick anything, though he did glance about for a target. Finally, in a bemused voice, he said, "You and Mrs. Lister. I'm tryin' to see Mrs. Lister throw a blanket over old Gordie and tie him up, but my brain's havin' a hassle providin' the picture. And who's gonna drive the car to Denver?"

"We can take a taxicab," said Mrs. Lister haughtily.

Beef chuckled softly. "In your head," he said. He thought he heard Ginny sob, but when she looked at him, he could see she had laughed against her will.

In pantomime, he struggled under the weight of a body on his shoulder. "Taxi!" he yelled.

Ginny could not keep from laughing.

"Well, if we can just go on havin' fun," said Beef, "maybe we can all keep out of trouble."

"I don't see what's so funny," said Mrs. Lister.

"You'll help us, won't you, Bomba?" said Ginny. She opened the front door and looked for Gordon.

"I'll help you keep your asses out of the soup, but that's *all* I'll help you with."

"Fair enough," said Ginny, still looking through the open door. She said it as though closing a deal, but Beef was far from being the party of the second part.

"That don't mean I'm about to kidnap Gordie."

"You can't kidnap your own son."

"He ain't *my* son. God, if he was I'd be glad he got married and out of the house."

"Here he comes!" she whispered. "Get into the closet, you two."

"Wait a minute," said Beef. Mrs. Lister was already stepping into the closet.

"Not now, Bomba, please," said Ginny, pushing him.

Beef allowed himself to be put in the closet. "This still don't mean I'm in on your crazy stunt," he said as the door was shut on him and Mrs. Lister.

"There's a blanket in there," said Ginny. She tried to look casual for Gordon's return. She noticed Mrs. Lister's cane and rushed to throw it into the closet after her. "Now don't make a peep," she whispered to them. She shut the closet door as Gordon walked into the apartment.

"Hello, Mother," said Gordon. He hesitantly walked across the room to kiss her.

"Why, hi there, stranger, where have you been keeping your-self?"

"One of the guys got sick. I volunteered for a double watch." He took off his holster and went toward the closet.

She quickly intercepted him. "I'll do it," she said. She took the holster and his cap to the closet and handed them to Beef, who gave her his most disapproving look. Mrs. Lister covered her mouth with her hands, containing her mischievous glee. Ginny shut the door on them and turned back to her son, who was now sitting on the recliner.

"You couldn't call?" she said.

"Sorry."

"Well, even if you worked a double . . ."

"Where's the paper?" he asked her.

Usually she would get it for him. "In the bathroom," she said. When he went to get it, she went into the kitchen and poured some milk into a saucepan and put it on the stove. She dropped six of her sleeping pills into an empty coffee mug. Gordon sat down again and pretended to read the paper.

"You seem overwrought tonight, Gordie."

"Overwrought is right."

"I'm making you some hot milk."

"No, thanks."

"It will relax you."

"I never drink hot milk."

"That's why you're so overwrought."

"No, it's not, Mother."

"Well, would you like to tell me about it?"

"I'd love to. We never have quiet, rational talks about our problems."

"If that's so, it's because we have no problems."

Gordon laughed in one syllable. "No, it's because you get angry and start cutting me off in the middle of sentences."

"I confess to having a temper, but you'd be amazed at how well I've been controlling it lately. Is there something you want to tell me, Gordie?"

Gordon faltered. "Yes, I believe there is."

"Oh?"

"I hope . . . isn't your milk burning?"

She rushed into the kitchen and turned off the stove. She skimmed the solidifying top off the milk and poured the rest into the coffee mug. She stirred it with a spoon to dissolve the pills.

"I hope you'll be fair about this," said Gordon from the living room.

"Your milk's almost ready," she answered. She brought the spoon up with the pills in it. They were too slow dissolving. She tried to mash them.

In the closet Beef and Mrs. Lister were having trouble breathing. Mrs. Lister had already slipped to a sitting position. Beef fanned her, fearing she would lose consciousness soon. The space, in total darkness, was not ventilated. The dusty, bitter smell of the vacuum cleaner, whose space they shared, lodged in their throats and made them silently gag.

Ginny took the milk to Gordon and said, "Drink this, we'll talk later."

"I think we have to talk now. I think we've been avoiding an honest talk for too long."

"I said *drink* it," she said menacingly.

"And you wonder why we have trouble communicating."

"I'm communicating perfectly. I took the trouble to make that, you better drink it."

Gordon took a sip of the milk. He picked a few particles of sleeping pills off his tongue. He rose out of his chair and looked at his fingertips in astonishment. "Mom, are you trying to *drug* me?"

She rushed for the box at the far end of the sofa, ran back to Gordon, and threw into his face the shreds of his personal pictorial history. He stood still for a few seconds, then brushed the confetti from his shoulders. "You already knew," he said in a defeated voice.

Just then, Mrs. Lister came rolling out of the closet, semiconscious. The stale air rushed out of her lungs with a dry, crackling rattle. In a moment, Beef crawled out on hands and knees, soaked in sweat. He looked up at Gordon and said with difficulty, "Hyuh, Gordie buddy."

Mrs. Lister came around and gasped, "It was awful in there, awful! I thought I was buried alive!"

Gordon ran out of the apartment, his hands in front of him, as though prepared for obstacles. He was heard to mutter something. Perhaps it was closer to crying. Closer still to screaming. He did not return that night.

9

The warm weather was over, and with it Beef's job. He gave some thought to leaving town, maybe to Texas or California, but finally had to confess that he did not want to leave the Springs. It was a happy place for him. He found another job, better than the first. He became a roofer.

"You can't bend a rufin' nail," he told Mae, by way of explaining his choice of the new occupation.

There was something immensely gratifying in laying a fresh roof. With the initial layer of tar paper, in overlapping strips perfectly parallel, he'd see the first promise of watertight integrity and would feel good for the family that would gather below a roof of his making. The rectangles of insulation went down practically by themselves, now warmth, next summer—coolness. Again he would shoulder rolls of tar paper and carry them up the ladder for a second layer. With this layer stapled down and trimmed, he would carry up bales of shingles with growing excitement—as preparation for the reward: sitting high above the ground, nailing in the sheets of shingles between his widely spread legs, watching the protective covering spread step-fashion, a bold challenge to the elements. The orderly progression of shingle overlapping shingle, hiding his nailheads, pleased him, and he'd often wish the roof could go on and on and on.

By the time he would get back to Mae's place, she would be on her way to the Pines. He'd clean up and drop in for a few beers before going over to Ginny's for dinner. Sometimes he would nap at Ginny's, patiently waiting for her grudge against Maria to dissipate. By 2 A.M. he would be back at the Pines to see Mae home. God, he liked his life then! Why couldn't he have nailed it down as firm as a sheet of shingles?

When the plan to kidnap Gordon failed, and entrenched him deeper in the enemy camp, Ginny once again turned her thoughts to an ultimate solution.

"I only wish she'd leave me out of it," Beef told Mae. "She's a good old gal, but I think this thing has shook a few studs loose."

Mae's tired feet seemed of greater interest to her.

"And Gordie, he sure ain't your ordinary kind of cop, that guy."

She took one of those tired feet, pulled it to her, and massaged it. "These people," she said, "they don't know what real problems are."

"He's married, right? And they're gonna have a kid, but he spends every other night on the Hide A Bed in Mama's place. She still wants him to spend *every* night with her. She's scared to death to be alone. You want to know where I was that night last week?"

"What night last week?"

"The night I wasn't here, for crissake."

"Oh, yeah, where was you?"

"She wouldn't let me go. She was afraid her daughter-in-law would come over and kill her."

"I thought it was her who wanted to kill her daughter-in-law," said Mae.

Beef nodded. "Wantin' to is okay, I only wish she'd shut up about it."

"Some Mexican girl, right?"

"She wouldn't let me go. She made me stay there and sleep in Gordon's bed."

"You boff her?"

"Shit, Mae."

"I'm the jealous type," she kidded him.

"I woke up in the morning to find Gordie with his gun up my goddamn nose."

Mae laughed.

"You don't believe me? Check my underwear. I've been the long way over the hill and seen me my share of weird individuals, but Gordie boy is somethin' special. It wouldn't of surprised me a bit to see him shoot a bullet up my nose."

Again Mae laughed.

"Thanks, you cunt." Beef got to his knees and made a gun barrel of his finger. " 'Get out of my bed,' he says, whispering so I can hardly hear him."

"Didn't want to wake up his mama," said Mae.

"Shit, she was so knocked out with those pills she takes the place coulda burned down around her."

"Did you get out of his bed?"

"I got out of the apartment. I don't trust that son-of-a-bitch with that gun. I trust her way beyond what I trust him. She's just a lot of talk. He don't say nothin'."

"He probably thought you were boffin' dear old Mom."

"You know, I think he did . . . does. I tried to tell him that sure ain't the case. She don't even want it."

"You ask her?"

"You can tell she don't."

"How come?"

"Maybe she figures she's had her share."

Mae laughed.

"I don't know," he said. "She's got a lot on her mind. Lonely. She's afraid loneliness will kill her. Hell, I know what all of that is about. That's why I put up with it."

"What about the wife?" asked Mae.

"I never even seen her."

"She puts up with it?"

"I guess so. I guess she don't have much choice. Ginny said she was married once before, so maybe she figures this is her last chance."

"These people," said Mae, "these friends of yours, they make trouble for themselves. They bring it on themselves."

"That don't make it any less hard."

He rubbed her calves. He massaged her feet between his massive hands.

"Ah, baby, that feels so good," she said.

She bent forward to hold for a moment his cock, limp and resting, as a gesture of gratitude. Then she lay back on the bed.

"One of these days," she said, "I'm gonna buy a chest of drawers, if I can find one in pretty good shape."

"What's wrong with this here one?" said Beef, pointing to the bureau against the wall.

"Aw, that one's no good. I'm talkin' about one of my own, that I can keep my underwear in and things."

It was her own apartment and as such rose above the total

cheerlessness of the room in the Folding he had moved out of. Nothing in it, however, belonged to her, save for the large calendar on the wall that displayed a small portrait of every U.S. President. Even that she got for free, but she had already determined she would take it with her when she moved on.

"Sometimes I wonder why I hang around," he said on his way to the bathroom. "I should go on down the road."

"I've been thinking of Utah," she said.

It was a state that held no fascination for him. "Why Utah?"

"I don't know. People don't drink so much in Utah. They're all Mormons or something."

Mae was often cold. Her blanket was safety-pinned to the corners of her sheet to cut down the chances of its slipping away during the night. With Beef in her bed, she pressed against his huge warm back. When he stepped out of it, she huddled next to the heat register and waited for him.

He came out of the bathroom saying, "I should tell them all to kiss my rosy red ass. Maybe not in those words."

"Do it then."

"I'm gonna do it. You think I'm gonna hang around with a couple of old ladies with wild schemes on their mind all the time? Who the hell am I?"

Mae was sniffling. She hugged herself and shivered.

"A lot of talk," he said. "Talk, talk, talk. Whaddaya think?"

"If you want to know what some people will do, you're talkin' to the wrong chick. I never been able to figure it out."

"A lot of talk."

"C'mere and give me a hug, will you?"

Beef enfolded her in his arms. "Thing is, I really like the old gal. I worry about her. You know the way you like some people, even though they're gonna give you headaches? It's like God tappin' you on the shoulder and sayin', 'You're it.' What we oughta do is get out of the game, pull up stakes and head for Utah, you and me." He added, to delay their departure, "We'll become Mormons."

She was quiet for a moment. Maybe she hadn't heard.

"Sooner or later you'd take off," she said at last, "stickin' me with the overdue rent."

"I ain't like that."

Mae looked at him.

"Not anymore," he said.

"Let's get back in bed, okay? I'm freezing."

10

Colorado College was playing its first home football game of the season, and Gordon went to see it. He *said* that was where he was going, but Ginny had her doubts because he wormed out of taking the rest of the family along. So she called a cab and the three of them went after him, to see if he was taking Maria to the game. Gordon was married, that was a clear and legal fact, but Ginny hoped to convince him to travel the paths of annulment or divorce that she knew well herself to be easy. For his part, Gordon rather liked the idea of being married. He found himself at greater ease with the other men on the force, now that he was married like them. He began to anticipate the birth of a son, his own special act of fathering. Most important, he was becoming affectionate. He had brought his wife to orgasm once, in the common manner. He hoped that if he could keep his mother at stalemate until the baby was born, she would be won over by grandmaternal instincts, and be powerless against the new Gordon.

It was clear to Beef the night of the game that Ginny had suffered a setback in her battle for control of her son.

"My philosophy," said Beef to ease Ginny Mom's suffering, "is that every setback is a lesson learned."

"A setback is a setback. Have enough of them and you're out of business, simple as that."

"Won't believe it," said Beef.

"The more setbacks you have, the more desperate you are to succeed. And let me tell you, desperation is an enemy."

"Now, *that* I know for a fact. Any pool shooter knows that."

Beef relished these intelligent discussions. Mae never wanted to talk about anything important.

Ginny paid for the tickets and bought Mrs. Lister a bag of warm peanuts, which she nibbled like a squirrel even though she knew her digestive system was not equal to them.

For the entire first quarter they walked the track around the field, searching the bleachers in hope of finding Gordon with his arm around his wife. Ginny said that when they found them she would grab Maria by the hair and drag her down the steps of the bleachers. Beef said, "Now, now." Mrs. Lister worried her peanuts.

"Gordie's going to be twenty-five soon," said Ginny. "That's a milestone in a boy's life, and a crisis for his mother. God, his twenty-first birthday was just awful."

"My, the years fly, don't they?" said Mrs. Lister.

"Only if you let them, old lady, only if you let them."

"You don't have to be mean."

"What are you getting Gordie for his birthday?" asked Beef.

"You're being impertinent today, Bomba."

"I don't mean no offense."

"I don't have to call you for impertinence. For that I can dial a number at random."

The two women searched in earnest, but Beef found himself becoming interested in the game. He had not played since the service and his dream of becoming a pro was no longer a dream, would soon no longer be even a memory.

They were an odd parade, like some esoteric object lesson on time, sex, and the generations: yesterday's hulking lineman with Mother on one arm, Granny on the other, both struggling to keep from flying when he became aroused by the action on the gridiron. They passed in front of the same fans for the third time, looking up at their faces, and they were greeted by uniform expressions of incredulity and ripples of mocking laughter.

By the end of the first quarter Ginny was convinced that Gordon was not in the stadium. He had told her another lie just to get out of the house, to service that south-of-the-border bitch.

"Maybe he likes to sleep with pregnant women," she said. "There are men like that. I think it's disgusting. Do you think he's doing it to spite me?"

"Is he a spiteful boy?" asked Beef.

"I know that's why he married her in the first place. I told him not to, so he did. I should have insisted that he marry her, maybe then he wouldn't have."

"Reverse psychology, they call it," he said.

They took a seat in the bleachers to rest their tired feet. Mrs. Lister feared that one day the overexertion of keeping up with Ginny Wynn and Bomba would kill her.

"I need at least ten of them now to get to sleep," said Ginny, "and when I do I sleep so badly."

"You better take it easy on those things," said Beef.

"He doesn't care," she said.

Beef was well into the game now and as he watched the action he explained the positions and object of the contest to the two ladies. At times he became excited and shouted and jabbed them both in the ribs, once knocking frail Mrs. Lister off the bleacher seat and onto the back of another spectator.

"A bit of deportment, please, Bomba," said Mrs. Lister, nestling down again.

Catching Beef's enthusiasm, the two ladies could not help becoming involved in the game themselves. They *oof*-ed whenever someone was soundly blocked or tackled, they rose to their feet when the others did, they seconded Beef's displeasure at an official's call. In between, Ginny talked into Beef's unlistening ears about Gordon's extravagant gift of a TV set to Maria, the check stub for which she had found while looking through Gordie's checkbook.

"She better enjoy it while she can," said Ginny.

"Huh?" asked Beef, responding to the threatening tone.

"Once he does leave her she's going to find it hard to get credit in this town."

"How come?"

"Well, I've gone to all the department stores and a number of smaller merchants. Told 'em not to let her charge anything because it would only go to dope and nigger boys."

"Aw, Ginny, I wish you hadn't done that," said Beef. "What if she finds out?"

"She knows. I told her."

"You told her?"

"One of the benefits of insomnia is that three o'clock in the morning means nothing to you."

"You better watch yourself, Ginny. She can make a complaint to the phone company."

"The phone company? Do you think that at this stage in my life there's a way in which the phone company can intimidate me?"

"I hope you don't do it every night."

"If I miss one, I make it up the next. Why shouldn't I?"

"Well, it don't seem to be doin' much good."

She sighed. "No, no, it doesn't."

Beef pulled a pint of Old Grand-Dad from inside his jacket and was about to take a nip. He handed the bottle to Ginny and said, "Sorry, ladies first."

Ginny looked at the bottle disapprovingly. She wrinkled her nose. "Bomba, I'm surprised at you."

Beef took a swig and said, "Just to keep the chill off." He handed the bottle to Mrs. Lister and said, "Missus?"

Mrs. Lister took it and said to Ginny, "It *is* cold out here."

She put the bottle to her lips and tilted it. She shuddered once, handed the bottle back to Beef, and fanned her mouth, trying to cool it.

"Oh, my," she said, "I see stars."

"Well, if you two aren't a *sight,*" said Ginny.

Beef and Mrs. Lister passed the pint back and forth like two old drinking buddies until it was empty. Beef dropped the dead soldier through the bleachers to the ground. By game's end, Mrs. Lister was fast asleep, sitting in an upright position, her head against Beef's shoulder. Beef had to carry her out to catch a cab, an encore comedy for the delighted spectators.

They stretched her out on the back seat of the cab, her head on Ginny's lap, her feet on Beef's. They were driven to Maria's apartment, and there on the corner was Gordon's car.

They helped Mrs. Lister out of the cab. Ginny paid the driver and walked over to the car. She brought her handbag back and slammed the roof with it. She unlocked the door and they put Mrs. Lister in the back seat.

"You'd better stay here with her, Bomba."

"Where're you going?"

"Why, I'm going to see why Gordie lied to me, naturally."

"Don't start up a lot of trouble, Ginny Mom, it ain't worth it."

"Stay with Mrs. Lister," she said, and she walked away toward the apartment house.

Beef got into the front seat of the car.

A light was on in the living room. Ginny rapped on the door, her rage falling over her like handfuls of rice at a wedding. She looked into her handbag for a possible weapon. She found a ball-point pen and gripped it tightly, determined to ram it into Maria's throat as soon as she opened the door.

But no one answered her knock. She rapped louder and said, "I know you're in there. Open the door this instant!"

The landlady stuck her head out of her door and said, "Leave the young people alone."

"This is a family matter, dear landlady, thank you very much."

Gordon finally opened the door. His clothes looked hastily put on. He was not wearing shoes or socks. He was exasperated to see his mother there. "Mother, we cannot go on like this."

Maria's voice came from behind him. "Let her in, darling."

In the car, Beef said to Mrs. Lister, "Every family has its squabbles, ain't?"

"It's just the way people are," she said, like an agreeable drunk.

"My own family's a mess. I gotta admit it."

"But it's awful to live alone. There's nothing to keep you from getting bored."

Beef turned and looked for Ginny. Evidently she had gained entrance.

"Ginny, though," he said, "she don't know when to stop."

"She's a go-getter."

"Like saying she wants to kill old Maria. She shouldn't talk like that. Somebody might take her serious."

"She *is* serious."

"C'mon!"

"You don't know Ginny."

"I seen enough movies to know that when you murder someone you do it in a way so they don't find out it was you done it."

But it made Beef think. Anyone who ever slept under a newspaper knows that the world's gone crazy.

"I'm gonna see what's keeping her." He got out of the car and walked to the apartment.

By the time he turned the corner and faced the units, the meeting had gone to invective. "You scheming little bitch!" screamed Ginny. He could hear Gordon's voice, high-pitched like a frightened child's, but he could not distinguish his words. The landlady opened her window when she saw Beef and said, "I'm going to call the police. I won't have this sort of thing."

"Don't do that," he said. "She's leaving now."

Ginny stormed toward him, but she turned and stamped her foot and called, "Gordon!"

Gordon came out of the apartment carrying one shoe. He stopped to try to put it on. Maria appeared behind him and stopped, framed by the doorway. Beef felt his heart rise. Inevitably, he compared her to Mae, oppressed by the betrayal.

"Maria," Beef whispered, like a lover.

"Come on, Gordon!" Ginny shouted shrilly.

"Mother, keep your voice down," said Gordon, in a forced whisper.

"Well, hurry up."

"Gordon," said Maria, "you can't have a wife and a mother in the same person." Professionally, she had often been an objective third party to other family disputes. She tried to bring the same objectivity to this one, but here she ran the risk of victimization and all prior training became useless.

Beef heard her voice for the first time. He wanted to lose himself in it.

"I will leave Gordon to interpret *that* remark for himself," said Ginny, sensing a victory of sorts.

Gordon looked up from tying his shoelace, a pained and indignant look on his face. "That remark wasn't necessary, Maria. I'm doing the best I can."

"You're doing what she tells you."

"She's not always like this," said Gordon. "I'll take her home."

"He was never deceitful before he met you," said Ginny.

"You provided the need," said Maria, sick of being bullied.

"He learned that from you, you little slut."

"Other things, Mrs. Wynn, he learned other things from me." Her voice cracked. "Things you couldn't teach him, things you made sure to drive out of him, to make him helpless."

"Well, I . . ."

"Look," said Gordon, "let's just stop now before one of us says something we're sorry for."

"Gordon, if you go now, you'll despise yourself for it," said Maria, pleading, as much for him as for the both of them.

"Listen to that, Gordie, that's your so-called *wife*. She'd like to see me dead."

Maria lashed out. "Isn't the feeling mutual!"

"There!" screamed Ginny. "I told you!"

"Maria, what a thing to say."

She leaned against the doorframe. Beef wanted to engulf her in his arms.

"Why wouldn't I?" she said, on the edge of exhaustion. "She threatens me every day. Oh, Gordon, make her stop. I can't stand it anymore."

Gordon walked back to her. Beef wanted him to stay and yet

he wanted her for himself, if only in dreams.

"I will, I promise," said Gordon. "I have to get her away from here, calm her down. I'll call you tomorrow."

"Stay!" she shouted. Then softly, "Please stay."

"I can't, look at her."

Ginny stamped her foot and said, "That's enough! I want to go home."

Gordon left Maria crying in the doorway.

Beef saw her cover her face with her hands. He wanted to punch Gordon.

They walked past him, toward the car. Beef looked at Gordon with contempt. He took the first step toward Maria. He wanted in some way to comfort her, to offer her support, to offer her whatever she would have from him. She saw him move toward her. Their eyes met. Beef recognized the fear in her face and he stopped short, asking for no more than the right to protect her. Crying, she slowly backed into her apartment and shut the door.

He was sure he had fallen in love with her.

"Bomba, come along!" snapped Ginny.

Automatically, he turned and trotted after her.

11

Beef enjoyed all the symptoms of an adolescent in love. He was reminded of when life was truly felt in the deepest parts, when one dreamily submitted to total surrender, unreasonable, unexplainable, unconditional surrender, not caring should it prove painful.

She was always in his thoughts, but frequently there was room for nothing else. He yielded cheerfully to the power of her presence, devoting himself to it. Sometimes it would come upon him as he roofed a house, and he would stop his work and gaze over the neighboring rooftops as though they were so many stepping-stones.

Although he was not unwilling to make love to Mae, he had lost the desire. She seldom initiated their lovemaking anyway, and he remained free to dream. He found himself falling asleep in her presence. He told her he might be coming down with the flu.

He hoped that Maria had not had many lovers. He wanted to be the one she would remember. Her husband Gordon did not count. He was an insect, a slug. Beef wanted to squash him under his foot.

When Ginny approached him with a new solution to her

problems, Beef quickly agreed to help. No one was going to kill Maria, not with him around. Others would die first, he promised ominously. He did not tell Ginny this, however. As far as she was concerned he was still the slow-witted Salvation Army day worker become roofing man, living illicitly with a snaggletoothed bar-maid above the Goodyear tire shop. That fit his plans better than having her know his true identity: a man in love. His goal? To cherish.

He played the dummy. He drove her and Mrs. Lister to Pueblo, the seat of the neighboring county, knowing they were about to commit a felony. But he was smart enough to know that if it kept Ginny away from Maria a felony was but a minor risk to take. And would a dummy be able to big-deal a hundred-dollar price for the job?

"Didn't you ever hear of marriage by proxy," said Ginny Wynn, "where they get a substitute to stand in and get married for somebody else?"

"Yeah, sure," said Beef, watching the road ahead of him as he drove.

"Well, this is annulment by proxy. I guess when you come right down to it," she continued, "they'd probably prefer you to do it the proper way, but, hell, Bomba, you never did anything the least bit *improper?*"

"I gotta admit I have, but nine times outa ten I wound up with a world of hurt from it."

Mrs. Lister sat quietly in the back seat looking off to the Rockies and her memories.

"Bomba, the little improper things in life are what keeps it spinning around. The first man who threw chili in the beans was doing something improper. And he wasn't even getting any one hundred bucks."

"Got some good eats, though, didn't he?" said Beef, laughing and shaking his head.

She rumpled his hair.

He felt the familiar sense of comradeship and anxiety that always foreran any illegitimate enterprise. "Why do we have to go to another county?" he asked. "That's what I'd like to know. What's wrong with the Springs?"

"Oh, *Bomba,*" said Ginny, exasperated.

"Yes, oh, *Bomba,*" said Mrs. Lister, aping her.

"We've got to protect Gordie's reputation, don't we? Now, all you got to do is look like a young fellow who was tricked into marrying an old bag like me and now sure is sorry about it."

"Hey, hold on there, Ginny Mom, let's back up a little there. You ain't no old bag. You got a couple polkas left in you yet."

She put a maternal hand on his knee. "You're sweet. Look sorry anyway. Don't say a thing unless you're asked a question and then answer yes or no as seems sensible for the situation. Same goes for you, Auntie, don't you volunteer a thing."

Mrs. Lister began to get excited about her role in the venture.

"Just remember, Bomba, your name is Gordon Wynn, W-y-n-n. And I'm your wife Maria."

"Who am I again?" asked Mrs. Lister.

"Why, you're my aunt, dear."

In the Pueblo County Courthouse, amid the trappings of justice, Beef felt the usual pain at the base of his stomach, knowing it was too late for out, but encouraged at least by the greater role he was playing in Maria's safety.

Mrs. Lister was as nervous as he, but Ginny was perfectly at ease and chatted brightly with the lawyer.

Finally the judge called, "Wynn versus Wynn."

The lawyer stood and said, "That is ready, your honor."

103

Beef was called to the witness stand, and he trudged there like the accused, expecting a long contract from a judge who was sick to death of his type. He had never seen a civil matter.

The clerk swore him in and asked, "Your name is Gordon Wynn?"

"Yes," he said, and in that breath he had committed perjury for the woman he loved and $100 to spend on her, if she would let him.

The lawyer said, "This matter, if I may say to the court, comes on pursuant to a stipulation and waiver, which is on file herein." Then he turned to Beef and said, "Mr. Wynn, you are the plaintiff in this action for an annulment of your marriage to Maria Wynn, is that true?"

"The what, sir?" asked Beef.

"The plaintiff. You are seeking the annulment, isn't that correct?"

"Yeah, that's right."

"You and Maria did go through a formal marriage ceremony at Colorado Springs, Colorado, is that true?"

"Yes, sir."

"You and she never lived together as man and wife, is that true?"

"Yes, sir."

"As I understand it, when you questioned her in regard to that she said she just wanted to be married but she never intended to go through with the marriage? Is that true and correct?"

"Yes, sir," said Beef.

"Had you known that she intended to never live with you as man and wife, Mr. Wynn, would you have ever married Mrs. Wynn?"

Beef asked for a repeat of the question and then answered, "No, sir."

The lawyer turned to the judge and said, "Well, I think that is all, your honor."

"The decree is granted," said the judge, without lifting his eyes from his bench.

In the car, though she had been somber as could be during the court proceedings, Ginny bounced up and down on the seat and clapped her hands like a little girl. "We did it!" she cried. "We did it! At last!" She threw her arms around Beef and kissed him. "You were just fine, Bomba. What a load off my mind. At last, that stupid marriage is over."

"You're sure that's legal?" asked Beef, knowing full well it was not and knowing there was now another county he must stay out of. Worth it.

"Legal, smegal, in a couple of days I'll have a piece of paper in my hand that will say to anyone who sees it that my Gordie is not married to that bitch."

Beef wished that he could believe in that false piece of paper as much as Ginny would. He wanted Maria free of that cop, her husband.

"I'm sure glad this here worked out," he said, "and everybody's happy as hell now. I believe you got something to give me, Ginny Mom."

She took a bill out of her purse, folded it, and slipped it into his shirt pocket, patting the spot after she had placed the bill.

He pulled out the bill with two fingers and looked at it. "This is a twenty. We said a hundred."

"Lordy, boy, you don't think I carry that kind of cash around, do you? A little old lady like me? Somebody'd hit me over the head for it. Don't you worry, Ginny will make good on the balance."

Beef put the twenty back into his breast pocket. Twenty cents on the dollar. People have been buying him all his life for twenty cents on the dollar.

12

The dissolution of her son's marriage existed only in Ginny's mind and, fraudulently, in the Pueblo County Hall of Records. In a new apartment unknown to his mother, Gordon continued to divide his domestic life, against daily conciliatory promises. Ginny felt the need to tell someone about the annulment, to reaffirm the truth of what she had done.

In Gordie's dresser drawer she discovered, for the second time, a form for a change of beneficiary for his insurance policy, naming Maria in place of her. She had destroyed the first one. Furious, she destroyed this one as well, but not before she discovered that it contained Maria's new address. She would go over there and prove a thing or two.

"What's the point, Ginny Mom?" asked Beef, who, of course, had to come, along with Mrs. Lister. By this time Mrs. Lister had begun to take her impersonation seriously and thought of Ginny as her dead sister's eldest girl.

"You should let Gordie and Maria come to some kind of agreement. Water seeks its own level," he counseled, relying once again on a phenomenon he adored, taught him by his father, who while in his cups imagined himself a plumber and a poet.

"I'd like to stick her head under water," said Ginny; even harmless aphorisms suggested weapons.

They walked arm in arm, Beef in the middle. Mrs. Lister slowed them down. At one point they had to stop entirely so that she could catch her breath.

"Do you want I should carry you piggyback?" asked Beef.

"That would look silly," said Ginny.

He bent over and Mrs. Lister crawled upon his broad back. Mrs. Lister ignored all stares and jeers except for when she shouted after a carful of roaring teen-agers, "Wait till you get old! See how funny it is then!"

The landlady was a landlady. All three had had lifetimes of commerce with the type: suspicious, snoopy, self-righteous. Their eyes always narrowed when you mentioned a dog, a cat, a parakeet. They were experts on cleanliness, physical and moral. Noise was an invention and pastime of those on welfare. They were wells of tea and sympathy until the rent came due and then they were as hard and dry as desert rocks. Ginny and Mrs. Lister knew them so well, and had dreamt so many times of becoming landladies themselves.

Ginny identified herself as Gordon Wynn's mother, surprising him with a visit. She wanted to be let into the apartment to wait for him. The landlady was skeptical, even after Ginny presented identification. She called the owner of the apartment house and asked for permission to go into the apartment.

"You're a very cautious landlady," said Ginny.

"In this business, you got to be."

"Funny, as cautious as you seem to be you don't know that they are not married. They are living in sin."

"I don't know anything about that. Don't care to."

When Ginny and Beef followed the landlady up the stairs in

the courtyard to the balcony facing the apartment, Mrs. Lister stayed behind. She avoided stairs whenever possible.

She unlocked the door and said, in the custom of landladies everywhere, "It's quite a nice apartment for the price."

"Yeah?" said Beef. "What's it rent for?" He had a longing to move in and assume the rent.

Ginny brushed them aside and raced into the living room. She saw the hated TV set, comfort to the enemy, and wanted nothing more than to put her foot through it.

The landlady watched her apprehensively, with growing awareness of the mistake it was to allow this woman and this man into one of her units.

"Easy now, Ginny Mom," said Beef. "Relax now."

She ran into the bedroom and threw open the closet doors. "Look here," she said. "One, two, three shirts. One pair of pants. Does that sound like a permanent resident to you? You are mistaken, my dear landlady, you have no Mr. and Mrs. Wynn here."

Beef looked at the bed. Her pillow, he thought. This is where she lies down to sleep.

Ginny had in her hands one of Maria's dresses. She held it at the neck, as though preparing to tear it to shreds.

"What's going on?" said the landlady. "I thought you wanted to surprise your son."

"I wanted to surprise *you*, dear landlady. You don't have any Mr. and Mrs. living here. You've got a beaner shacking up."

Unnoticed in the tension, Beef filched a barrette from the top of the dressing table and dropped it into his shirt pocket.

"Look, put the dress back and come downstairs and I'll make you some tea," said the landlady, with the calmness one musters when faced with a couple of lunatics. "I'm afraid you're going to tear the dress, and that wouldn't be nice. I'm responsible for this apartment, and I think we should go downstairs for some tea."

"That sounds like a good idea to me," said Beef. He wanted to make good his escape with the treasure in his pocket.

"Tear the dress? I'll tear out her heart and feed it to the dogs!"

"Ginny Mom," said Beef, "shit on that talk." He took the dress away from her and hung it in the closet, furtively running his hand over it as he shut the door.

"I'd like to use the bathroom, please," said Ginny softly.

The landlady seemed swept by a wave of revulsion. "Come downstairs and you can use mine," she said.

"But I need a bathroom now."

"Well, I think you can hold it in for the minute it takes to go downstairs," said the landlady. "I'll make you some tea."

Ginny did not use the bathroom; the landlady did not make any tea.

When they got back to the landlady's apartment they saw Mrs. Lister sitting in a corner talking to herself, her lips moving slightly.

Ginny turned to the landlady and said, "They are not married."

"All I know is they came here as Mr. and Mrs. and he paid the rent and as far as I'm concerned they're just another couple in one of the units."

"Then you don't know very much. Did you know she takes dope?"

"Seems like a sweet girl to me," said the landlady.

Ah, the sweetest of all, thought Beef, and beautiful too.

"She goes down to Fort Carson and sleeps with GIs," said Ginny.

"I think you better go now," said the landlady.

"I think so too," said Beef.

"I've half a mind to buy this place and fire you and give my

110

aunt here your job. You're not a very good manager."

"Well, fine, you do that," said the landlady. "Good-bye."

"Maybe you'd like to go down to Pueblo and look at the courthouse records and see for yourself that their marriage was annulled. She married him just to brag to her friends that she hooked a white man, so he dumped her."

Beef was stunned and frightened to hear her talk freely of their crime, a bona fide felony that could put them all behind bars.

"Well, I don't believe that either," said the landlady.

"Why don't you just see for yourself?" insisted Ginny.

"Look, if you don't go, I'm calling the police," she said, at the end of her patience.

"Oh, I'll get her," said Ginny. "And I'll get you." Then a very grand gesture involving extended hands and a body stretched to its limit, a presidential gesture, an evangelistic gesture. "I'll get everyone!"

"The hell with it, Ginny Mom," said Beef.

"I will kill her if it's the last thing I do!" she yelled.

"Talkin' like that'll just get you all curdled up in the stomach."

"She means it," said Mrs. Lister.

But she fails to reckon with me, thought Beef.

There are things sadder than a man who lurks outside the apartment of the woman he loves, knowing she is inside with her husband, whom she loves instead of him, unaccountably. There are no doubt numerous things sadder than this, and Beef tried to think what they might be as he withdrew into the shadows, that night of the day he had gone into her apartment with Ginny.

Inside, Gordon and Maria stood on opposite sides of the kitchen counter. Gordon was in uniform and Maria wore a robe. She was trying to tell him something, but apparently was having difficulty finding the words. She clasped her hands in front of her, struggled for her breath, then came out with it. Beef recognized the pained expression on Gordon's face. He asked her a question, she answered it. He asked another. She replied. He had heard enough, lowering his head into his hands more in embarrassment than despair, but she had more to say . . . more to say . . . until she cried out. She was leaning over the sink, crying into a paper towel. The man would not comfort her. He would not get off his stool. He would not take his head out of his hands, nor his unhappy wife into his arms.

Beef, who had never hurt anyone deliberately, said to himself, "If he don't stop making her cry, I'm gonna kill the son-of-a-bitch."

BOOK 2

BOOK I

1

Wednesday, the day before Thanksgiving, the district attorney of Pueblo County, Ralph Ferguson, received a visit from attorney Roger Glover, who said that he had a hypothetical case to try out on him.

The district attorney, "Fergie" to his friends and occasionally to the press, leaned back in his chair and smiled. "Hypothetical" cases to a lawyer informally consulting the DA were like "this friend of mine" to a neurotic consulting a psychiatrist at a cocktail party. He hooked one thumb over his old-fashioned suspenders, crossed a leg over a knee, and scratched his ankle.

"Go ahead," he said to Glover.

"Well, supposing a man and a woman, along with a much older woman, an aunt, come into an attorney's office and want an annulment of their marriage. The lawyer prepares the papers, they go to court, and the decree is granted, because they admit to never living together as man and wife and she admits she had no intention of doing so."

"Go on," said the district attorney.

"The lawyer then learns that the two people who got the annulment were not even married, were not who they claimed to be. They were getting the annulment for another couple, against their desires, that is, against the desires of the couple that actually *are* married."

"That's called a fraudulent annulment," said the DA, who relished words like home cooking and wasted not.

"What would you do, as DA, if this annulment took place in Pueblo County?"

"I'd prosecute," said Ferguson.

"What if one of the people involved was a young police officer?"

"I'd still prosecute. I've never believed in protecting cops, or anyone else. That's what keeps butchers in hospital operating rooms."

"The officer is one of the innocent parties."

"Then he has nothing to worry about."

"The thing is, Ralph, it was his mother who got it."

Ferguson rocked forward and leaned his arms on his desk. The situation was no longer just a fraudulent annulment. It was a symptom, a warning. "I think you better tell me what you know," he said.

Roger Glover folded his hands over his stomach. So much for hypothetical cases.

"It seems this young policeman from the Springs got married to a girl his mother disapproved of. Old story, right? Happens hundreds of times every day, right? Only in this case Mother is so steamed she gets somebody to impersonate her son, she impersonates her own daughter-in-law, an old crony impersonates her aunt, and they come down here to Pueblo and annul the marriage. I think it's her way of making the strongest complaint possible against her son's choice of wives."

There is a stronger complaint possible, thought Ferguson, but he said, "Who granted the decree?"

"Barry Winston. I've just come from his office. He thinks it's possible to call her on contempt of court and save the son from what could be a bad blow to his reputation and career. It's a felony, you know."

Ferguson smiled. "Who are these people, Roger?"

"Well, that's part of my problem. I was the lawyer they contacted, as you've guessed, I'm sure. I think this falls under the client-lawyer confidence."

"In this case, I believe not."

"Have you researched the point?"

"I will," said Ferguson.

"I've talked to the son. Naturally, he was terribly upset about it. My feeling is that ethically I've done what I'm obliged to do. It's now his duty to see Winston and you. He told me he would see Judge Winston Monday, after the Thanksgiving weekend, and I'm sure Winston will send him right over here."

Ferguson flipped the leaves on his calendar pad to the following Monday and wrote "Annulment."

"What's this policeman's name, Roger?"

"He'll be coming to see you Monday."

"Just in case he doesn't."

"I can't tell you, Ralph. It's probably a whacky old possessive mother. The woods are full of them. We'd be sick if it finished the kid as a cop."

2

Beef got Tessie Maguire to fill in for Mae at the Ponderosa Pines and together they honky-tonked the night away. "Let's go out and have some fun, dammit," was Beef's proposal. They shot eight ball, they threw darts, they rolled dice. They tried their luck at the bowling machine and the shuffleboard. Beef won beers for the house, first by swallowing a whole hard-boiled egg in one clean gulp and then by lifting a barstool upright from the floor by only one of its four legs. They danced the pony. "If that's a pony," yelled another honky-tonker, "I'm dyin' to see the bull moose!" They laughed. "See," said Beef, "I knew I could make you laugh." They sang. "Good-bye, cruel world, I'm off to join the circus . . ." They staggered from one joint to another, supporting each other along the way. They ended the night weaving in front of a bar with no name, sharing a pickled pork hock. "Live life to its fullest, that's my philosophy," said Beef, licking his fingers. "The hell with heartaches."

Somehow he got her home, but in the darkness they both stumbled and sprawled across the floor. Mae grumbled, "Oh, fuck," and Beef tried to suppress his laughter.

They lay there, neither bothering to get up to turn on a light.

"You wanna cup of coffee?" Beef asked her. She did not reply. They lay quietly for a few more minutes.

"Mae, she won't let up." The joy of the evening fell out of his voice.

Mae said nothing.

"She ain't foolin' around, let's face it, sooner or later she'll find somebody who'll do it. Well, I can't let her. Wouldn't matter to me if Maria was as ugly as a mud fence, I still wouldn't stand by and let her die. But *some*body is gonna die soon, and I have a feelin' I'll have a hand in it. Don't get me wrong on this, I never killed anybody in my life. I never even liked huntin' much when I was a kid. Fishin' was for me. Hell, a fish don't feel nothin'. But I wonder, is there a killer in me too, Mae? That ain't like me. I'll tell you what I'm like. I like to have fun. Didn't we have fun tonight? Didn't we? What I'd like outa life is two nights a week like this here, maybe Wednesday and Saturday, and a good steady job that I can count on and that I can show what I can do, and a decent woman to come home to . . . a couple kids . . . I'd like to buy a pickup and take them all campin'. You know, Mae, I never voted. Never had a bank account or a listing in the phone book. So what, right? So something, is my whole point here. Look, is there a killer somewhere in me, Mae? Is there a killer somewhere in everybody? Mae?"

He took her cheeks between his hands and turned her face toward him, her mouth like a fish's. She looked like every other girl in his life, including the one he married. "Mae?" She was unconscious.

Mae had not been invited to Thanksgiving dinner at Ginny Mom's. Since the meal was to be served at one o'clock and Mae always slept deeper into the afternoon than that, Beef slipped out of the apartment alone, promising himself to take her to dinner that evening, when she would have a better stomach for it.

Mrs. Lister was there, as always, but Gordon was not, and he had promised he would be. "If he doesn't come . . ." said Ginny, ". . . if he doesn't come . . ." but she never said what would happen if he didn't come. And he didn't.

Her mashed potatoes were instant, her peas and her cranberry sauce were canned, her rolls were out of a cellophane package. But the turkey was her own show, and she had left it in the oven for as long as she dared. Gordon would evidently rather dine with his pregnant Mexican wife than with his mother, a preference Ginny found insulting.

Beef helped Mrs. Lister sit at the dining table. He uncorked a bottle of wine. "Ain't this nice?" he said. Ginny fetched the turkey. Hoping for the perfect bird, she opened the oven door, and like a dragon it belched a ball of fire at her. Frozen in the instant, Beef was struck by the sickening thought that life would be better for him, and Maria, and Gordon, and Mrs. Lister, if she were consumed by the flame.

Ginny slammed the open door shut, killing the fire, but her hair was still burning. She screamed, "They're trying to kill me!" Beef tore off the tablecloth and knocked over Mrs. Lister as he dived at Ginny, covering her head. Her screams were muffled under cover of the tablecloth. Mrs. Lister lay on the floor near her overturned chair, stunned from overexcitement and the pain of her own fall. Beef slowly removed the tablecloth from Ginny's head. Her eyebrows were singed away. What was left of her hair was man's length. The pungency of burned hair filled the room.

"They tried to murder me!" she cried. "You're both my witnesses!"

"It was an accident," said Beef. "Let me look at your neck,

Ginny Mom. Are you burned anywhere?"

Mrs. Lister had risen to her knees and from that posture began whimpering.

"She put him up to it," moaned Ginny. "He rigged that turkey. That's why he's not here. She'll pay for this!"

"My God, Ginny Mom, can't you see it was an accident!"

"Kill or be killed!" shrieked Ginny.

"You stop it!" said Beef and he slapped her face, dashing her into numbed silence. She lay on her side on the kitchen floor, eyes staring at nothing.

Mrs. Lister made it to her feet. She took her cane and in a daze started shuffling toward the door. Beef watched her until she left the apartment and shut the door behind her, without a word.

"I'm sorry, Ginny Mom," said Beef. "You were hysterical."

"Are you in it with them? Do your job and get it over with."

"Stop talking crazy. C'mon, get off the floor." He tried to lift her up, but she resisted. She wanted to lie where she had fallen, on the cold kitchen tile.

"Nobody loves me," she said.

"Gordie loves you. Relax."

"Nobody does."

"Gordie does," said Beef, "and in some cockamamie way I guess the hell *I* do."

It seemed to help her, if not him. "My pills," she said, "get my pills. I want to sleep."

Beef got them for her. He gave her a glassful of water. "Easy with those things," he said when he saw how many she was taking. He took the pill bottle and put it on the counter.

He got her a pillow and spread a blanket over her. "I want to sleep," she mumbled, burrowing under the blanket.

Beef waited until she was asleep. Then he dropped the mashed potatoes into a pot, poured the peas on top of the potatoes and the cranberry sauce on top of the peas. He twisted both drumsticks off the burned turkey and dropped them into the pot, which in twenty minutes sat on the bed between him and Mae, both of them bare-ass naked.

"Give thanks," he said.

"Thanks," said Mae.

Monday came and went, and the young policeman who was supposed to did not appear in the office of Pueblo's district attorney. Tuesday, Ralph Ferguson called Judge Barry Winston and asked him for the name of the people involved in the fraudulent annulment which took place in his courtroom. The judge refused, claiming a concern for the reputation of the young man, who had that morning conferred with him, and an uncertainty about the ethics involved. What he didn't say, but what the district attorney understood clearly, was that he considered Ralph Ferguson a ruthless prosecutor who took every minor crime committed in his district as a personal injury, who believed that the only sound way to prevent crime was to make the punishment for it quick and severe. There had been a running feud in the newspapers during Ferguson's entire tenure, twelve years, between the DA's office and the county judges, whom he accused of being lenient to the point of malfeasance.

He ended his fruitless conversation with Judge Winston and called Roger Glover, hoping to pressure him into revealing the names of the principals, since the cop he was so sure would contact the DA did not show. Roger Glover had gone on vacation and would be gone for a week.

"Chickenshit," said Ralph Ferguson. He drummed his fingers on the desk and said to himself, "So here I am. A felony's been committed in the county court. A cop knows. An attorney knows. A judge knows. It seems the only one who doesn't know is the district attorney."

He wrote a memo to a staff secretary to check the court records and make a list of all annulments granted during the previous two months. It was a bother, but conceivably, in the long run, worth it.

3

A wise gardener plants a patch separate, away from his main crop, a patch for the rabbits and other wild marauders. He makes a deal with them: This is your patch and you may eat from it freely. But venture into the main garden and you're dead, as a lesson to the others. And if the others don't learn the lesson, the patch will be taken away and you can all starve to death.

If God is a gardener, then the earth is his rabbit patch. If man had the power to do likewise, he would make a deal with cancer.

City planners are familiar with this principle and conscientiously, though discreetly, practice it. They know that any community, no matter how respectable, how scenic, how clean, is going to have its number of nasties. They need their square block. Give it to them and draw the borders clearly. Within this square the police will carry a light stick, but mind your skull should you truck outside. Citizens, go there if you must. Buy a temporary tour through blessed oblivion, purchase a moment's contact with warm flesh, double your money on the turn of a card or the angle of an eight ball. What you do there and see there, you leave there.

In the Springs the block formed by Nevada, Colorado, Tejon,

and Cucharras filled this need. It was right across the street from the courthouse.

The Panama Club was there, hip to hip with the Ponderosa Pines and the Elbow Room. Its only apparent distinction from the other two establishments was that instead of Hank Williams and Ernest Tubb, its jukebox spun out Jorge Negrete and José Alfredo Jiménez, to whose heartbreaking melodies patrons would add the excruciating Mexican song-laugh, followed by someone in the crowd yelling, "Call Immigration!"

On a busy Friday night the pursuit of happiness there approached carnage, and the interns who drew the duty that night approached their vigil with both dread and excitement, wondering what new surgical challenges might be sent them courtesy of the Panama Club.

Naturally there were those idealistic citizens of Colorado Springs who wanted the place closed. The police who came regularly to take pictures of the aftermath would tell the proprietor, Juan Barrajas, that he was skating on thin ice. The Liquor Control agents told him the same thing. He was skating on thin ice. He wondered what it meant.

Ginny Wynn had for some time been attracted to the Panama Club, as she was to the whole neighborhood, initially because Gordie had told her of the many arrests he made there. It gave her a thrill to think that her son was feared there. But beyond that, the Panama fascinated her for its own dark promises, and she wished she were a man so that she might openly dally in such places.

So it came as no small pleasure to learn that Juan Barrajas himself had been arrested, and by Gordon. It seemed that receipts from Coors beer were hardly enough to keep the Panama solvent, and other enterprises were demanded, specifically the sale of transistor radios previously burglarized from a local store.

The pinch was for receiving stolen property. Juan managed to make the bail and was back at his bar, but the outlook was that he would have to do some time.

Ginny wasted none of her own time. Her singed head wrapped in a bandana, eyebrows penciled in, she took Mrs. Lister to lunch on Wednesday to Howard's, because she knew that Howard's was closed on Wednesdays. Faced with the locked door, she suggested they walk down Colorado Avenue and find some other suitable place. They passed several places and wondered aloud that anyone could possibly put into his mouth any item that touched those grills.

They passed the Folding, where Beef lived when he first came to town. They turned the corner and soon were in front of the Panama Club.

"Let's go in here, Mrs. Lister."

"This doesn't look like a restaurant to me, Ginny."

"Well, maybe they'll know where to go around here for a good lunch."

Ginny tentatively opened the door. A curtain blocked the view of the interior, in the custom of bars like the Panama which appeal to every man's desire to know what's beyond the veil. From the inside, the curtain serves to keep natural light out of an unnatural atmosphere, no matter how many people move from outside to inside, inside to outside.

Ginny drew aside the curtain and ushered Mrs. Lister into the stale darkness.

Juan Barrajas was seated behind the bar washing beer glasses.

If misery is a destination, Juan wore all the directions on his face. His eyes were shadowed and watery from lack of sleep, from darkness, from smoke, from the things they had seen. His face, tight and deeply creased, was turning sallow. One side of his upper lip was twisted and on his chin was a one-inch scar. His hair was brittle black, turning gray. Tuberculosis had settled in his wasted body. He looked on the verge of his last mortal cry.

He automatically turned toward the rustle of the curtain. "Yes, ladies, what can I do for you?" He did not assume they had popped in for their first beer of the day.

"Do you serve coffee here, señor?" asked Ginny Wynn.

"Yes, I have coffee. Do you want to sit at the table?"

They sat next to the jukebox and Juan Barrajas served them coffee. He was pleased to have respectable people sitting in his establishment. He tried to smile at them. If he could have his way, he would have nothing but nice customers, ladies and gentlemen, but this was only desire, not reality.

Ginny looked up at him and said, "I hear you're in a bit of trouble."

Juan felt a cramp in his stomach. What's going to happen to me now, he wondered.

"Trouble, yes. I know about trouble. What do you know about it?"

Ginny opened her wallet and showed him a picture of Gordon in uniform. "My *hijo*," she said.

"This man, your son, is not my friend," said Juan.

"I have a message from him," said Ginny.

"What message?"

"There is a very bad woman. A bitch. A *puta*, who has made my son marry her."

"That is the message? I do not understand it."

Ginny took a sip of the bitter coffee.

"She has become a problem to him."

127

The old man shrugged.

"You have a problem too."

The old man cocked his head. When did he not have a problem, when in the course of nearly seventy years was there a day without a problem?

"Now you may have to go to prison."

"It is unfair!" said Juan. "I told them they could keep some stuff in my back room. I did not know it was not theirs. Then your son comes here . . ."

"You help him with his problem, he will help you with yours."

"He? Help me? It was him that did this to me."

"He will testify at your trial that you are innocent. He will fix it so there is no trial, so you are left alone."

"He can do this?" asked Juan hopefully.

"Is he not an officer of the police?"

"Why would he want to do that for Juan Barrajas?"

"He needs your help."

"What can I do?"

"This bitch, do you have some friends who would help me get her out of the way? I will pay well for the job."

There was a boy, Danny Yanez, who sometimes helped out at the bar. He had a friend, Rudy Montalvo, who was a fry cook once but quit.

"There are some boys," Juan told her. "I know them. I don't know if they want to talk to you or not."

"Could you ask them?"

"Yes, I will ask them to talk to you. I don't know if they will want to."

"I'll pay well. Can you ask for tomorrow, here?"

"I will ask them," said Juan. "That is all I will do. For this your son will . . . ?"

"Sí, sí," said Ginny, taking Mrs. Lister by the elbow and leaving quickly before he could change his mind.

Forty miles to the south Ralph Ferguson was reminding a girl named Peggy that she was to check the court records for annulments granted over the past two months. Peggy did not know he was in such a hurry for the information. She promised to put aside her other work and get right on it.

4

They met for lunch at Manitou Springs, near the hotel they went to as man and wife, when Maria thought they would have a good life together. She wondered now what made her believe it. She did not feel like eating and suggested a walk instead. They stopped at a window and inspected some Navajo turquoise rings. "Would you like one?" he asked.

"Gordon," she said, "it's not going to happen."

There was no need to ask what she was talking about. "Just for a while longer," he said.

"Have you done anything?"

"When the baby is born you'll see a miracle. You'll see her maternal instincts come out."

"She has more than her share of maternal instincts already."

"Is that supposed to be a joke?"

"She's sick, Gordon. I mean, my landlady can tell she's sick, why can't you? Her and Mrs. Lister and that horrid muscleman she keeps around."

"Bomba the Jungle Boy."

Maria shuddered. "Your mother is one thing, but that one . . . he frightens me."

"He's harmless. He's just a dumb drifter looking for a home. They mother him."

"There's a psychiatrist I know, I've talked to him about her."

"She's been to a psychiatrist."

Maria was surprised and encouraged. "What did he say?"

"That she was perfectly normal. I think he liked her."

She turned away from him. She felt like a woman in love with a married man. "I don't like knowing my mother-in-law can come and take away my husband any time she pleases."

"You saw what condition she was in that night. She was out of control."

"I'm practically in hiding."

"I'm doing what I can," said Gordon. "I want to make it work. I *have* to! What do you want me to do, lock her up?"

"Yes!" she yelled.

Gordon looked down at the sidewalk. "Toss her in the loony bin, right?"

"A hospital, Gordon, where sick people are cared for."

He had hoped for something to happen when he became a husband; he was sure it would, once he became the father of a son, who would be a boy like other boys, who would grow to be like other men.

When he did not speak, Maria said, "Maybe I should go to New Mexico. I have relatives there."

"Please, don't," he said.

"I don't have much of a choice."

"I'll do it," he said. "I'll do it and get it over with."

She turned around and faced the street. "When?" she asked.

For one horrible, unforgettable moment he wanted to push her through the storefront window. He quickly pulled her to him.

"Right away," he said. "I'll get the papers, I'll do whatever I have to do."

She took his hand in both of hers and laid it against her face.

Ginny and Mrs. Lister returned to lower Nevada Avenue and sat at the same table, next to the jukebox, whose internal workings were exposed to the examination of a repairman. A man was sweeping the floor, another was wiping down the bar. Helpers.

Juan Barrajas came out of the kitchen and walked to their table. Ginny tilted her head in the direction of the helpers. Juan nodded, affirmatively. Ginny rose and walked toward the bar, leaving Mrs. Lister at the table. Juan said to the helpers, "This is the cop's mother, who wanted to talk to you."

Rudy Montalvo leaned his broom against the wall. Danny Yanez came from behind the bar. Ginny tried to choose the dominant one, and thought it might be Montalvo because of his fresh good looks. The other was ugly. She threw an arm around each of them.

"*Muchachos!*" she said, leading them to stools. "Señor Barrajas, I want to buy these two boys a drink."

"I'll have a Pepsi," said Montalvo.

"Me too," said Danny Yanez.

"Pepsi it is for my two young *amigos*. How old are you boys?"

"Nineteen," said Montalvo.

"Twenty-six," said Yanez.

"Well, if you want my advice, get old quick. Youth is a curse."

Montalvo laughed politely and in two or three beats Yanez followed. Ginny guessed that Montalvo was the dominant one.

Juan served them and retreated to his kitchen, the favor done. He sat next to the stove and tried to think of other things.

Ginny sat at the bar, between the two helpers.

"You two boys interested in making some good money?" she asked.

"Juan said about a job," said Rudy Montalvo.

"You bet," said Ginny cheerfully.

"Your son is a cop, huh?"

"Gordon Wynn."

"I heard about him."

"I'm his mother."

"I heard he ain't too bad."

"What kind of job he want done?" asked Yanez.

She made no effort to lower her voice or conceal their conversation. "Well, there's this woman who tricked my son into marrying her. A real bitch with a bag full of tricks. I want to show you two *amigos* something."

From her purse she took a handful of check stubs and scattered them on the bar. Rudy Montalvo examined them like a junior accountant; Danny Yanez turned on his barstool to watch the jukebox repairman at his work and called to him, "Give us a few free ones, huh, when you go."

"Sure," said the repairman.

"These are checks that my son Gordon wrote out to her," said Ginny. "Payoffs."

"Sounds bad," said Montalvo, as a journeyman mechanic might say into the hood cavity of an old automobile out of his province.

"I'd like somebody to give her a good scare, know what I mean?"

"Old Goose here," said Montalvo, indicating Danny Yanez, "could scare the pants off of the Pope."

Ginny grabbed Yanez by the back of the neck and shook him playfully. "Goose, huh?"

133

Yanez smiled boyishly and Ginny saw in him a resemblance to Jerry Lewis. She mentioned it to him and he beamed and did a minute of his Jerry Lewis routine. Ginny laughed loudly. Rudy Montalvo, who had seen the routine many times, smiled indulgently and paternally.

"Think that'll scare your daughter-in-law?" asked Rudy.

"Well, if I wanted her to die laughing, old Goose here could do the job. But it's not exactly what I had in mind."

"What do you have in mind?"

"I'd like her out of the way . . . like far out of the way."

"You want us to kidnap her?"

There was nothing in his voice to indicate he was unwilling.

"*Amigo*, I want you to kill her."

"Oh, I see," said Montalvo.

Danny Yanez seemed to be listening but he had a difficult time shifting his attention from the fascinating work of the jukebox repairman. With all those wires, how could he know which did what?

"I'm the kind of woman who puts her cards on the table," said Ginny.

"This is good."

"Naturally, I expect you two boys to be as open and honest with me."

"You can trust us," said Montalvo. "What I want to know is, does your son . . . is he in favor of this?"

"Of course he is," said Ginny, "and I don't have to remind you he's an officer of the law."

"How come he ain't down here then?" asked Montalvo.

"Good God, boy! He's got a reputation to mind. If you were an officer, would you come down here to negotiate for yourself?"

Rudy admitted that he probably would not.

"Of course not."

Juan Barrajas took a cup of coffee to Mrs. Lister, who sat at her table alone, looking at Ginny and the two men, her lips moving slightly. He placed the coffee in front of her and whispered, "I think the boys will help her. Anyway, I did what she asked, didn't I?"

"Do you have a bathroom?" asked Mrs. Lister.

At the bar, Montalvo lowered his head toward Ginny and said, "What's the pay for this job?"

"Well, what do you think it's worth?"

"This is the sort of thing that should cost a lot of money," said Montalvo, as though wearing a white cap and giving her an estimate for painting a badly flaked porch. "Right away, we'd need some gloves and things, a weapon, a car . . ."

"I have the car, I have everything you'll need. I have . . ."

"I don't think we should use your car or anything, because we shouldn't give anyone a chance to link us together."

"Good thinking! What do you think of your pal here, Goose, isn't he smart?"

"If he's so smart, why ain't he rich?" said Danny Yanez, believing he had delivered the zinger of the week. He made a comic face and left the conversation to peer over the shoulder of the repairman. He could resist no longer.

"Talking about rich . . ." said Montalvo.

"Young fella, I am prepared to make you three thousand dollars richer by this job. *Mucho dinero.*"

"Mrs. Wynn, that's very nice, but you gotta remember that with a job like this, there's a lot of risk."

Montalvo had an appealing baby face and now seemed to pout, having to bargain with the mother of a cop.

"Well, you name a figure then."

135

"I think the job should be worth at least five thousand dollars."

"That's a lot of money, an awful lot of money." She thought about it. "But you're a good boy. I believe I can trust you."

"We'll keep up our end of the bargain," he promised.

"Okay, five thousand dollars, but I can't pay it all at once."

"Oh, that's all right, you can make payments."

"How about half when the job is done and half in three months?" asked Ginny.

"That's fine, only thing is we have to have a little now, to buy the things I said and everything. Like a hundred and a half, at least."

Ginny was hesitant to make a cash down payment.

"Don't worry, we'll deliver on our end," Montalvo reassured her.

She had that morning closed her savings account, pawned the last of her wedding rings, found the $7 she had hidden in various places about the kitchen, and sneaked $3 out of Gordie's wallet. Unless she overlooked a stray dollar or two on the bottom of her purse, the total came to $120.

"What's today?" said Rudy Montalvo. "Thursday? We'll probably do it over the weekend, so we would need the money like today."

"You wait right here."

Ginny went back to join Mrs. Lister. She looked into her handbag and counted the bills she had put there that morning. "Damn," she said. "Do you have any money, dearie?"

"The bathroom is *filthy*," whispered Mrs. Lister.

"Yes, yes, do you have any money?" Ginny reached across the table and took her purse.

The jukebox repairman gathered up his tools and left, making good on his promise to play a few free ones. An Anglo number with a heavy, hard beat began to play and Danny Yanez took the floor to do his famous Jerry Lewis dance imitation. Mrs. Lister covered her ears with her hands.

Ginny walked back to the bar and said, "Would you settle for a hundred and twenty-five? I can probably get another twenty-five dollars tomorrow."

Montalvo took the cash and said, "That's okay, just if you could give us half of what's left when we finish the job."

"I have a secret account in Denver. I'll wire and have it for you."

Montalvo gave a twenty-dollar bill to Danny Yanez and said, "We're gonna do the job on the witch, Goose. Save enough of this to buy us some gloves."

Yanez folded the bill into a tiny square. He popped it into his mouth, pulled his ear, and pretended to swallow it, rolling his eyes as it went down.

Ginny clapped him on the shoulder and said, "Boy, you should be on television!"

"Someday I'm gonna be!" declared Danny Yanez.

"All right, I think we better work out a plan," said Montalvo, and the three of them moved their heads closer together, Danny Yanez trying hard to act serious, but unable to keep from smiling, no matter how hard and earnestly he nodded to whatever they said.

"I think," said Ginny, "you should get her good and doped up. I have hundreds of sleeping pills. Take her somewhere and get rid of her. But make sure you cover her face and her fingertips with acid, so if they find her they won't be able to tell who she is. And don't forget the teeth. They always use the teeth to identify 'em.

Get plenty of acid on the teeth."

"I say no to that," said Yanez, placing his palms on the bar and straightening his back.

Ginny expected him to follow with a gag. "It's not right to mutilate a person's face and his teeth," he said.

"Well, do what you think is right," said Ginny.

Danny nodded gravely to indicate loyalty to his personal ethics.

"Where does she live?" asked Rudy.

Ginny wrote the address on a slip of paper and gave it to him.

"Okay, well, we'll probably get around to it this weekend. We'll call you when the job is done," said Montalvo.

"Look, I want to keep Gordon out of this as much as possible. You understand, don't you? If he answers when you call, just say . . . say you're Annie's nephew and you're calling for Annie."

Danny Yanez laughed at Annie.

Montalvo said, "Annie can be a code name with us."

"Let's make it Little Orphan Annie," said Yanez, to honor one of his favorite comic book friends.

Next door, in the Ponderosa Pines, Beef Buddusky was having a lunch of beer, beef jerky, and barbecue-flavored potato chips. He was reviewing his life, trying to find that point in his history when he felt the stirrings of love as strongly as he did now. There must have been another time when he regularly hung around some girl's house, hoping to catch sight of her, hoping more that she would see him and the miracle occur, prepared to do anything for her.

This new feeling had put a wedge between Mae and him, and he looked for some good excuse for walking out on her, in spite of knowing he would miss her when he left.

He was surprised to see Ginny and Mrs. Lister pass in front of the hazy streaked window of the Pines. He ran outside to catch them. "Hey, what are you two doin' down here?" he yelled behind them. Both women jerked around quickly as though caught in a crime. Ginny covered her heart with relief when she saw who it was.

"You gave me such a fright," she said.

"You're a little outa your territory, ain'tcha?"

Ginny was too excited to keep it a secret. She jabbed Mrs. Lister, then shook her, laughing and saying, "I got two boys to do it!"

"Do what?" asked Beef.

"You know what," said Mrs. Lister, trying to ward off Ginny's playful slaps with her cane. "Ginny, if you want me to walk alongside of you, you'll have to act your age," she scolded. "She just hired two Mexicans to do it," she told Beef. "In that place there. You should see the bathroom."

Ginny started to pommel Beef, for the sheer joy of it. "I *knew* I could do it!" she cried.

He pinned her arms to her sides.

"Get this straight, you *ain't* gonna do it. I ain't gonna let you."

"Ha! Try and stop me."

"Well, that's exactly what I'm gonna do."

"Behave yourself, Bomba, I could make a package deal with those two."

Beef released her arms. She stood there smiling brightly. It took him a moment to accept the knowledge that Ginny Mom, his best friend in life, had just threatened to kill him.

"You and me are through," he said, and he walked toward the Panama Club.

She shouted after him, "Don't kid yourself!"

5

Beef went into the Panama Club. Juan Barrajas was alone behind the bar. "Where's the two was just talking to Ginny Wynn?" he demanded.

He backed up in terror. "Are you a cop?"

"Shit, no, and it's a good thing for you I ain't. Where are they?"

"Out the back door. I don't know where they went. All I did was introduce them."

Beef ran through the kitchen to the back door and looked up and down the deserted alley. Maybe the deal, like many others, was only in Ginny's mind. The Mexicans probably agreed to nothing. Maybe they humored her and she believed them. But maybe, maybe they were on their way to do it. He would be there first.

He waited for some time outside the apartment, unsure of his mission. Bewildered, really, as in a dream. Something told him that she *would* respond to the feeling that stirred him, she would, or else life and the world were badly arranged. He could not talk himself out of it. Finally he knocked.

She opened the door, a look of recognition on her face. Before she could say anything, Beef said, "Maria, I know your husband Gordie."

She recognized him, Beef knew, and associated him with Ginny. The entrance to the apartment was a sliding glass door. She closed it to a two-inch opening. "My husband isn't here now," she said.

"It's you I have to talk to."

"But he'll be home in a few minutes."

"Good, I might as well talk to him too. This thing is goin' too far."

Uneasily and in silence, they looked through the door at each other.

"What thing?" she asked at last, though the question was not necessary.

"Ginny Mom. Your mother-in-law."

The words themselves, when now uttered, were synonymous with embarrassing problems involving poor mental health.

"Something has to be done about her," Beef added.

Maria nodded in understanding. She slid open the door. "Would you like to come in?"

Beauty responds to selflessness, his instincts told him. If he loved her in the proper way, she would put herself in his care.

"Thanks," he said, stepping inside. "Nice place."

"Can I get you something?"

"No, thanks."

"Would you like to sit down?"

"Buddusky's my name. People call me Beef."

She sat on one of the two occasional chairs. Beef remained standing, self-conscious about what he hoped he could say. Why shouldn't a guy say what's on his mind? If he hadn't come out and asked for it, would Mae have ever thrown it his way? But this was beyond fucking. This was a whole other thing, and there was no time to take with it.

"You a Catholic?" he asked.

"Yes," she answered, her brow wrinkling in confusion.

"Me too."

"Aren't you a close friend of Gordon's mother?" she asked.

"I guess I am, but she sure is stretching it. The things she says about you . . ."

"Sit down, please," she said, "you're making me nervous."

He sat on the sofa. "Like takin' dope and running around . . ."

"All lies." She relaxed for a moment. The interview was becoming more comfortable for her. Perhaps she felt the presence of an ally, the best of allies, one who has come over from the other side.

"Oh, sure, I know that. I knew that from the first minute I laid eyes on you."

"She's a very sick woman," said Maria.

"She's not that kind of girl, I said to myself. I *know* that other kind of girl, I said. But this girl is something special."

"I can't understand what's keeping Gordon," Maria said, anxious again. That last was a sexual message, she believed.

"Dividin' his time like he does, it's either his mother or you always wonderin' what's keepin' him. He shoulda been twins." Beef laughed at his joke. "Sorry," he said.

"It should be funny," she said. "It's a very funny situation, if it's not you in the middle of it."

"I'm real sorry. It ain't funny at all. Maybe once, but not with her . . . Look, do you love him, honest?"

Maria drew back in her chair. "What?"

"Gordie. Do you really love him?" he asked, in lover's despair.

"Of course I love him," she said. She tried to lead him to safer ground. "Now you said you had something to say about Mrs. Wynn."

"How can you love him?" he asked. "He makes you cry, he . . ."

"You'd better come back when he's here."

"He should be here *now.* She wants to kill you."

"She's insane."

He could see he was frightening her and yet he could do nothing about it. Why couldn't he say the right things, as others do with such ease?

"That just makes it all the easier for her to do it. How am I gonna protect you?"

"Protect me?"

"We got to get you out of here somewhere. Utah, maybe. Pennsylvania."

He moved off the sofa and stood in front of her. He could see that his presence towering over her was sending her into terror. He squatted down, to bring his head below hers.

"A safe place," he said, "where you can have your baby and live in peace."

Her expression was one of mixed pity, revulsion, and fear. He realized like an awakening that what he felt for her could never, under any circumstances, ever be returned.

"You want me to leave?" he asked, hoping she might not. If only she would offer him something again, he would stay and have a cup of coffee and let her do all the talking.

"Please!" she said, and she started to cry. Every time he extended his hand she shrank back. He despised himself. Another man would have known what to do. He rushed out of the apartment, anguished to be the cause of further suffering.

The jukebox blared, ". . . *my son calls another man daddy . . .*" and Beef covered his eyes with his hand. The old woman next to him wanted to cry too for such an ox so sentimental, or else she had her own thing to cry about, because she sure enough started crying. He drank his beer from the bottle, drinking as though each swig were the last of the final bottle. He rolled his shoulders and looked around him for begrudgers and belittlers.

"Fuck you all," he announced, spreading his sour mood evenly over the entire establishment.

"Be the best one you ever had," the old floozy boasted through her tears.

Hardhats just off the job came in for some beer and pool before going home. They ribbed each other good-naturedly and drank with great relish, they played eight ball with boyish enthusiasm and ate chips noisily, like men thoroughly satisfied with themselves, knowing where their next lay and pay were coming from, caring little for the rest of it.

Beef grabbed his beer and drank it viciously, sending a spurt of it up his nose.

In spite of the proof that he messed up his own life, Beef's father held a few fine values, one of which was a lesson he drummed often into his son: "You got your health? Then count your wealth in the friends you have." Beef remembered these wise words every New Year's Eve when he took stock of himself and found he hadn't a friend in the world.

"This shit has got to cease," he said. "It's got to come to a screeching halt."

Mae would be behind the bar in little more than an hour. He remembered the night she was too sick to get out of bed and he had to go down to the Ponderosa Pines and push beers in her place so that she wouldn't lose her job. He hated it. It was the wrong side of the bar for him. Having to work the bar made him hate Mae, but then at two-thirty in the morning he returned to the apartment to find she had fixed him something exquisite, two grilled bacon and cheese sandwiches. She gave him a blow job as he ate them. He had her the following morning as she leaned against the stove, making a pepper and onion omelet. He could be a lucky man, if he could keep from going crazy.

"I'll see you later, Ed," he said to the bartender, rising and going to the door.

"You make sure Mae's ass is down here by six," said Ed. "I ain't hangin' around here all night waiting."

"Listen, you don't say nothin' about her ass, I'll take care of her ass by my ownself."

He hurried to the apartment and found her sitting on the floor near the heat register, a blanket around her shoulders. Her eyes were watery, her nose was running.

"What's the matter, you got a cold?" he asked, taking off his shirt.

"Yeah," she said. "Look, you got any money?"

"I got something better than money, baby. I got *plans.*" He took off his shoes. "We got to see what we can make of us." He took off his pants.

"I ain't feelin' so hot," said Mae.

"I got to take a pee," said Beef on his way to the bathroom. "C'mon, hop in bed. Give you anything you want."

"Money," she said weakly as Beef shut the bathroom door behind him. He urinated and was peeling off his shorts when he noticed the broken eyedropper on the floor beneath the sink. He knelt down carefully to pick up the pieces. A bit of tape dangled from the underside of the sink. Beef lowered his head and saw the rest of her fix kit taped to the sink.

His plans or his plan to have plans drifted for a moment, then disappeared into thin air.

He rose and put his hands on his naked body, as though feeling for the poison that might have passed to him.

He opened the bathroom door and stood above her. "Bitch," he said. "As if things wasn't bad enough."

The pathetic creature he saw aroused a cruelty in him. He wanted to hurt her, to humiliate her sexually, to give her what she must have been used to.

"I guess you think I'm pretty dumb," he said.

"I ain't too smart either," she said.

"You said it, lady. I'll give you this, you don't lie."

The hell with it, his anger went nowhere but inward. He picked up his clothes and put them on. He went into the bedroom and threw his few things into his canvas bag.

"I'm leavin'," he said on his way past her.

She did not look up to see him go.

He checked into the Folding Hotel with half a gallon of cheap Burgundy. It wasn't his old room but it might as well have been. He took the Burgundy to bed and a pint through it began to miss the way Mae pinned her sheet to her blanket.

Someone's radio played country music from KPIK. When he woke up there was no more music. With his hangover as companion he missed her less. He resumed drinking, and soon he missed her more. The radio came on again. The wine was gone.

6

Rudy Montalvo was a baby-faced secret lover of music, who first ate the county's chow at age twelve, for drinking wine and smoking marijuana with the big kids. Since then he had never been out of custody for more than a few months at a stretch, and he was currently on parole. Most of his arrests had been on drug-related charges, and though he had pulled some armed robbery jobs, he had never been caught on anything stiffer than breaking and entering.

His pal, Danny "Goose" Yanez, was six inches taller than he, seven years older than he, and about eight beats slower than he. Although Yanez had participated in many illegal endeavors without fear or remorse, he had never been arrested and was never a problem to anyone, not his teachers, his family, or the neighborhood. He was a major problem to his wife, who kicked him out, but in this he was not conspicuous among his wedded contemporaries. In truth everybody liked him. He was fun to be around.

In all their lives, neither of them had ever been sought out to perform a service, unless you count Yanez's draft notice as a solicitation, so they were rather pleased with themselves at landing so effortlessly a $5000 commission on which they now held a $125 retainer.

The contract killers knew that to handle the affair properly they would need a car.

"Let's hot-wire one," said Yanez. "Let's get us a big fuckin' Cadillac."

"Do you know how to hot-wire cars, Goose?"

Sometimes Rudy made him feel inadequate. "My cousin Hector does," he said in his own defense.

"Oh, fine. Tell your cousin Hector to get us a Cadillac. Listen, tell him to bring his girlfriend too. Does he have a sister?"

"Sure, he has three sisters. Carmen, Teresa, and Lucy."

"Well, tell him to bring Carmen, Teresa, and Lucy along too."

"Hector lives in Arizona," said Goose.

They did what Rudy intended to do from the start: borrow Lupe Martinez's car. She was the wife of a friend of his, who was currently serving time. They paid her $20 to use the car for a few days. It was a 1947 Buick, a source of many memories for its three previous owners, but a pain in the ass to Lupe. She called it her taco wagon—no spare tire, no jack, the original spark plugs.

They walked into Sears, where Rudy bought two pairs of gloves and Goose boosted a roll of adhesive tape.

They drove Lupe's car to a snooker parlor, where they called into the alley a man they knew, for the purpose of borrowing the gun they knew he carried. They were going to Denver, they explained, and needed it to pull a few jobs. They gave him $10 for the use of it, and he gave them the gun. Neither Rudy nor Goose knew the caliber of it. It was a gun.

So there they were, standing on Nevada Avenue, the logistics of the operation covered, with $90.04 left to spare. Rudy shifted the gun to another part of his waistline.

"What'll we do now?" asked Goose.

Rudy thought about it for some time and Goose waited patiently for his decision.

"You want to catch a movie?" asked Rudy.

When Gordon checked in from his watch the desk sergeant told him, "There was a call for you." He shuffled about some papers. Mother, thought Gordon. He would forever be a station house joke. "Here it is," said the sergeant. "The DA at Pueblo wants you to call."

"Oh, shit!"

"What's the beef, Wynn?"

None of your fucking business, he thought, but said, "Just something I forgot to follow through on."

Gordon went back to the locker room and sat down. He was faced with somehow saving his mother, his marriage, and his job, all at once. He wondered which would be the first to fall, and would the rest come tumbling after. The judge had told him that as distasteful as it would be, he would have to go to the district attorney to iron out the fraudulent annulment his mother had committed. The judge was willing to let his mother and Bomba off with a reprimand, but the DA, he warned, might be harder to convince. "The impetuous action of a mentally ill woman now institutionalized," was the phrase that came to Gordon. He wanted to feed it to the DA. Surely he would not press charges. The problem was that Gordon knew he could never institutionalize his mother. He picked up the phone to call the DA. He even deposited his dime, but the phone became lead in his hand and he put it down. He would call him Monday.

Ralph Ferguson, who was distracted by other duties, did not remember until he was getting into bed that night that Gordon Wynn had failed to return his call. That was inexcusable. If Wynn did not call by ten o'clock Monday morning, he would simply place his mother under arrest, and quite possibly, depending upon the attitude of this young policeman, report him to his superiors for discipline.

About the time Ralph Ferguson was settling down to sleep, Beef Buddusky rolled his bulk out of bed. He wore only one sock but hadn't the courage to go looking for the other, not with his head pounding the way it was. He was afraid that if he lowered his head the top of it would pop right off. He took off his sock and tossed it away to find its own mate. He put on a fresh pair, full of the self-contempt of a man out of his own control.

He went down to the Panama Club. The place was crowded and noisy and the talk was in Spanish. Juan Barrajas was behind the bar, unhappy to see Beef again. He ordered a Coors to put the old man at ease, and because he wanted one very much. He poured half a glassful and drank, spitting out tiny pieces of ice that had been in the glass.

"Don't like that," he said aloud.

The rest he drank from the bottle, then he ordered another. The cold beer brought his mouth back to life. By his third bottle he could again appreciate the advantages of being alive. The fourth made him long for Maria. The fifth made him miss Mae. The sixth made him resentful of the cesspool called life. Midway through the seventh he was loaded again and ready to fight.

"Hey," he said to Juan Barrajas, "where's those two boys of yours?"

"Not my boys," he said, constantly worried.

"Where are they? I want a talk with 'em."

"They were here early. They went somewhere."

"Well, you tell 'em for me I'll kick their asses they don't watch out."

Then it landed on Beef and all but sobered him. If they went somewhere, maybe they went to kill Maria.

He ran out of the Panama and all the way to her apartment house. He sweat away the beer by the time he arrived. The cold air chilled his damp body. The windows of her apartment were dark. There was no sign of the two Mexicans. He crossed the street and leaned against a small tree, where he had a good view of her apartment. Show up here, you'll wish you hadn't, Beef promised them.

He stayed there for half an hour. Finally a car driven by a young woman pulled to the curb in front of Maria's place. Maria herself got out of the car, carrying a shopping bag. She waved good-bye as the car pulled away.

She should know she was in need of him.

"I love you," he whispered as she climbed the steps to her apartment.

The lights in her apartment came on. He would stay as long as it took.

In another apartment, at an angle behind him and three stories above him, an old woman pulled aside her curtain with two withered fingers and spied on Beef. She believed him to be the thing she feared most, an arsonist, a madman who sets your building on fire, then warms himself in the glow of the flames in which you crackle and sputter like a rasher. An emergency rope fire ladder was rolled up in her closet, sitting next to an Ansul dry chemical fire extinguisher. It would not happen to her. She watched Beef for twenty minutes. He did not move. The number was taped to her telephone. She dialed. "Police?"

He lost track of how long he had stood there, watching Maria's apartment, but finally a squad car pulled to a stop in front of him and the outboard officer said, "What're you doing out here?"

Beef lowered his head to see if the driver might be Gordie. It wasn't. He had the impulse to tell them he was standing guard over a pregnant woman in danger of her life. He had the impulse to tell them everything. He wanted to tell them everything and then give them a chance to ask him many questions which he would answer truthfully. Instead he said, "Just walkin' home."

"How long you been here?"

"I don't know."

Both cops got out of the car.

"Hands against the car."

Beef leaned forward, putting his hands on the roof of the car. He spread his legs. He knew what to do, he had done it before. The cop searched him.

"Got any identification?"

Beef gave him his driver's license. He looked at the guns in their holsters. He wanted one.

One cop took the license into the car, and the other said, "Stretch your arms to the side."

He did it.

"Now shut your eyes."

"What for?"

"Shut them, you big shit."

He shut his eyes.

"Now touch your nose with both fingertips."

He brought both forefingers to the tip of his nose. He was

152

apparently sober. "We had a call about a prowler out here," the cop explained.

"One?" asked Beef. Maybe someone had seen the two Mexican boys.

The cop looked at him quizzically. "Unless you got a turd in your pocket."

The other cop came out of the car and said there were no outstanding warrants on Harold Buddusky.

"Where you live?"

"Folding Hotel."

"What the hell you doin' way over here?"

"Takin' a walk. I got a lot on my mind."

The two cops thought that was a pretty good joke.

"Get in the car."

Beef got into the back seat and sat with his two hands between his legs, as if he were in handcuffs already. They drove in silence. Maria must have seen him and called the police. Why did she refuse to understand? He might as well tell the cops about Ginny hiring two Mexican boys to murder Maria. He was in jail anyway.

But they pulled up to the Folding and one cop reached around and opened Beef's door. "Out," he said.

Wait a minute! There's gonna be a murder. Go to Ginny Mom Wynn and tell her it's not allowed except in dreams, call up Maria and tell her who I am, who I really am. Yeah, I'm involved. Okay, I'll do my time, but go to Ginny, call Maria . . .

Beef looked out at the sad entrance to the Folding, feeling peculiarly misused, and got out of the car without a word. He went up to his room with nothing left of the seven beers he had downed but a full bladder. He relieved himself in the bathroom at the end of the hall. He walked back toward his room. One of the doors opened and an old wino poked his head out, fear on his face of the indecisiveness of life, the fidelity of death.

"Would you like to join me in a drink?" he asked, like a gentleman, holding up a nearly full bottle of T-bird.

He was of indeterminable age, like most winos. Scabby, his clothes wrinkled from sleeping in them, parts of his beard three days old, parts four, he stood tottering in the doorway and yearning for some human contact to distract him from reveries of the things he had lost along the way to dreams unattainable. Is this my father, thought Beef, will I be him?

"Sure," Beef said, and followed him into his room.

During the intermission between features, Rudy said, "We should pack her bag and take it so it would look like she left town."

"Good idea," said Goose. "You want a Jujy Fruit? I got two left."

Rudy extended his hand and Goose gave him the black one.

"We should take her south somewhere," said Rudy, as though some unwritten code specified it.

"Okay. Can we give her a good screwing?"

"You ain't even seen her yet. What if she's ugly?"

"What if she is?"

Rudy laughed at him.

"When do we get started?" asked Danny.

"You got the balls for it, we can do it tonight."

"I got grapefruits."

"Okay, after the flick. We'll see your grapefruits shrink to raisins."

"What're we gonna do with her?" asked Goose.

"I don't know. Shoot her, I guess, and bury her somewhere."

"You still got the gun?"

Rudy lifted up his jacket to show him. Then the house darkened and the film began.

Leaving the theater Goose said, "I had a bitch like that once. Fucked like a machine."

"C'mon, not like that."

"Yeah, only she had black hair."

"And was built different, right?"

"Maybe a little bit fatter."

"C'mon, Romeo, we got a date."

They cut across a vacant field to the car. Midway they heard a dog whining. The dog was lying on his side, badly injured. He was a mongrel, terrier size, who had evidently been in a fight with a much bigger dog. The tip of an ear was gone. Blood oozed from several wounds.

"Jesus, Rudy, maybe you better plug 'im and put the poor guy out of his misery."

Rudy bent over the dog. "Easy boy, good doggy, I ain't gonna hurt you."

The dog looked frightened of him but had no power left to resist. Rudy caressed the dog's head for a moment, then carefully lifted him and cradled him to his chest.

They took him to a veterinarian. No one was there but the kennelboy, who called the doctor. Rudy and Goose waited until he arrived and stayed in his waiting room while he worked on the dog.

"Did he have a collar on him?" asked Goose.

"No."

"He's our dog then, right?"

"Let's give him to Lupe. Her kids can take care of him."

"Can we call him Chico?"

"Sure."

The doctor finished with him and Chico seemed much better for it. His eyes conned them for sympathy with the streetwise technique of a mongrel on his own. They paid the doctor $12.50 out of the money Mrs. Wynn had given them to do a job which for the time being they had forgotten. They carried the dog to the car and drove him to Lupe Martinez's house.

Beef raised the window in the wino's room, put both hands on the sill, and leaned out, looking at the distance from him to the cold, hard concrete.

"You wouldn't take a dive on me, young fella, would you?" said the wino from his bed.

"Sometimes it occurs to me," answered Beef.

"A man would be a damn fool to do it by jumpin' out a window."

"What could be easier than crawlin' out of a hole? Hell, that's how I got here. Seems a fittin' way to go."

"What happens if you change your mind once you're on the way down?"

"Huh?"

"Let's say you crawl out of that window and you see the ground coming up at you fast, and you decide that life is sweet and you don't want to die?"

"Won't matter. In a second it'd be all over."

"But I got a feeling that would be the longest second any man ever lived."

Beef backed slowly away from the open window, too aware of an eternity in that isolated second.

"You want my advice," said the wino, "get yourself a single-barrel shotgun, grab the end of it in your mouth like it was your sweetheart's nipple, and pull the trigger. There's no time then to change your mind. You wouldn't even hear the shot."

Beef went to pour a drink. "Shut the window," he told the wino, who got out of bed and did it. He looked down before he shut it. "Diving don't appeal to me," he said.

"What's your name, dad?"

"Straight," said the wino, smiling with the remnants of his teeth.

Beef shook his head and had to laugh. "Straight Arrow?" he asked. "You some kind of Indian?"

"Marvin Straight," said the wino.

Beef laughed himself from the dresser to the rickety wooden chair to the stained linoleum floor.

Rudy Montalvo and Danny Yanez saw still another movie. Danny ate three boxes of buttered popcorn, frequently wiping his greasy fingers on his jeans. Rudy furtively drank half a pint of blackberry brandy.

Outside, they leaned against parking meters for a time, smoking cigarettes and watching the sparse traffic on Nevada Avenue. Out of boredom Danny put both hands on top of a parking meter, leapt, and cleared it. Rudy said, "I know a jerk tried that and left his balls hanging on the crank."

It did not frighten Danny because he did not believe it. He repeated the performance. "The wild goose flies again!" he cried as he went over the top.

The usher set up a ladder and began to change the letters on the marquee. They watched him for a while, amused at how he tried to make use of the letters already there from last week's feature, to save himself the work of going down and up the ladder.

"You still have the rod?" asked Danny.

Rudy opened his jacket to show it to him.

"We should knock this place over," said Danny. "There's only this guy and the ticket girl and the candy girl."

"For what? A lousy hundred bucks?"

Danny did not think there would be that much. It sounded fine to him.

"One of these days you're gonna get your ass caught in the wringer," said Rudy. "We got a job for five grand and you want to fuck around for peanuts."

"So let's get the five big ones."

Rudy unfolded the slip of paper on which Ginny Wynn had written her daughter-in-law's address. He flicked his finger at it.

"Half for you and half for me, right, Rudy?"

"Right down the middle, *amigo.*"

"You know what I'm gonna do with my share? I'm gonna get a set of wheels."

"First we got to do what we said we'd do."

"I ain't afraid."

"You don't see me sweatin' it, do you?" said Rudy.

Beef Buddusky sat on the wooden chair, his left leg crossed over his right, his left elbow on his leg, his forehead resting on his flat palm. "I opened myself up to her," he was telling Straight. "I didn't ask for nothin'. All I wanted was to love her and protect her, her and her baby both. But she was sick that she had to look at me, Straight. I got a right to be mad, don't I?" He took another swallow of wine. "A man's got a right to be mad when he opens himself up to a woman and she pushes it all back in his puss. So I'm just gonna sit here and be mad. I'm gonna think of Number One from now on."

"There's a lid for every pot," observed Straight.

"Huh?"

"She wasn't meant for you."

"I always knew that. But I thought I was meant for her."

"It don't work that way, son. Don't worry, you're still young."

"I had a girl was crazy for me. But somehow it was never the same once I got this feeling for the other girl."

And so Beef told him all about Mae, and Straight thought he was listening to another cunt-whipped kid. Straight set him straight. In their wine-soaked tour of many hours' duration, Straight had told him the things he needed to know.

"Didn't I tell you the proper way to suicide yourself?" asked Straight.

"Much obliged," said Beef.

"Well, now I'm telling you something more important than that: a good woman is hard to find, pissant."

"I already know that. You think I don't know that?"

"So you walk out on a good woman just because she's got a habit and you got the hots for somebody else's woman. You oughta be ashamed."

"Well, shame's been comin' on me slow but sure."

"Now you don't have either one of them."

"I didn't have a choice. There's more to it than I told you."

"So tell me more."

"I got my secrets," said Beef.

"And soon you'll have a lot of regrets too."

"Whaddaya mean by that, Straight?"

"A good woman is hard to find!" shouted Straight impatiently.

He harped on the subject so insistently that Beef finally said he would take Mae back, if she promised to kick the shit and rid her body of the dreaded poison. "And I'm gonna help you do it," said Straight, who pushed his bony shoulder into Beef's armpit and helped him stagger to the street. There he was sick in the gutter and had to go back to the room. Beef went on alone to the Ponderosa Pines.

He leaned against the bar. Ed was tending.

"Well," said Beef, "where the hell is she?"

"She ain't been in. She's gonna get her ass canned."

Beef imagined the man on the next stool laughing at him. He shoved him into the bar. The man, who had some size even on Beef, threw a right hook, which Beef blocked and countered, knocking him to the floor. Beef was summarily eighty-sixed from the Ponderosa Pines. He told Ed to stick the crummy place up his ass. He nursed his sore hand drinking T-bird with Straight.

Rudy Montalvo and Danny Yanez drove to the address on the slip of paper. Yanez got into the back seat and curled up, his face against the back cushion.

"This is it, baby," said Rudy, giving him the opportunity to chicken out.

"I'm ready."

"Yeah," said Rudy, the first hint of nervousness in his voice. He walked into the courtyard and up the steps. He could see her moving around in the apartment. One pair of the gloves he had bought for the job stuck out of his hip pocket. Goose had lost the other pair only hours after receiving them.

Maria went to the glass door. She looked at him, but was not afraid.

"Yes?" she asked, sliding open the door.

Rudy was taken off guard. He did not expect to see a Chicana.

"Are you Mrs. Wynn?"

"Yes, I am."

His first impulse was to excuse himself and go down to the car to discuss this new development with Goose. Ginny never told them the girl was a Chicana, and since she was married to a cop, Rudy never considered she was, in spite of the name Maria. It was a complication he resented, and he was angry with Ginny for failing to be entirely forthright. Unfortunately, he could not think fast enough to say anything other than what he had planned.

"I was having some drinks with your husband downtown in a bar and he's pretty drunk. He asked me to drive him home. Anyhow, he's passed out down in the car. Can you give me a hand with him?"

"Oh, my goodness," she said.

She looked for her bedroom slippers. She was dressed for bed and wore a robe over her pajamas, but she had been walking around the apartment in bare feet. She stepped into the slippers and said, *"¿Está bien?"*

He was nearly disarmed by the intimacy of their common first language. *"Sí, tomó mucho."*

Rudy tried to laugh but his throat was too dry. If he let her get down to the car he would have to go through with this thing.

She followed him down the stairs, without sliding shut the door to her apartment. They walked to the car side by side. When Rudy bent forward to open the rear door he paused and looked back over his shoulder at the stranger named Maria. *"¿Qué pasa?"* she asked.

She leaned into the back of the car with her arms stretched forward to shake her drunken husband awake. Yanez spun over, grabbed her hands, and pulled her into the car. At the same time Rudy Montalvo hit her on the back of the head with his gun and slammed the door. He raced around the car and got behind the wheel and pulled away.

"Son-of-a-bitch," said Yanez.

"Oh, man," cried Rudy. "I didn't think we would, Goose!"

She was not knocked unconscious. She fought with Yanez and screamed, "She's done it! She's actually done it! *!Mi Dios, me está matando!*"

She thought then of her baby who would never have a life outside of her own body, and in that moment entered into insanity. Her strength redoubled in madness, even as the blood streamed down her neck.

"Shut her up, Goose! *Please!*"

Montalvo sped through the deserted streets of the city, making for Route 25. Yanez wrestled with her, hitting her repeatedly in the face with his fist until her face was covered with blood, but still she did not weaken and she would not stop screaming.

"Rudy, Rudy! I can't hold her!" yelled Yanez.

They were out of the town. Montalvo pulled to the side of the road. He turned around so that he was on his knees, pointed the gun at her heart, and pulled the trigger. When he heard the click, he pulled the trigger again. Now for the first time he broke open the gun and discovered it had come without bullets. He hit her over the head with the pistol. The handle came apart. Rudy looked at the useless weapon and threw it down next to him. He pulled back onto the highway and sped south.

She moaned softly, but struggled no more. Yanez taped her hands in front of her and taped her mouth shut, but it did not silence the plaintive moaning. He did not want to rape her. He wanted to be away from her.

"Can't we dump her here on the side of the road, Rudy?" he asked.

"They'd find her."

"I don't care, man."

"She's still alive."

"Shit, Rudy . . . oh, shit, Rudy."

Twenty miles out of town, in barren and deserted cow country, the car started to miss and sputter.

"This thing ain't gonna get us very far," said Rudy.

"We shoulda hot-wired one," said Yanez.

"Shut the fuck up!"

"Shut the fuck up yourself," said Yanez. "You're so goddamn smart. Here we are in a car about to shit out and we got a woman not dead or alive with us, and . . . oh, *shit.*"

Outside it started to snow.

"All right, all right," said Rudy, "we got to find a place to get rid of her—quick."

They could see the Pike's Peak Turf Club off to their right. Rudy wanted to get out of sight of it. No place along the road offered enough concealment. They were forced to drive on. Maria was slowly regaining consciousness. Her moans became louder.

"Rudy, get us out of this!" pleaded Yanez. "I can't listen to her anymore."

He left Route 25 at County Line Road and circled under the highway to the other side, out of sight of traffic. They found a deep dry wash and pulled the car to the side, killing the engine and lights.

They carried her out of the car and down into the wash. Her moans made her heavier. Thirty yards back from the road was a railroad trestle. They dragged her toward it.

"We can bury her under that," said Rudy.

She began to kick and struggle again and fought to scream through her taped mouth. Her hair was caked with blood, some of which had hardened around her eyes.

"She's strong as hell, for a lady," said Goose Yanez.

"Go get a rock and bash her head in," said Rudy.

Maria's eyes flared wide in terror. They laid her on the ground and held down her struggling shoulders and legs.

Yanez looked around him. "It's too damn dark out here to find a good rock," he said. "You wanna bash her head in, find a rock yourself."

"All right, all right, pick her up. Let's get her under cover."

The snow was beginning to fall heavily. They dragged her, still fighting, under the trestle. On the other side of it they could see the lights of a ranch house far off in the distance. Yanez sat behind her and held her in a hammerlock, trying to cut off her air. Rudy began digging a hole, first with a stick, then with his hands. They heard the mooing of cattle. It took a long time to make any progress without a shovel.

"Goddamn," said Yanez, "I never knew it was so hard to kill a person."

"You want to dig for a while?" asked Rudy. "See how easy *this* is."

So they traded places. Rudy took over the hammerlock on Maria, and Yanez began digging with his hands.

"Why won't she die?" said Rudy.

They traded twice again before they decided the grave was deep enough. By that time she was motionless.

Goose's hands were raw and the left one was bruised and sore from the pounding he had given her face. From the grave he had dug, he called to Rudy in a whisper, "Is she gone?"

Montalvo relaxed his grip and moved away from her, letting her fall flat to the ground. His biceps were weary and sore. He knelt beside her and laid his ear against her breast.

"Can you hear it?" asked Yanez.

"Keep quiet. *Shhhhhhh.*"

Rudy heard something. He looked at Goose. "Yeah, I hear it too." It was a train, and in a moment it was roaring above their heads, sending them huddling against the walls of their refuge like two shell-shocked veterans.

When it had passed and they were able to compose themselves, Rudy went back to Maria.

Danny Yanez squatted next to the grave, waiting.

Though the train had gone, the sound of it remained in their ears. "Hell, how are you supposed to hear it?" said Rudy.

"Take her pulse," said Yanez.

"I could never find pulses. You do it, you were in the Army," said Montalvo, attributing to military experience vast stores of practical knowledge otherwise unattainable.

Danny Yanez had never taken a pulse in his life, but he enjoyed Rudy's assuming his expertise in the practice. He bent over her and took her thin, pale, bound wrists in hand, narrowing his eyes like a medic.

"Finished off," he said.

In the long, endless corridors of madness and in the ease and calm and peace that foreran death, she felt a weight upon her breast and later heard the words spoken, as from a great distance and about another person: "Finished off."

Goose took the legs, Rudy the arms, and together they carried her to the trench and covered her with dirt. There was a witness to the crime. One curious steer that had strayed from the herd.

Real killers now, they drove back toward the Springs through the snow, their hands and clothes wet and dirty and bloody, their world changed irrevocably. Goose looked behind him at the bloodstained upholstery and saw one of Maria's slippers on the floor. He threw it out the window.

Rudy's arms were shaking and he had trouble holding the wheel steady. "Light me a cigarette, baby, I gotta have a cigarette," he said.

"Me too," said Goose. "Christ, I gotta have a cigarette too."

Though the night was very cold they were sweating and felt as though hot air were being pumped into their veins, floating them away. Goose lit the cigarettes. They puffed rapidly.

"Don't cop out to nothing, Goose. That's all you gotta remember. Can you remember that?"

"I can remember, Rudy. I ain't gonna cop out to nothin'."

Reluctant to look at each other, like first-time adulterers, they sat nervous, scared, and silent for nearly fifteen minutes, until Rudy wet his forefinger, reached over, and reamed Goose's ear. Goose brought his foot up and slammed it against Rudy's thigh. It caused him to floor the accelerator for an instant, and they fishtailed in the snow.

"Watch the fuckin' gas, birdbrain," laughed Rudy, straightening out the slide of the car.

Goose farted and said, "There's some gas for you, *pato*," and reached over to grab Rudy at his crotch. Rudy elbowed him in the ribs and said, "Watch the goddamn car! I'm drivin' a car here, you silly son-of-a-bitch."

Goose mimicked his words in his Jerry Lewis voice and ran his hands over his contorted face.

They found themselves elated, swept up in the matchless emotion of having to keep the ultimate of secrets, and they insulted each other and grabbed at each other's crotch all the way back to Colorado Springs.

BOOK 3

1

Midnight. Gordon wanted to be with the warm, loving woman he believed was still waiting for him. Instead, he hovered in the doorway, looking at his mother. The light behind him extended only to the foot of her bed. Tomorrow new arrangements must exist, he thought, or . . . they must exist. The stalemate must be broken.

"Mother?" he whispered. "You awake?"

"Yes, dear."

"I have an idea."

She was not eager to hear it. Lately all his ideas had three angles. She smiled in the dark. They would shortly take on a different shape. "What is it?" she said.

"Can you keep an open mind?"

"Well, I always try."

"What would you say to a larger apartment?"

"But the expense . . ."

"It would be cheaper than maintaining two apartments."

She still would not believe that that other apartment was in any way his, and consequently could not understand his proposal.

"A big place," he said, "with two bedrooms. It would require real effort in the beginning, I know, but if we all enter it in the spirit of good will, there's no reason . . ."

"Are you suggesting . . . ?"

". . . why we can't have some sort of happy, normal family life."

"Are you suggesting that we take in that . . . that . . ."

"An open mind, Mother, remember?"

The anger coiled tightly in every part of her body, and she wanted to call that other one by the proper names and describe the fitting fate for her, but for what? It was in the offing anyway, and now the less said about her the better.

A wonderful opportunity presented itself. She could be magnanimous and at no real risk.

She pretended to cry softly. "Gordie, do you think it could work out?"

"I believe it could, if we all gave it an honest try."

"Do you think your . . . do you think she would be willing?"

Gordon took one step into the bedroom. "She's a very understanding girl, Mom, I'm sure she would try to be friends. She's always wanted to be friends with you. She doesn't want to take me out of your life, she never did."

"Lord knows, we can't go on like this."

Gordon did not want to push too eagerly. "On that we all agree." He held his breath, waiting for her decision. He *knew* that if he didn't rush things, she'd eventually come around.

"I'm willing if she is," said Ginny, and she found herself shedding real tears. She liked this role of the great peacemaker. She had never before compromised, and now with the first, the graciousness and the humility of the act made her feel rather good. She had the fleeting thought of making it real. In any case, the tears were real, and they confounded her.

"Gordie?"

He went to her and found her hand in the darkness.

"You're the only thing in this life I've ever really loved, Son."

"I know, Mom, I know."

Real, the tears were real.

In the morning, the landlady discovered in her routine chore of sweeping the snow off the balcony walkways that Maria's door was open and the lights still on.

"Maria?" she called through the doorway.

It was a cold morning and had been a cold night. She stepped inside the apartment, but did not close the door behind her.

"Maria?"

Everyone has family problems. People are always threatening those they hate. Nothing ever comes of it. But she found herself too afraid to open the bedroom door. She knocked on it.

"Maria?"

She sensed someone behind her and her heart seemed to rise inside her. She spun around and saw Gordon. Weakened by fright, she leaned against the bedroom door.

"What are you doing in here?" he asked. He slid the door shut behind him. "My God, this place is freezing."

She had to catch her breath. "Mr. Wynn, the door was open and, look, the lights are on. I was worried."

"Where's Maria?"

"I called."

Gordon brushed past her and opened the bedroom door. The lights were on, the bed neatly made.

"Where is she?" asked Gordon.

"Don't you know?" asked the landlady.

He called her office. She had not arrived, they said. He went back into the bedroom to look for her suitcases. They were in the closet.

"Where could she be?" he said.

Suddenly the landlady was screaming at him. "Ask your *mother!* Ask your *mother!*"

For a moment he hadn't a notion what she was ranting about.

Rudy Montalvo and Danny Yanez managed to get a few hours' sleep in Danny's room. They threw their bloodstained clothes into a neighbor's garbage can and drove the old Buick to a barranca, where they tore the bloodstained rear upholstery out of the car. They sprayed the area with a can of black paint they had bought at an auto parts store.

They drove to the snooker parlor and explained to their friend that they had to bash in the head of a gas station attendant with his gun and the gun proved second best. They gave him the pieces and twenty dollars for a new one.

They returned the car to Lupe Martinez. She was in the midst of a birthday party for one of her children, and the house was full of kids, the little dog Chico happily begging from all of them. Rudy gave the birthday boy $5. He and Danny led Lupe away from the party and showed her the damage to her car.

"Oh, *shit.*"

"One of us flipped a cigarette out," explained Rudy, "and it blew back there, set it on fire. We were lucky we could pull the stuff out before the whole car went up in smoke. It don't look so bad now."

"Shit it don't," said Lupe. "When Hernandez gets out of jail he's going to break your arms." She looked from them to the car.

"Assholes," she said. "See if you get to borrow it again."

"We're gonna have some money soon," said Goose. "We'll have it reupholstered for you. Hernandez won't know the difference." He did not want his arms broken.

Lupe called them several more uncomplimentary names, and that out of her system invited them to have cake and ice cream with the rest of the ten-year-olds.

Goose performed a number of his Jerry Lewis routines for the children. He had them dropping their punch and rolling on the floor. Later that day he learned his estranged wife had given birth to a baby girl in Pueblo. He hitched down there to try to see them and his other two children.

Gordon ordered Mrs. Lister to go home. He had to speak with his mother alone. Ginny told her to stay, she had no secrets from her old friend.

"Well, am I going or am I staying?" asked Mrs. Lister.

"You're going, goddammit!" shouted Gordon, and Mrs. Lister wasted no time in saying so long.

"You shouldn't yell at her like that," said Ginny. "The poor thing's afraid of you the way it is."

"Why does she have to be around here all the time?"

"Company . . ."

"I'm sick of seeing her. She should be in a home somewhere, old as she is. Why don't you make friends your own age? You're either with an old biddy on the far side of senility or someone twenty years younger than you."

"If you're referring to Bomba the Jungle Boy, he's no twenty years younger than me. Why, when I had you I was only . . ."

"Sit down, Mother."

"What a mood you're in! After last night I thought your disposition might change. I don't know what else I can do to please you."

"Sit down."

"I've given in to all your demands."

"Please sit down."

Reluctantly, she took a seat, but she would not look at him. She folded her arms in front of her and rebelliously escaped his attempts at eye contact.

He grabbed her face between his hands and anchored it inches from his own. "Maria is missing," he said. He watched her carefully for her first reaction.

It was of true disbelief, and Gordon thought he detected an element of sorrow. For a moment he allowed himself some hope. He released his hold on her.

"She probably ran off with another man," she said.

The momentary hope he enjoyed plummeted and was replaced by a fear he had never known before. Had any man ever known such a fear? Had any other man ever lost his wife at the hand of his mother?

He could hardly speak. "Honey, if something's happened to her, I don't know what I'll do."

"You'll do just fine."

"Listen close," he said. "This is a time we have to have the absolute truth between us, maybe for the first time in our lives."

"What do you mean by that? We always . . ."

"Now, don't interrupt me, Mother. Not this time. You killed her, didn't you?"

"No," she answered, without a second's hesitation. "But I'm not sorry she's dead."

"What do you mean, dead? A minute ago she was off with another man."

"Well, you're the one who said 'killed.'"

"Tell me, Mom. God, let me know now."

"I was here with you last night."

"Did you have someone kill her? Bomba the Jungle Boy?"

Ginny laughed. "What an imagination you have! Bomba couldn't kill a fly if it landed on his nose."

"He went through that annulment with you, maybe he did this for you."

Ginny jumped to her feet, angry. "Who told you about that? Did she tell you that?"

"Her landlady told her and she told me. By now half the people in town must know about it. But forget about that. I don't care about that. What I want to know is, did you kill her? If ever you loved me, tell me the truth."

A lie could not have come so quickly, thought Gordon.

"I hate her, but I didn't kill her."

And yet he still could not believe her.

"What about all those threats?"

"Just talk," she said.

Gordon felt a strange calmness settle over him. He could not explain it, especially since in his heart he knew his wife was dead and his mother was the cause. His fear had vanished. He even imagined his body temperature dropping rapidly and his movements slowing down. Soon he would be without any feelings of any sort, save self-preservation.

"Well, then," he said, "I guess I better go in and report this."

"Why do you have to do that? I mean, why don't you wait a few days and see if she comes back?"

"I better do it before the landlady does."

He stopped once more at the apartment before going back to the station house. The carpet in front of the door was wet where some snow had blown in and melted. The door was undamaged. Nothing in the apartment itself had been disturbed. He looked in the living room closet. Her heavy car coat was there. She would not have gone out on so cold a night without it. He looked in the bedroom closet but could not tell what clothes, if any, were missing. He tried to clear his mind as he sat on the bed and looked into the open closet. His eyes fell upon the closet floor. The bedroom slippers were missing.

He looked all over the apartment, including the wastebaskets, for those slippers. He sat down again. All right, then, she was wearing bedroom slippers. If that was the case, what else might she be wearing? Up again, he looked for her robe and could not find it.

Dressed in slippers and robe, she must have answered a knock on the door or opened it for some other reason, for there was no forced entry. He looked for a safe conclusion. Could she have opened the door, left it open, and dashed to a neighbor's apartment? She could have, but they knew none of the neighbors. Could she have run a quick errand somewhere else? But where, dressed like that? And why didn't she close the door, unless she intended to carry something out or in that would require both hands? Whatever the reason for her leaving the apartment, she obviously did not return. Clearly, someone had taken her away. He felt his limbs hang like dead things.

At the station, upon stepping inside, he knew that the entire place had changed and because of him. The usual noises ceased as soon as he came inside. One cop who was on his way outside found reason to divert to the bulletin board. The desk sergeant,

Sergeant Murphy, looked up from his work, conscious of the change in atmosphere.

"Hey, Wynn, c'mere."

Gordon went over to him.

"What the fuck is going on, Wynn?"

"What are you talking about?"

"Well, for one thing the DA's office in Pueblo keeps calling for you."

"Christ, I'll take care of that."

"Yeah, now what about this other thing?"

"What other thing?"

"The skinny here is that your old lady is missing."

At first Gordon thought he meant his mother.

"I just came in to file a missing persons report."

"We already had two citizen calls on it. The chief wants to talk to you and your mother."

"Why my mother?"

Murphy looked at him in a great show of confusion. "I don't know what to make of you, Wynn. I never did."

"Look, Murphy, you got something to say, say it."

"You mean, like man to man?" he asked sarcastically.

"Yeah," said Gordon.

"With *you?*"

It was a short step and a jump to the elevated desk. Gordon got him by the shirt front and pulled him over the top and to the floor, where he dropped his knee into Murphy's groin. The other cops dragged him off Murphy and into the chief's office.

Ginny Wynn and Mrs. Lister met Rudy Montalvo at Woolworth's.

"Can I buy you a sandwich?" she asked brightly.

"The job is done," he said in a whisper, ominously, like a killer.

Ginny smiled and closed her eyes for a few seconds. "How did you do it?"

"We just did it, you don't have to know how. I'm not feeling very proud about this."

"I knew you could do it."

"Just let me have the money, please."

Three five-and-dime shoppers, they ambled the aisles of Woolworth's, fingering the goods. Ginny read the labels of various bottles of cheap perfume, her back to Montalvo. "I've got some money for you, boy," she said. "You know Ginny isn't going to stick you."

He picked up a toy racer and tested its friction motor along the flat of his hand. "I hope not, 'cause we did our job and now we'd like our payday."

Down the aisle, Mrs. Lister said, "I remember when you could buy a good paring knife for a nickel."

Ginny turned around and stood next to Rudy and touched him with her shoulder. "How'd you do it?" she asked.

"Never mind," he said.

They walked to the next counter and looked at key cases, wallets, and imitation leather goods.

"Did you use acid, like I said?"

"No."

"Why not? Did you dope her up?"

"Mrs. Wynn, I don't want to talk about it, can't you see?"

"Do you feel all right?"

"Fine."

"Are you sure?"

"Sure, I feel fine."

"You're not irregular?"

178

"Hey, Mrs. Wynn . . ."

"Go to the next counter," she said and they walked, stopping to examine the notions. "Because if you are irregular I'd recommend prune juice. If that doesn't work, try Phillips Milk of Magnesia."

"I don't pay attention. I don't know if I'm regular or I ain't."

"You shouldn't ignore these things."

"Look," he said, "all I want is the rest of the money and then you'll never see me again."

"Patience, my sweet beaner."

"Mrs. Wynn, don't come around with that shit."

"I'm only kidding, for goodness' sake. Foreigners are always so sensitive."

"I was born in Yuma, Arizona," said Montalvo.

"Well, who wasn't?" answered Ginny. "Here."

She slipped $50 into his hand. He gave it a quick count. He had expected considerably more. "What's this?" he asked.

"That, my *amigo*, is the monthly payment on my refrigerator."

He looked at the money in his hand like a drought-defeated farmer feeling for rain.

"Well, when do I get more? When do I get it all?"

"I wired the bank in Denver," she said. "I touched bases with my bank in Chicago. The Kansas City bank has promised an early reply, and I have a call in to the bank in Seattle. But these things take time. Be patient."

She quickly walked out of Woolworth's, Mrs. Lister struggling to keep up. Rudy watched them go, and suffered his first misgivings about Mrs. Wynn's honesty.

On the first day of his hangover, Beef Buddusky could not get out of bed. He made it to work on the second, but he threw up on some man's roof and had to take the rest of the day off.

He stopped at a bar and got himself back into shape. At the hotel he took a hot bath and shaved. He looked into the mirror and somehow felt justified in feeling sorry for himself. Things had simply gone to shit.

He rehearsed a long heart-to-heart talk he was going to have with Ginny. If he could get nowhere with her (and he already expected that would be the case) he would tell it to Gordon. He would apologize to Maria. He would talk to Mae. Somehow he would straighten everything out. He should have done it long ago. Enough is enough.

He was intercepted on the sidewalk by a breathless Mrs. Lister, who panted and leaned on her cane and said, "We can't go up there, Bomba. The police are there. I saw them."

Suddenly there was nothing in his mind. "How come?" he asked.

"How come? They killed Maria, those two boys."

Beef grabbed her by the shoulder and shook her. "They didn't!"

"Oh, yes, they did!" she said, her teeth rattling.

He held her shoulders and felt himself sinking like a raw egg in a glass of beer. He walked backward, bowing like a Chinese servant as he retreated down the sidewalk. Every time Mrs. Lister tried to tell him more, he raised his hand to stop her.

"Got *bad* hearing," he said.

Beef went back to his hotel, settled his account, and packed his bag. He dropped his swimming trunks into the wastebasket, as sad as rootlessness. On his dresser was the barrette he had stolen in Maria's apartment. He could not throw it away. He put it into his pocket and slung his bag like guilt over his shoulder. He walked to Route 25, dropped his bag to the ground, and extended his thumb to the south. He gave one long, last, wistful look at the Springs, where once he thought he had found a home.

2

The man in the wrinkled suit who stepped into the Colorado Springs Police Station was a man familiar with such places. He had graduated from one. He knew instinctively when there was a major crisis in the station itself. What he sensed here was occasioned by one of two things, in his experience: either a cop had been killed or a cop had committed a major crime.

He presented himself to the desk sergeant and said, "You have an officer named Wynn. Is he around now?"

"You a reporter?" The sergeant was in a foul mood.

The man showed him his identification. "Martin Lowell, chief investigator, Pueblo County DA's office."

The sergeant's features softened. "Christ, man, c'mon with me."

It was almost 9 P.M. before Martin Lowell returned to Pueblo. He came into the office and sat down in a chair like a man who had spent the past several hours listening to things for which only cops could have ears.

District Attorney Ferguson leaned back and waited for him to speak.

When he did, he said, "You know, the Springs is a helluva pretty town. It's easy to see why people like to retire there."

"But?" asked Ferguson.

"But I think the shit's about to hit the fan there. A girl has disappeared without a trace. The one who got the annulment was her mother-in-law. When that didn't bust up the marriage I think she cooled the girl."

Ferguson flipped back through his calendar pad to find the word *Annulment* written there. He wrinkled his brow, angry at himself and once again doubtful of the nobility of man. A woman had boldly demonstrated her capability of acting out deep hatred, and no one picked up the cue.

"Goddammit," he said, "I should have arrested them as soon as I learned their names. What about the son?"

"It wouldn't surprise the rest of the fuzz to learn he had a hand in it. They don't like him much there. But they got nothing on him. All the evidence they have, which isn't so much, points to the mother."

"What are they doing?"

"They're in a tailspin. They're walking around the station talking to themselves."

"Did they book her?"

"They don't even *have* her. They had to let her go."

"What!"

Ferguson reached for the telephone and located the DA of El Paso County still in his office.

"Hello, Fred, this is Ferguson in Pueblo."

"Why, hello, Ralph, how are you?"

"What's the story on this Wynn case?"

"Christ, bad news travels fast. How did you hear about it?"

"I have an interest. What's going on?"

"Well, the word around town is that the mother of one of our cops hired some local talent to murder her daughter-in-law. The girl is missing, under unusual circumstances. She denied it, of course, but she finally said she was the victim of extortion on the part of two Mexicans who are working for an old guy named Barrajas, who owns a local eyesore."

"Why the extortion?" asked Ferguson.

"Threats against her son, she claims, because he arrested Barrajas in a case involving receiving stolen property. Anyway, she picked one of the Mexicans out of the mug book, a bad boy named Rudy Montalvo. We questioned him and he denied even knowing Mrs. Wynn. We picked up Barrajas and he admitted knowing Montalvo and his friend, a kid named Yanez who's supposed to be down there in Pueblo right now. We're looking for him. But he doesn't admit to anything else. Then we find out that Mrs. Wynn was always in the company of a little old lady named Mrs. Lister and a big thug they called Bomba the Jungle Boy. Getting interesting?"

"Go on," said Ferguson.

"Looks like Bomba the Jungle Boy has run, but they bring in Mrs. Lister, who right off the bat tells them she can't say anything or else she'll go to the gas chamber. They asked her who told her that, and she said Ginny Wynn. They reassured her that only murderers go to the gas chamber. She breathes a sigh of relief and tells them two Mexican boys murdered Maria Wynn, the policeman's wife. We bring in Barrajas again and this time he admits to introducing Mrs. Wynn to Montalvo and Yanez. Beyond that, he says he knows nothing."

"My man tells me you let Mrs. Wynn go."

"I had to, Ralph. All we had was Mrs. Lister, and if you could listen to her you'd know she'd be next to worthless as a witness.

Barrajas could possibly be an accomplice, so he's no help. We need a body and then some, or we're in real trouble with this one. All we've got now is a senile old lady. And I'm afraid they might all run."

"They will run," said Ferguson. "Do you want me to put her on ice for you?"

"Can you?"

Ferguson told him about the annulment.

"Christ," he said, "this is getting peculiarer and peculiarer. You take her, Ralph, and I'll find some way to nab Montalvo and Yanez. Can you boost the bail on her?"

"I can try."

When he hung up the phone, Ferguson looked at Lowell, who asked, "What's the oldest sin, chief?"

"Stealing apples," said the DA.

Lowell thought about it for a moment, and said, "I guess you're right at that."

Ferguson waited in his office until he heard that Mrs. Wynn was safely in the custody of the County of Pueblo. He had a strong impulse to go down and have a look at her, but he overcame it. The real case was in the Springs, and welcome to it.

3

In Colorado Springs, Juan Barrajas finally admitted to interrogators that he introduced Ginny Wynn to Montalvo and Yanez for the purpose of doing some sort of job for her. He did not know what kind of job, he said. Yes, the boys borrowed a car to do the job. The car belonged to Lupe Martinez, who was questioned and freely admitted that she had lent her car to Rudy. She showed it to the detectives.

"See what they did to it," she said, still peeved at them.

There were some bloodstains that the spray paint did not cover.

They arrested Montalvo and charged him with violation of his parole: driving an automobile.

The police picked up Yanez in Pueblo and took him to the Springs for questioning. The name Ginny Wynn did strike a familiar note with him, but he could not place the lady. Ah, maybe it was in the Panama Club that he had met her, but the memory was vague. Well, she could have propositioned them to commit murder, but they sure wouldn't take her up on it.

They could get him no further than that, but they were sure he would be the first to weaken and tell all, if they could only keep him in jail for a while. Unfortunately, there was nothing to charge him with, and he had no criminal record.

The El Paso County DA called Ferguson and asked him if he thought, since Yanez was from his county, that he could arrest him for something.

"I'm sure of it," answered Ferguson. He did some checking, found Yanez was delinquent in his child support payments, and arrested him for that.

All three of them were now behind bars, but unless a body and a confession were forthcoming, it would be hard to keep them there for long. Montalvo and Yanez could be held easily enough, but Mrs. Wynn might have the resources to make bail.

Ferguson filed a complaint against Ginny before Judge Barry Winston, the same judge who had earlier been duped into granting a fraudulent annulment, charging her with bribing a witness (Bomba the Jungle Boy), fraudulently preparing a document to deceive the court, forgery of Maria Wynn's signature, and aiding and abetting the commitment of perjury. To Gordon's great surprise, the judge followed the district attorney's recommendation and set the bail at $50,000. Gordon could not raise it, nor could he get it reduced.

The chief of police put Gordon on a two-week suspension for striking a superior officer. After that, he advised, Gordon would be wise to take his vacation time. Gordon knew there was no way they could make him take a vacation; he had done nothing wrong. But he also knew he could not serve with men who looked at him the way they did. His days as a cop in Colorado Springs, if not elsewhere, were over.

His only concern now was his mother. He could not get her out of jail. He set out to find a lawyer who could.

Ginny kept to her story. If Maria Wynn was murdered, it was in retaliation for Ginny's not paying extortion money. She said that it was her belief, however, that Gordon's wife pulled this disappearing act in order to give her husband a lot of bad publicity. Gordon defended her to the press, supporting the lie that his wife had often threatened to leave like that, mysteriously and without a word. He insulated himself against memories of Maria and hopes for their child. What might have been did not become. He would permit himself no emotion contrary to the defense of his mother. He would not look to any future beyond saving her life. He was, and probably would be, neither trapped nor free.

Rudy Montalvo would say nothing at all. His friend Goose Yanez kept indicating that he would like to talk, but just couldn't bring himself to do so.

Mrs. Lister became a local celebrity and was only too willing to tell all she knew, down to the finest detail she could invent. She liked the attention. For her own protection, the police sponsored a vacation for her at a hot springs resort, where she spent her days soaking with a third-degree black belt in karate.

Juan Barrajas, an inch at a time, finally allowed that he knew the boys were to be hired for something comparable to murder, but he had no alternative. He did not want to go to prison at his age. He had been advised by a disbarred lawyer who frequently loitered around the Panama Club to refuse to testify unless he was offered immunity from prosecution as an accessory or accomplice. This advice cost him one bottle of beer, but it was worth considerably more.

The annual Christmas party for the courthouse offices was winding down. Earlier there had been the sharing of a multitude of gripes concerning pay scales, seniority, politics, job titles, bureaucracy, and all the other irritations of government employment. Shortly thereafter followed the customary quick assignations in cloakrooms and closets, offering youthful thrills but no promise of fulfillment. Santa arrived on the scene and distributed goodies to all assembled. Now Santa lay passed out in a corner, his beard over his eyes, two of yesterday's darlings asleep on either side of him; the resident legal bunny had made her selection for this winter's night and departed; and a community realization that another year was nearing its end, thrusting them into a new and uncertain one, settled over the celebration and all but stilled the laughter.

Martin Lowell was rounding the last turn to a mean drunk. There was no satisfaction in having three killers behind bars, if only on piddling charges. It offended his sense of enclosure to be without a corpse or confession. The Springs authorities in charge of the case had made only two trips down to Pueblo to question Yanez and the mother.

Ralph Ferguson stopped to talk to him on his way out of the party.

"Good night, Marty."

" 'Night, chief."

"You feeling all right?"

"Yeah, I'm fine."

"If you feel like it, go and talk to Yanez. Maybe you can help out the Springs."

"Okay, maybe I will. Nobody up there's moving his ass."

Ronnie Fischer, a sheriff's deputy, wandered up to them.

"Take Ronnie here with you," said Ferguson. "He doesn't seem to be enjoying himself either."

Ronnie Fischer had recently flunked another exam for promotion. An ex-Navy signalman, he did not drink, having sworn off after causing $2000 worth of damage in a Honolulu bar and sending two Marines to the hospital with serious jaw fractures. He was demoted for this, and his future in the Navy looked weak, which is why he mustered out. Like so many men whose entire adult life had been spent in the military, he sought police work upon discharge. He worried that he would not get very far in the sheriff's department either.

Lowell and Fischer went downstairs to an interrogation room and called for Yanez to be brought to them.

"You want to be the good guy or the bad guy?" asked Lowell.

"Makes no difference to me," said Fischer.

"I'll flip you for it."

"You don't have to."

"Okay," said Lowell, "I'll be the bad guy."

Yanez was brought into the room. Neither Lowell nor Fischer paid any attention to him. He stood a moment, then helped himself to a chair.

Fischer sat behind the desk. Lowell sat on a corner of the desk and said to him, "Why don't you and the old lady come over some Sunday after the New Year and I'll barbecue something?"

"Good idea."

"I got a recipe for chili I'd like to try out on you."

"Sounds good."

"It'll rip you a new asshole."

Danny Yanez sat smiling, looking from one to the other, as though he expected them to invite him.

"What are you smiling for, punk, you glad you killed a defenseless girl?" said Lowell.

Yanez looked deeply hurt. He stared between his knees and said nothing.

"Montalvo squealed," said Lowell. "He says you did it. The old lady says the same thing, says it was all your idea."

Yanez said nothing until Martin Lowell kicked his feet and

almost sent him flying off his chair, and then he said, "C'mon, man."

"How's the new baby, Goose?" asked Fischer, offering him a cigarette.

"Okay, I guess. She didn't even let me see her."

"Your kids are gonna be real proud of their papa when they grow up. You want them to follow in your footsteps, lady-killer?" asked Lowell.

Yanez took a drag on his cigarette and said, "You're a real bastard."

Lowell kicked his feet again.

"Hey, man, I'm gonna go back to my cell there. I don't have to talk to you guys."

"Ease off, Marty," said Fischer. "Goose is gonna do what's right. He's a good boy. Ask anyone in town."

"Yeah?" asked Yanez, not realizing he was so popular.

"Sure, everybody around here says you're a good kid, wouldn't hurt a fly."

"This chili I make," said Lowell to Fischer, "I use three different kinds of chilis at once."

Yanez let his head hang down. "I'd like to help you guys, you know that. You, Fischer, not this other guy. He ain't my friend."

"Well, I'll be your friend," said Fischer, "but you gotta level with me, like friends always do."

Poker, seduction, and the third degree, thought Fischer, they're all the same.

"Can I have a coffee?" asked Yanez.

"Sure, kid," said Fischer, rising.

"No! Don't leave me with him. Let him go get it."

"Okay, punk," said Lowell, leaving the office. "I'll get your goddamn coffee for you."

"He really is a bastard," said Yanez. "Been drinking too, looks like. You stay with me, Fischer, or the son-of-a-bitch will kill me."

"I think I can keep him off you, but he's feeling mean because he keeps wondering where this poor girl is, her and her poor little baby, where they're lying tonight."

Yanez's mouth opened wide in terror. "What baby?" He gripped the arms of his chair.

"Goose, the girl was pregnant."

Danny Yanez held onto his seat and howled so loudly that Lowell ran back into the office thinking Fischer had hit him. Fischer motioned Lowell to leave again.

"I *love* kids!" cried Goose. "I got three kids."

"Why don't you tell me the whole story, Goose, you'll feel better then."

"We didn't know about no baby. She was a witch. That's what we were told. A witch!"

"Who told you that?"

"That lady, the cop's mom. Oh, shit, man, shit . . ."

"She was going to have a baby."

"Oh, man . . ." Yanez started to cry. "I'm no fuckin' good."

"Why don't you tell me everything you know, Goose?"

Yanez jumped out of his chair, and Fischer with him, in case he would have to bring him down. "I'll do it for my kids!" he cried. "I'll tell the truth about everything."

Fischer eased him back into his chair and called Martin Lowell into the office. They gave Yanez a cup of coffee and Fischer sat behind the desk, a yellow pad in front of him. He clicked the button of his ball-point pen several times and said, "Okay, Goose, go ahead."

"She was gonna have a baby?"

"I'm afraid so."

"You gotta believe me, we didn't know about the baby."

"We believe you, Goose. Nobody would kill a baby if he knew. You just tell us what happened."

Yanez had an unclear recollection of that meeting at the Panama Club. Juan Barrajas had told them there was a lady with a lot of money and someone was in her way. She was with an old lady. A guy was fixing the jukebox, he remembered. Soon, he forgot his remorse and struggled to recall details.

He told them of seeing the movies several times before getting around to going over to Maria's house. He described pulling her into the car and trying to subdue her. He told of how hard she fought.

"On top of everything else," he said, "the damn car was givin' us trouble. That car was a loser. I had a car once, boy, before they repossessed it, a Thunderbird. That was some car. It was a French car."

"A Thunderbird ain't a French car, Goose," said Fischer.

"This one was. The tires was always going down on me!" Yanez followed with, "Yuk, yuk, yuk, yuk!" and twisted his mouth and nose to one side of his face in imitation of his hero Jerry Lewis.

Lowell and Fischer laughed at him, and Fischer had to put down his pen for a moment to crack his knuckles and wipe his eyes.

"You're too much, Goose," said Fischer.

"Everybody says I should be on television," said Yanez.

"I can guarantee it. By tomorrow you'll be on all the channels."

It took a moment for Yanez to understand. The irony of his achievement did not diminish his pride in it.

He told them of passing the Pike's Peak Turf Club trying to find a spot to drop her. He told them of pulling off the road, going under the main highway and burying her under a railroad trestle.

Lowell and Fischer looked at each other, a silent tension in their faces.

"Tell us again where you buried her."

Yanez described the spot.

"What exit was this from the highway?" asked Lowell.

"I don't remember," said Yanez.

"Well, think, dammit."

"I *am* thinking."

"Was it called County Line Road?" asked Fischer.

"That's it."

"And you're sure she was alive when you were digging the grave?" asked Lowell.

"Yeah."

"You killed her in Pueblo County," said Lowell.

"So?" asked Yanez.

"So that makes it Fergie's case," explained Fischer.

Yanez was still not interested. Until Lowell said, "You're one dead goose."

4

Beef Buddusky endured the sermon, fighting his own fatigue and boredom at being told once again that every day he continues his low-down ways, salvation slips further and further out of his reach. The captive congregation could sense from the rhythm of the zealot's voice that he was building to his conclusion. Derelicts about the room elbowed their neighbors awake. As anticipated, he made one last plea to seek Jesus Christ, ". . . the Son of God, who taught us all to pray . . ." At last he gestured them to their feet and they bowed their heads and mumbled the half-forgotten phrases of the Lord's Prayer. Then they were given their beans and cornbread.

Beef was in Los Angeles, stopping at still another mission. He had made it to Mexico, where all he did was watch and listen to the mariachis. They don't slough off. They can be singing to two drunk gringos, one with his head dead on the table, and they still give it all they got. You wonder what it means to them. The one fella could be out cold and his friend could be wishing they'd all go away, but the mariachis don't slough off.

Maria's presence weighed too heavily on him in Mexico. He wanted to try for Peru. If he could only get to Peru, he was sure, he would be able to start a new life. But instead he went drifting northward again. Thanks to Ginny and Mae, he had become too domesticated in the Springs ever to find comfort and freedom in the road. He wished he had something to insulate him from his loneliness: an obsession or a talent or a purpose in life. Some of what the mariachis had.

Someone had left a newspaper on the table. He spread it out in front of him and saw the headline on the bottom right corner: SALVATION ARMY HANDYMAN SOUGHT FOR ROLE IN GIRL'S DISAPPEARANCE, *Man Posed as Policeman.*

He had never thought of himself as posing as a cop. That meant something different from what he had actually done. He was not sure he could pass himself off as a cop, but that's what it said in the paper. He boxed his own ears for the despicable pride he felt. The wasted men sitting on either side of him drifted away, accustomed to crazies who beat their own heads.

The newspaper account made much of the man who allegedly impersonated Gordon Wynn in the illegal annulment. He was known alternately as "Beef" and "Bomba the Jungle Boy," and the story suggested that some sort of hedonistic cultism may be involved.

"I never hurt nobody!" he sobbed. "God, I was born to lose," he quoted the tattoo on his bulging bicep. Somebody called the goons, who invited Beef to seek salvation elsewhere.

He claimed his bag and walked to an entrance of the Harbor Freeway. He extended his thumb. "Might as well be in hell," he muttered.

A caravan of cars followed Danny Yanez down Route 25. Manacled, he sat in the back seat between a priest and Ronnie Fischer, the only officer he would trust.

He directed the driver off the highway and told him where to stop. Fischer helped him walk through the snow to the railroad trestle. Newsmen and police from two counties clustered behind them. Yanez had no difficulty finding the spot. He broke down and had to be taken aside and comforted by the priest, who put his arm around his shoulders. After a few moments Danny stepped forward and pointed down to the ground. He was helped back up to the car by Ronnie Fischer. The priest stayed behind. With the first shovelful of dirt they found her.

5

Beef had colored his hair black with shoe dye and had touched up his newly grown moustache, still sparse, with black eyebrow pencil. He wore a pair of fake eyeglasses. He bought two bottles of aspirin and the evening papers at a drugstore and took them back to the room he had rented near the Pueblo County Courthouse.

Being on the lam was not abnormal to his prior way of life, and being in Pueblo was not in itself so unsafe. The fugitive runs, he does not stay within sight of the court that wants him. But safety was an unsatisfactory reason for his presence there, and he had no other explanation, no more than the singed moth who returns to the flame to be burned crisply.

Nobody would have listened to him, he reasoned. Why would anybody take his word, a drifter with a record, against the word of a cop's mother? Maybe, though, if he had gone to the cops, they would have at least talked to her about it and that might have been enough to scare her away from killing Maria. Ginny could have then pressed charges against Beef for slander or something. Still, a girl would be alive today. Hell, people are dying every day from being in the wrong place at the wrong time. Innocent people, beautiful people, pregnant people. Old suicidal fantasies offered small comfort.

He went out into the hall and called the Ponderosa Pines in Colorado Springs. He would take Mae back on her terms, on any terms. He needed an ally and she was the only one to whom he could turn. Maybe they could get a little back of what they once had.

"Ponderosa Pines."

"Is Mae there?"

"Mae don't work here no more."

"Oh, yeah? Where's she work?"

"I don't know. She left town."

"Where'd she go?"

"Utah, I think."

"Ed? This you?"

"Naw, Ed don't work here no more either."

"Well, where the hell is *he?*"

"Jail."

He was going to have to see this through on his own. He went back to his room and opened the paper.

MARIA'S BODY FOUND IN PUEBLO COUNTY: POLICEMAN'S WIFE BEATEN, STRANGLED. *Suspect Admits Murder for Hire.*

There was a large picture of the grave site. Her partially uncovered and decomposed body was hardly discernible. The story included the late-breaking news that the coroner's autopsy indicated Maria might have been buried alive.

He studied the picture of her corpse, still half in the ground, and he remembered seeing her for the first time and knowing he would love her, and knowing how much. He took a handful of aspirins for his headache.

It was a mistake to bury Maria under that particular railroad trestle, a mistake her killers could not have anticipated, a mistake they could not appreciate even after their arrests. It put the crime in the jurisdiction of Ralph Ferguson, district attorney of Pueblo County.

Ferguson was a bent and frail man who wore mismatched clothes and kept his pants up with suspenders passed down from an earlier generation. He looked quasi-official, almost agricultural, like a pig farmer who also happens to be president of the school board.

But he was a giant-killer and a local hero. Even Beef, who had never done Colorado time, knew "Fergie" from talks with those who had. His was one of the most respected names in the joints, and when ex-cons got together to fantasize about future jobs, they made a wide circle around Pueblo County. There was no making a deal with Fergie, there was no measure of mercy when he prosecuted. Pueblo County was a hostile environment for criminals.

Upon discovery of the body, Ferguson, who was hounded by the press, issued a statement.

A crime has been committed in Colorado, one of such frightening brutality, of such devious premeditation, that we must move as quickly and as forcefully as possible to assure that the perpetrators are meted out punishment in kind. There will be those who will rise to the defense of these ruthless killers, who will try to find excuses for their despicable behavior, but will anyone speak for the beautiful young girl and her unborn child who were beaten and put into the ground still fighting for life? If ever society were called upon to accept the role of retaliator, this is the case.

Beef read the statement and said to his empty room, "This man wants Ginny Mom and the two Mexican kids dead."

District Attorney Ferguson, Beef read, made $17,500 a year and was in office for his tenth year. He had been a defense attorney and reportedly ran for DA because he thought it was too easy to win cases against the county. It was rumored that he successfully defended a child molester he knew to be guilty, and when his client smiled and extended his hand after his acquittal, Ferguson said, "Get away from me, you son-of-a-bitch." Shortly after, a political unknown and a recent transplant from Michigan, he was elected district attorney by a landslide.

He was first in his class as an undergraduate and first in his class at law school. After his first year in office Pueblo County topped the state with its conviction rate, 97.4 per cent. During nine years in office he was number one in conviction rate six times. He always appeared alone and unaided in important cases, and he never lost a jury trial. Never.

In the previous year only one of 196 offenders was found innocent by a jury, and one of Ferguson's deputies lost that case. During his tenure he prosecuted five capital cases, and all five eventually paid for their crimes in the gas chamber.

"*Woi Yesus!*" said Beef Buddusky. Reading about the district attorney sent him into a panic he believed was on Ginny's behalf. Then he faced the unthinkable. "What if he wants *me* dead?"

If Ginny's lawyer was intimidated by the district attorney she did not reveal it to the press. In interviews she ridiculed him and his statement, claiming he had a "vengeful God complex." When reporters tried to promote a pre-trial feud, Ferguson said coolly, "I'll deal with Miss Ryan and her client in court."

Sally Ryan was one of a handful of American lawyers who had transcended the practice of law to become personalities in their own right, newsworthy people who could be called upon at a moment's notice to fill a vacancy on a TV talk show, nothing to promote but themselves.

Expert showmen all, who charged exorbitant legal fees to those who could afford them, they would take a case without a fee and fight it for years if it had the potential for staying in the news. One of Sally's East Coast colleagues had won so much publicity as a personality that he hardly practiced law at all, preferring to spend most of his time playing the part of a lawyer or judge in TV dramas and feature films. Some say the man's heart broke when he tried to get the lead in *On the Waterfront* but found he had been typecast and inferior actors like Brando were picking up the meaningful roles.

Sally Ryan was severe in dress and manner; everything about her seemed battened down and under lock and key. If she wore make-up, it was not enough to make a difference. And yet she had a fine figure and very good legs, though one knew instinctively that she had never lain with another human being. Perhaps only one, if you cared to invest in her a mystery and seek an explanation for the way she was.

She was head of her own busy firm and had an enormous number of clients. Her method of fee setting frequently got her into trouble with the bar, which suspected her of usury, but she took advantage of the bar's notorious reluctance to speak ill of one of its own and always escaped with a mild rebuke.

She was the darling and champion of Denver homosexuals. She would visit the jail, agree to defend the recent men's room violator at a nominal fee, if he would agree to bring her five others similarly charged whom she could defend on a sliding scale, at an average of $20 per month for an average of five years. She was the only lawyer in Denver with a secretarial pool of nothing but homosexual males, past clients, who toiled for subsistence wages, working off their fees.

She was anywhere from forty-five to sixty years of age, and though she had lost several capital cases no client of hers had ever said farewell from the gas chamber. She contacted Gordon Wynn, who had inexplicably already been turned down by a long list of other prominent attorneys, and he was quick to agree to her terms. Sally Ryan would defend Gordon's mother to the final disposition of the case in return for 100 per cent of the publication rights to the Wynn story (hard-cover, soft-cover, foreign, domestic, magazine, newspaper) and 100 per cent of the film rights, TV rights, recording rights, and other rights to technical advancements still to be invented. In addition, Gordon turned over to her the registration for his car, and he agreed to work in her office as investigator for a period of three years, at subsistence wages.

6

Beef's mother had come through with some cash. It was Christmas, after all. Always before, wherever he was, and once he was in prison, Beef tried to create a sense of Christmas for himself. It did not take much. An eggnog with some barroom cronies was sufficient. Once he was part of a family, and a family is never so good as on Christmas and the lack of one never harder than then. Traditionally, his family would have a goose stuffed with an exquisite mixture of sauerkraut, boiled potatoes, and caraway seeds. The anticipation of the feast was so great, the smell of the house so rich, that he and his father had to take a long walk through the strippings and into the woods before dinner, and this too became a tradition. Then when his father disappeared the tradition went with him. Still, the memories were there, and with them the memories of two Christmases with the family of his own making, and every year he tried to keep Christmas in some small personal way. But not this one.

He made instant coffee in his room, and for dinner a piece of baloney on two pieces of dry bread. This brought back memories only of the drunk tank, where he and the others would stand at the bars with both shaky hands outstretched. The bull would walk down the line, placing a piece of bread on each hand. He would make a second trip to put a piece of baloney on every other slice of bread. The drunks would slap their hands together like one muted unit of applause and sit back against the wall to dine.

By Christmas Day, after Yanez had confessed and Maria's body was exhumed, Rudy Montalvo still refused to talk. He had been transferred from Colorado Springs to Pueblo and booked for murder. He was spending his fourth Christmas in the custody of the People.

Martin Lowell and Ronnie Fischer spent a good part of their holiday with him, urging him to confess to his part in the crime.

"Don't you guys have families? I got nothing to say," said Montalvo.

"You should see your pal Goose," said Lowell. "He's calm and happy and sleeps like a puppy. He's got nothing on his chest."

"But pimples," said Montalvo.

Lowell started cleaning his fingernails with a paper clip. "You may think he's dumb, but old Goose has outsmarted you. He's gonna come out on top and let you and the old lady suck up the gas. Hell, he's only a poor *re*tard led around by you and Ginny Mom."

"The man upstairs knows I'm innocent."

"You're getting the shaft, pal," said Lowell. "The grand jury meets day after tomorrow. You'd better get in under the wire."

"I'm making book that the other two'll beat it."

"Fuck you."

After a long silence, Fischer said, "The girl was Catholic, you know. I wonder if that means her baby will go to hell, not being baptized and all. Of course, the baby wasn't born yet, but you'd have to say it was alive. It was a little girl, the coroner said. I wonder if she will go to hell. I wonder what they do with her in this case. I mean, do they embalm the little girl and bury her in the same coffin as her mother or do they put her in a separate coffin or do they put her back inside the mother and sew her up or what? What do you think?"

Montalvo started to sniffle.

"Will the baby go to hell, Rudy? What's your opinion?"

Rudy covered his face with his hands and had to be returned to his cell. They waited until eleven that night and then Fischer called for him again. He asked him only one question: "Rudy, do you want a priest?"

"Yeah, I think I do."

Fischer called Father Cooper, one of two Catholic chaplains who regularly visited the jail. He arrived at eleven forty-five, excited because he knew from the newspapers and television who Montalvo was. Fischer shook hands with him and took him to the interrogation room and said only that the boy wanted to talk to him. Father Cooper was with Montalvo for forty-five minutes. When he opened the door to leave, Fischer could see Montalvo inside, praying on his knees. As Father Cooper passed Fischer, he clasped his hands together and said, "I think he's ripe."

Twenty minutes later Rudy Montalvo emerged from the room smiling sweetly. He asked Fischer, "Do you know how it feels to finally turn to your Saviour?"

"Good, huh?"

"The best."

Fischer offered him a cigarette and lit it for him. They leaned against opposite walls in the hallway and smoked.

"The circumstances," said Rudy, "are very, very unfortunate, and I am very, very sorry, but I know God has forgiven me and now I am ready to be judged by man."

Fischer led him to another room, called the captain and a

stenographer, and listened to Rudy's full confession.

Two days after Christmas the grand jury met to hear testimony regarding the death of Maria Wynn. Martin Lowell was the first witness. He identified photographs of Yanez, Barrajas, Virginia Wynn, Montalvo, and Mrs. Lister.

The coroner took the stand and dispassionately described the condition of Maria's body and testified that in his opinion death was not by natural causes or by self-inflicted wounds but by some human agency other than the victim.

Montalvo told of the crime from his point of view and Yanez followed with his. Mrs. Lister told her rambling story. Two landladies were called. Finally the last witness, Gordon Wynn, was called.

Ralph Ferguson did not bother rising. He questioned him from his table, methodically, and with a great deal of quiet contempt, revealing through his questioning that although Mrs. Wynn had been married once or twice during Gordon's adult life, she chose to live with her son rather than with her husband. Wasn't this an unusual state of affairs, wondered Ferguson. Gordon replied that he didn't think so.

Ferguson then stood up and asked, "At the time that you lived with your mother, did you ever sleep in the same bed with her?"

A few members of the grand jury leaned forward. Gordon turned to look at them before answering. "No, sir," he replied, unruffled.

"Never?"

"Never."

Ferguson had no further questions.

The grand jury deliberated for ten minutes and brought back an accusation against Virginia Wynn, Rodolfo Montalvo and Daniel Yanez of a felony, to wit, a violation of Chapter 40, Article

2, Sections 1 and 3 of the Penal Code, murder. In addition, Mrs. Wynn was indicted on four counts of felonies in connection with the fraudulent annulment. Also indicted, in absentia, on three counts of felonies was John Doe, alias "Bomba the Jungle Boy," alias "Beef."

7

It was late at night, early in the morning, and the few left in the place voted to unplug the jukebox and sing, Beef Buddusky among them, holding and swinging his bottle of Coors by its sweaty neck. *"Last Saturday night I got married, me and my wife settled down . . ."*

He was with good old aces he knew, though he had never seen a one of them before that night, men who spoke the same language as he, transplanted like him from a bed of gravel to a patch of sand. Honky-tonk men, juke-jointers, barflies; chips off the old block, heartaches to their mothers to see how like their fathers they have become, whiskey bass troubadours willing to face the action end of a broken beer bottle for the honor of a sodden chum or a Four Roses chippy, but unable as hell to raise a kind word to the only ones in the world who love them, against all common and uncommon sense.

He was with folks who gave their full sympathy unstintingly. Time and again he had sought and received their collective succor against the inequities of a landlady, a boss, a wife, an insensitive society, a D and D. On the other hand, they were equally willing to swoop down en masse with definitive condemnation upon those who have earned it and to suggest to the wheelers of fate what ought to be done about them. Communists ought to be sent to Russia; dissatisfied Negroes ought to be sent to Africa; crooked politicians ought to be shot; child molesters ought to be staked to an anthill. That sort of thing.

Mom Wynn, as she was now known, ought to be given the gas chamber. In the other seat they ought to put that dodo Yanez and on her lap ought to sit baby-face Montalvo.

Beef thanked the dear Jesus, Mary, and Joseph that they failed to include him in their vigilante fantasy.

"The son, too, they ought to cut off his copper balls, the goddamn lousy mama's boy," said one of the hairy-chested men.

"What balls?" asked another, well hung.

"He didn't have nothin' to do with it," offered Beef. "Montalvo said."

"That's a cover-up, can't you see? They're protectin' the little shit."

"He was a cop. He turned her in," said Beef. "You think he'd do that if he knew she was guilty?"

"Look at 'im, there's nothin' he wouldn't do."

"Now, wait a minute . . ."

"Hell, you heard what he told the grand jury."

"The way I read it . . ."

"Hell, boy, you don't know nothin.' "

"Well, maybe I don't know nothin', but I do know this here: in America a person's innocent till he's proven guilty or there ain't a cow in Texas."

"Maybe not, but there's a helluva lot of bull!"

The barflies Beef knew tended to reduce things to cat-and-mouse. If you can get away with it, fine; if you get caught, tough shit. Seldom were they vindictive toward a common captured criminal. If you get caught, you do your time, and no adrenalin is wasted on you. But this case was awakening in them a pristine savagery, an indignant alarm on behalf of the entire tribe.

They soundly condemned the killers and cursed as well those who knew about the impending murder but did not lift a finger to save the girl.

"Look here," Beef asked the most vocal of them, a small weasel-like man. "What would you do in that case?"

"I'd rat on them, quick as a shot," he answered.

"Easy to say," said Beef. "The old lady Lister was senile, the Mexican guy was afraid of gettin' sent to the joint, and Bomba had a record, how could they go to the cops?"

"Hell, I have a record, I'd of gone."

"That's easy to say." Beef braced himself for the ordeal of discussing himself in the third person. "What about Bomba the Jungle Boy?" he asked.

"They'll catch him. He'll get his."

"All he did was help her get an annulment."

"I hope the bastard can sleep nights."

Beef winced. He *couldn't* sleep nights. Would they forgive him if he told them that? "Seems to me he was only what they call an innocent victim of circumstances," he said. "You know, in the wrong place at the wrong time."

"Shit, boy."

"Don't call me no boy. I'm as old as you are."

"But you're dumb, boy. Anybody'd stand up for that bloodsucker and her crowd is as dumb as they come."

"For all you know, she was only a good mother," said Beef.

"She chewed his balls away. Call that a good mother?"

"She wanted to keep him out of trouble," Beef said. "What the hell is a mother for?"

"Anybody'd stand up for a ball chewer must like chewin' on them himself."

Beef lowered his head and said, "Cut it out."

"You hungry for balls?" continued the small weasel-like man. He pushed Beef and when he encountered no resistance pushed him again. Beef turned his back on him. The small man shoved him. "C'mon, tell us how you do it, you big tub of yellow shit."

Beef said nothing.

The small man grabbed his arm and pulled him to the door. "Get the hell out of here!" he yelled. He opened the door and forced Beef outside. "Come in here again and I'll kill you, you motherfucker!"

Out on the sidewalk, Beef heard them laughing and after a moment heard them singing wistfully again, of lonely trains that whistle by on moonless nights.

8

Beef believed he had done a good job of protecting Maria, up to his one lapse, when they killed her. If only she hadn't rejected him, called the police on him as he stood there guarding her, he would not have fallen into oblivion with Straight, drowning the ugly man's dream of loving a beautiful woman. Now, he must find some way to repay her for letting down his guard. God save him, he still loved her.

He recklessly made the rounds of the Pueblo honky tonks, seeking a merciful word for the accused and absolution for Bomba on the lam. In each smoky room the verdict was the same.

Some suggested that Bomba the Jungle Boy might even have been rubbed out because he knew too much. It made a kind of sense to Beef. He went back to his room and read again the long and complicated definition of schizophrenia that he had copied into his notebook at the public library. He wanted so badly not to be Bomba the Jungle Boy that he sometimes believed he was not that person. That may be why he thought he could go to court, like any other citizen, and watch the trial of Mom Wynn. Rudy and Yanez were each to receive separate, subsequent trials, this in exchange for their pleas of guilty and their testimonies against Ginny Wynn.

He did not expect it to be so crowded, especially during the early proceedings. The spectators lined up before dawn and the corridors swarmed with newsmen, who were calling the crime "the Silver Cord Murder Case." Beef did not know why; as far as he knew, no silver cord had been involved.

No one expected an acquittal. In fact, when Ginny pled "Not guilty," and Sally Ryan added, "And not guilty by reason of insanity," the spectators groaned.

It seemed a fair plea to Beef. If they did not catch him soon he would be able to cop the same plea himself. His hanging around this crowded courthouse, for instance, seemed not quite sane.

Gordon and Ginny walked into every court session arm in arm, through the hooting and the jeering of the many who waited in line. "Yoo-hoo, copper, mama's boy!" Beef would turn to those next to him and hiss, *"Shhhhhh!"* Neither Gordon nor Ginny ever looked their way.

Juan Barrajas, in the grip of consumption, had been secretly kept in a hospital by the DA's office and was helped into court by a nurse.

Mrs. Lister strolled into court every day on the arm of a bailiff. The DA chose not to consider her an accomplice. Likewise, Bomba the Jungle Boy, should he ever be found, would not be prosecuted except for his role in the fraudulent annulment. An accomplice, according to law, was someone who could be charged with the same crime as the defendant, and a defendant cannot be convicted solely on the testimonies of accomplices. This rule, at trial time, tends to cut down the number of accomplices.

Beef was momentarily relieved. He was not an accomplice. The

DA said so. That must make it so. Why couldn't he believe it?

The district attorney had in court a large map of Colorado Springs. Through the questioning of detectives he ascertained the locations of the Panama Club, Ginny's apartment, Maria's various apartments, and many other more incidental addresses connected with the case. The coroner and his assistant testified that the body found buried below that railroad trestle was indeed that of Maria Delgado Wynn, and that she died by other than natural causes, accident, or suicide. She died, he said, at the hands of another person or persons. The cause of death was one of three mechanisms: strangulation, suffocation, or brain damage. All so cold, the words.

Two landladies, Mrs. Rogers and Mrs. Shaw, testified to the disturbance created in their units by Mrs. Virginia Wynn.

Attorney Roger Glover was called and he testified about the fraudulent annulment. Sally Ryan tried to object to any testimony regarding another charge but Ralph Ferguson claimed that the annulment proved motive for the crime. Miss Ryan was overruled.

Montalvo and Yanez were called, in that order, and the jurors moved uncomfortably in their seats as they listened to their calm descriptions of the night they murdered Maria Wynn. Montalvo insisted that had they known she was pregnant she would be alive today, for both he and Yanez loved kids. He ended his testimony by saying that for the first time in his life he was happy, now that Jesus was in his corner.

Yanez's account was vague and uncertain, though he earnestly tried to answer each question in a dignified, intelligent manner.

Juan Barrajas testified in faltering English and was followed by Mrs. Lister, who testified for an entire day, sometimes growing so tired she almost fell asleep on the stand. She told long, rambling stories that often were incomprehensible and sometimes drew laughter from the audience and jurors alike.

During a recess, Beef left with the half of the audience that went out to the corridors for a smoke. The other half saved their seats for them. A woman with thick legs offered him a cup of coffee from her thermos.

"Ain't this the berries?" she said.

"Huh?"

"I used to come to court all the time, but it bored me to tears after a while. This one's a beaut, though. Old Fergie's gonna gas the dame."

"You think so?"

"Oh, sure. She'll be the first woman ever executed in the state of Colorado."

She seemed to take a perverse pride in the new ground broken.

"I look at her," said Beef, "and I can't see her killing somebody."

"Bighearted lug, ain't you?"

"What about Bomba the Jungle Boy?" he asked.

"What about him?"

"He didn't have anything to do with this."

"The hell you say."

"He's just another guy, like me, passing through one town on his way to another."

"So if he's innocent, why ain't he here to speak up?"

"Well, maybe he is," he said.

"Huh?"

The spectators began filing back into court.

"Thanks, missus, for the joe."

"You're welcome," she said, screwing the top back on the thermos. "She'll get the chamber, kiddo. Good for her."

When they resumed, the district attorney spilled onto a table the pieces of a tie Maria had given Gordon for his birthday and his mother had cut up. Mrs. Lister had saved the pieces.

Just like her, thought Beef.

9

Sally Ryan made no opening statement. She began her defense by questioning Ginny Wynn, one of only three witnesses for the defense.

That day the corridors were packed by 5:30 A.M. The courtroom door guardian was Deputy Sheriff Ralph Moran and it happened to be his birthday. A few of the girls got together and baked a cake. Others brought coffee in thermos bottles. Others brought paper plates and cups and napkins. Standing in the corridor, a piece of cake crumbling in his hand, Beef sang the encore with the others: *"Happy birthday, dear Deputy Ralph . . ."*

He shook the deputy's hand and said, "Many happy returns. How old are you, ace?"

"Thirty-nine," said the deputy, smiling.

"You and Jack Benny, huh?"

The deputy laughed. "Yeah, next year I start counting backward."

"Well, many happy returns. Whaddaya think of all this?" Beef took a big bite of cake.

"All in a day's work," said the deputy.

"Tasty stuff," said Beef, wiping crumbs off his mouth.

Everyone ate and enjoyed, many already worried about what they would do once the trial was over. They would miss each other.

Preferred places in line went up to $10.

Courthouse secretaries showed up for work at 6 A.M. and typed and filed and ran about industriously so that by nine-thirty they could have permission to slip through the judge's chambers and get the best seats in the house for the morning session.

The questioning began with minor details about her history and Gordon's childhood, adolescence, and young manhood, during which he always stayed in his own bed, she claimed, no matter how cold the morning or frightening the night.

She told of her suicide attempt and of later seeing Maria and Gordon together. She had no impression at all of Maria until it became clear that Gordon was serious about her. She admitted calling her once and accusing her of sleeping with Gordon, which Maria did not deny.

"Naturally I was quite upset over such goings-on," she said.

Miss Ryan led her through the stories the other witnesses had told. Yes, it was true that she went to Maria's apartment. Gordon was supposed to be at a football game and when Ginny saw that he wasn't there she became worried. But there was no argument. Gordon simply wanted to go home with her, and he did. Bomba the Jungle Boy was there. Ask him.

Another time she went to Maria's apartment to show the landlady that Gordon was not really living there. The landlady was very cooperative and let her into the apartment. Ask Bomba, he knows.

She admitted that she had concocted a plot to tie up Gordie and kidnap him for a few days, until he came to his senses.

She admitted mothering Bomba the Jungle Boy, but all he ever

219

did for her was wash some windows.

She admitted meeting Juan Barrajas quite by accident. She and Mrs. Lister had been looking for a place to eat. Mr. Barrajas had been standing at the doorway to his establishment and said, "Aren't you Gordon Wynn's mother?" Next thing she knew, she was the victim of extortion.

She admitted having no love for Maria but denied wanting to harm her.

She simply could not understand, she said, why all those people on the witness stand told lies about her.

When it came time for Ferguson to cross-examine her, he stood very close to her and looked right into her eyes. She looked right back at him, unflinching.

"As I understand it," he said, "you did not really dislike Maria, but you disapproved of Gordie marrying anyone, isn't that right?"

"At that time, yes," she said. "He was going to night school and still had a long way to go. He was in no position to get married."

"In other words, you didn't want Gordie married at that time to anyone?"

"Not at that time I didn't."

"And was your reason for that a concern for Gordie's future?"

"It was."

"You believed that Gordie could not support a wife and child?"

"No, not if he was to support me and go to school too."

"Is that why you told people that the baby Maria was carrying was not Gordie's?"

Gordon Wynn stood up in the audience and shouted, "Mr. Ferguson, my name is Gordon, not Gordie."

"Your honor," said Ferguson, "I ask that this man be ejected."

"You sit down please and keep quiet," the court warned Gordon.

"Well, he's right, your honor," said Ginny.

Sally Ryan stood and said, "Will the court request Mr. Ferguson to call the defendant's son 'Gordon' or 'Mr. Wynn'?"

"Your honor," said Ferguson, "testimony shows that this witness calls him 'Gordie' more often than 'Gordon.' I have a perfect right to call him 'Gordie.' "

"You can have some respect for him," said Sally Ryan.

"Why?" asked the district attorney.

Sally Ryan usually had a ready answer for everything.

He continued to call him "Gordie" throughout the trial. So did the public.

"Continue," the court demanded.

Ferguson turned back to Ginny and said, as though he had no real interest in the question, "Now, is it true that Gordie, your son, has lived with you all his life?"

"Yes."

"And he lived with you while you were married to James Powell?"

"James Powell?"

"Did Gordon Wynn live with you while you were married to James Powell?"

"What do you mean? I never lived with James Powell."

"Perhaps not, but did your son . . ."

"What does that have to do with it?"

The judge said, "Answer the question."

"I certainly have a right to know what he's driving at," said Ginny Wynn.

"Just answer the questions," said the judge.

"Did Gordie also continue to live with you while you were married to Clyde Smith?"

Sally Ryan rose and said, "We are going to object to that as incompetent, irrelevant, and immaterial."

"What's he doing?" asked Ginny Wynn.

"She told you," said Sally Ryan, "that Gordon Wynn has lived with her all his life. These questions are asked only to prejudice this jury."

"And to humiliate my son," added Ginny Wynn.

"The questions are incompetent, irrelevant, and immaterial," said Sally Ryan.

"And humiliating," said Ginny Wynn.

"The objection is overruled," said the judge.

"He has *always* lived with me," said Ginny Wynn. "He always will."

"Don't be too sure," said Ferguson.

"Your honor," said Sally Ryan, "the district attorney is taunting the witness."

"Mr. District Attorney?"

"I'm sorry, your honor. Mrs. Wynn, during all the time you were married to . . ."

"I told you!" she shouted.

". . . young Sam Leonard . . ."

"I told you!"

Sally Ryan rose again and said, "We are going to object to that upon the ground that it is incompetent, irrelevant, and immaterial, upon the further ground that it is an appeal to the prejudice of the jury, and upon the further ground that the question has been asked and answered."

Ferguson said, "I think I have a right to show that there was a peculiarly close relationship between mother and son in this instance. Despite the fact that the defendant was married to other persons at the time when her son was a grown man, she continued to live with her son rather than with her husbands. It would follow that her son, having married, would prefer to live with her rather than with his wife."

The judge asked, "What is the question that now is objected to?"

Ferguson answered, "The question that is specifically objected to by Miss Ryan is whether Mr. Gordie Wynn, the defendant's son, continued to live with her during her marriage to young Sam Leonard."

"Why do you have to keep calling him *young* Sam Leonard?" said Ginny in a loud, angry voice.

"He was, I believe, about your son's age."

"She has stated he lived with her all his life," said the judge. "That is sufficient."

"All right," said Ferguson, "I will withdraw that and ask another question. Gordie lived with you all his life, but when you married Samuel Leonard, Mr. Leonard did not live with you and Gordie, did he?"

"Objection," said Sally Ryan.

"The objection is sustained," said the judge.

"All right," said Ferguson, secure that the points had already been made. "Mrs. Wynn, you and Gordie occupy the same apartment, do you not?"

"We do."

"How many bedrooms are in this apartment?"

"One."

"And how many beds?"

"One."

"Isn't it true that you and Gordie share that bed together?"

"Absolutely not!"

Muted ripples of laughter spread through the audience.

"I'm on trial for my life!" Ginny yelled at the audience.

"Where does Gordie sleep, then?" asked the DA, as though she had never shouted.

Ginny grew angry and snapped at him, "Don't stand on top of me like that!"

Ferguson walked to the far end of the jury box.

"That's better," she said.

"I believe it is," said Ferguson.

Ginny took a deep breath and said, "You tried to trick me. I know what you're doing. Well, we have a sofa bed in our place, a sofa that opens up. That's where Gordie sleeps. You're disgusting!"

"Just answer the questions, Mrs. Wynn," cautioned the judge.

"Did you buy Gordie's clothes for him?" asked Ferguson.

She raised five fingers into the air.

"Selected the clothes he would wear?" asked the DA.

Again, she raised the five fingers.

"Would you mind explaining yourself?"

"Fifth Amendment," said Ginny, quite calmly.

It seemed all her life she had wanted to do that.

Exasperated, Ferguson requested the court to order her to answer, which it did. Sally Ryan also told her that she would have to answer the questions.

"Of course, I shopped for him," she said at last, "just like any other mother would."

The questioning of Ginny Wynn took three days. When it seemed no more could be learned from her, Ferguson said, "Well, let me ask you one more question. Maybe you can answer this simple question with a yes or no."

"Shoot."

"Pardon?"

"Ask your question."

"On the eve of Maria's murder, was there anything you wanted more than the death of your daughter-in-law?"

Ginny thought about it. She could find no way to answer that question.

"Yes or no," prompted the district attorney.

She held up five fingers.

The district attorney turned to the jury, sighed, and said, "That is all."

Gordon testified to his mother's pathological fear of being left alone. That is why she always had Mrs. Lister around, why she took in Bomba the Jungle Boy, why she couldn't stand to see Gordon marry and move out. He knew she would rather be dead than alone.

Sally Ryan walked closer to the witness stand to ask, "Was that why you kept your wedding a secret?"

"Yes."

"And when did you finally tell her?"

"The next night, after the wedding. I don't remember if I told her or if she already knew. Anyway, she was hysterical."

Hysterical? thought Beef; she threw the pieces of your baby pictures in your face.

"Nothing I could say could console her. I left her there and returned to my wife."

When me and Mrs. Lister came rolling out of the closet, thought Beef.

"Tell the jury why you continued to reside, part-time, with your mother during your marriage."

"I loved my mother." There was a gasp in the audience. "And I loved my wife."

"Then why did you leave her on your wedding night to run home to Mother?" asked Ralph Ferguson when he had his turn at Gordon.

"I did not leave Maria on our wedding night and I did not run home to Mother."

"You stayed with your wife all night?"

"On the night of our wedding, yes."

Clearly, Ralph Ferguson did not believe him. He paced for a moment and then asked, "You said that your mother was afraid of being alone; is that right?"

"Yes, sir."

"Was she also afraid of the dark?"

"Occasionally."

"And would you go to her on those occasions?"

"To which we object on the ground it is incompetent, irrelevant, and immaterial," said Miss Ryan.

"Your honor, I intend to show that an unusually powerful bond exists between this witness and his mother."

"Your honor, it is perfectly clear to everyone in this courtroom what the district attorney is trying to show. It might be well to remind him that this is no place for sleazy innuendoes."

"Objection overruled."

"The question was," said Ferguson, "on those occasions when your mother was afraid of the dark, did you go to her?"

"I'm not sure I know what you mean."

"Did you leave your bed and go to her?"

"For a moment perhaps, till she got over her fear or nightmare or whatever."

Beef sat in the audience and wondered what difference it made.

The testimony of the psychiatrist Sally Ryan had engaged to examine Ginny was anticlimactic. He diagnosed her as a sociopathic personality disturbance, anti-social reaction.

Beef respected the man for his wisdom. It was the line of work he would like for himself, given the necessary intelligence. Yet Ferguson, in his cross-examination, seemed to regard him as moronic.

"You are familiar, Doctor, are you not, with the Diagnostical and Statistical Manual on Mental Disorders published by the American Psychiatric Association?"

"Yes."

"And in it a sociopathic personality is defined as 'chronically anti-social individuals who are always in trouble, profiting neither from experience nor punishment, and maintaining no real loyalty to any person, group or code. They are frequently callous and hedonistic, showing marked emotional immaturity with lack of sense of responsibility, lack of judgment, and an ability to rationalize their behavior so that it appears warranted, reasonable and justified.' "

It rang a bell with Beef. He used to be one.

"Now, Doctor, does that describe a sociopath?"

"Yes, that is a fair description of the classification," said the psychiatrist.

"And isn't it true, Doctor, that most criminals fall under this category of disorder?"

"Well, yes, it does generally work out that most criminals are sociopaths."

"So what this term describes, Doctor, is a mean, wicked person who commits criminal acts, does it not? A person who doesn't profit from punishment or experience? Isn't 'sociopathic personality' a fancy name for plain old-fashioned meanness?"

"I believe that's an oversimplification."

"Do you?"

"Yes, I do," said the psychiatrist.

"I don't," said Ferguson. "That is all."

Mrs. Lister was recalled to the witness stand. She looked tired. Soon it would all be over, and she would be without the trial and Ginny both. It would be back to the rec center for her, and perhaps one more small wave of attention and then everyone would forget about her and dullness would settle over her again.

"Mrs. Lister, did you ever call upon Mrs. Wynn in her apartment early in the morning?"

"Yes."

"Did you ever see Gordie in bed as Mrs. Wynn discussed him?"

"Yes."

Here we go again, thought Beef.

Sally Ryan stood quickly and said, "We object to that as incompetent, irrelevant, and immaterial."

"What is the relevance of his being in bed, Mr. District Attorney?" asked the court.

"I am trying to establish the exact time of this witness's conversation with the defendant."

"Objection overruled."

"I had called on Mrs. Wynn early one morning," said Mrs. Lister. "Gordie was still in bed in the living room. I was afraid of waking him up."

"What did Mrs. Wynn say?"

"She said, 'Isn't he beautiful? Couldn't you just eat him?'"

"Thank you, Mrs. Lister, that will be all."

She was helped off the witness stand by the bailiff and ushered to her seat in the audience. Ginny glared at her, as she did at all the witnesses for the People. Just beyond the railing Mrs. Lister stopped, leaned forward on her bamboo cane, and squinted at Beef, who lowered his head.

"Oh, my," she said. "It's Bomba the Jungle Boy. How are you, Bomba? You look so different."

All eyes turned to Beef Buddusky, who involuntarily slid down in his seat and said softly, "Hyuh, Mrs. Lister."

The photographers were the first to come to their senses. They jumped over benches, railings, and each other to get a good shot of Bomba the Jungle Boy, who had to cover his eyes from the striking light of their flashbulbs.

The judge beat his gavel futilely for order. Finally Ralph Ferguson ordered a bailiff to place Beef under arrest.

Ginny turned to her attorney and said, "It doesn't rain but that it pours." Court was adjourned for the day.

11

After Beef's first day of testimony, in which he truthfully answered the DA's questions, his picture was once again in all the papers and on TV. The woman with swollen feet who had given him coffee in the corridor was interviewed and her life was now complete. The local honky-tonk people could only sputter at the strange twist of events. The small weasel-like man told everyone how he had recently thrown Beef out of a local bar, though no one believed him and he became bitter and frustrated. Deputy Sheriff Moran would tell no one that he had shaken Beef's hand.

Beef's cross-examination was brief.

"Mr. Buddusky, have you ever been convicted of a felony?"

"I have, ma'am."

"What felony?"

"Grand theft, auto."

"Any other felony?"

"No, ma'am, only the one that I'm up for now."

Beef put his hands together and leaned forward.

"That is the felony you pled guilty to in the Superior Court of this county?"

"That's right, ma'am."

"What felony was that?"

"Perjury, ma'am."

"You haven't been sentenced on that charge yet?"

"No, ma'am, I have not."

"That's all."

He was called on redirect to explain that no promises were made to him regarding his perjury charge. He was also questioned further on the one direct proposal to him to commit murder.

"Well, first she asked me if I'd like to earn three thousand dollars. I said sure. Then she said she wanted me to get rid of Maria."

"And what did you say to that?"

"I didn't believe she was serious. I told her if I thought she was, why, I would have to go away. Listen, I heard lots of people say they was going to kill someone, when they was mad at 'em. Ain't you?"

"What did she say?"

"I told her to keep quiet. We were having dinner in a place and I didn't want people to hear her. Thing is, I liked Mrs. Wynn. She was good to me. I didn't want any trouble and I didn't want nobody in any trouble. I figured she was just shooting off her mouth. She was like a mother to me."

"What happened then?"

"I got mad and walked out of the place. She and Mrs. Lister caught up with me and told me to forget the whole thing. And I did."

On recross-examination Sally Ryan asked him if he believed Mrs. Wynn really wanted to murder her daughter-in-law.

"How can anybody believe that? No, I didn't want to believe it. I didn't know what to believe."

"You said you wanted absolutely nothing to do with it?"

"Nothing. I didn't even want to hear about it."

"Yet you believed she was serious about it?"

"I did and I didn't. To this day I don't know what to believe. Even though it finally happened there's no really convincing me she was serious. She was a lady mad because her son went off and got married on her. So naturally she talked about how she'd like to kill the girl. I don't think she knows herself if she was serious."

"Nonetheless, it was serious enough for you to be concerned?"

"Sure."

"Then why didn't you go to the police?"

Beef remembered sitting in the back of the squad car. It was an opportunity missed, for which he would never forgive himself. "At that time, missus, as you know, I had come to Pueblo and committed perjury. I was open myself for a charge."

"Oh, I see. You were willing to let a girl be killed rather than put yourself in a position where some charge might be made against you because of what you did in Pueblo; is that right?"

It wasn't that simple. But Beef decided to stay on the ground he and a lawyer might understand.

"Normally, a man doesn't go and commit a crime and then go to the police, for any reason. I been in prison. I know what it's like. A year or two in prison and you forget who you are. You come out and you do crazy things that send you back to prison. Look, I knew when I helped with the annulment that it was a crime, but somehow I convinced myself that it was all right. Nobody gets hurt and I get a hundred dollars. It was crazy and it was stupid. I tried to talk to her myself, tried to tell her to let it alone, let it work itself out, but all she wanted was to see Maria dead."

"Liar!" shouted Ginny from the table.

"C'mon, Ginny Mom, what's the point?" said Beef.

"I wish I never heard your name, Bomba!"

"You never did, missus," he said sadly.

Beef Buddusky drew a sentence of one to three, and was delivered to the prison at Canon City.

BOOK 4

1

He lay on his bunk, his hands behind his head, looking at the bulge in the mattress above him.

"Knock-knock."

"Who's there?" Beef asked dutifully, but with no sense of play.

"Highway cop," from his cellmate, Norman, an armed robber.

"Highway cop who?"

"Highway cop every morning with a hard-on," said Norman, filling their tight cubicle with his own moist laughter.

Beef did not laugh. He had become as morose and moody as his old girl Mae, and only infrequently did Norman bother to take up again the challenge to amuse him. The best that could be said for him, according to Norman, was that he was short and soon another cellmate would replace him, one who might laugh once in a while and help pass the time away.

Beef dug under his flat and lifeless mattress and withdrew a dirty folded slip of paper. He unfolded it carefully; some daylight could be seen through one of the creases. He reviewed the list he had made months earlier.

With his meaty hand that could hardly tolerate a pencil, Beef had scrawled at the top of the list, "The Murder of Maria Wynn and Baby Girl Wynn." The inclusion of Baby Girl Wynn followed long, solitary debates during which he concluded that two lives were taken, in spite of the official one count of murder. So. At the head of the list, Ginny Wynn herself. Goes without saying. At any particular point in time she could have stopped it by letting the young people live their own lives.

Second, Rudy Montalvo and Danny Yanez, Montalvo first because Yanez was mentally retarded and needed a guiding influence for any action. Both were simple minds, even to Beef. They were used to being moved to action by more facile minds. The boys didn't know Ginny, they didn't know if they could trust her. All they knew was that she was a cop's mother. They certainly couldn't have given any thought to their prospects for getting caught.

Next on the list, Juan Barrajas. His guilt was much greater than his own, he reasoned. He arranged the meeting. He knew what she wanted. Why didn't he stop it or tell the police? Well, he was a sick, old man with poor command of the language, in debt and facing prison, whose only hope was that Gordon would quash the arrest.

Mrs. Lister was next on the list. If anyone was privy to all that was happening it was Mrs. Lister. At any time she could have gone to the police, but Ginny had a strange and powerful hold over her, the reason for which was unknown to Beef. Mrs. Lister was certainly as guilty as Barrajas. Almost equally guilty.

What of Gordon himself? Why didn't he protect his own wife? Could he not know what his mother was capable of doing? Or was he really . . . that way with his own mother? Beef could not believe it. That was an invention of the district attorney, to turn the jury against them.

There were nameless people on the list: two landladies who

heard threats, employees at the hospital. All knew and none would believe. Beef closed his eyes and imagined them in a small room; he would hardly be noticed.

At the bottom of the list was Maria's name. She knew Ginny wanted her dead. She knew and did not adequately protect herself and her child. Beef gave nights of thought in the closeness of his cell to the theory that a victim subconsciously is an accomplice to his own murder.

Beef had yet to write his own name on the list. A prerogative of the author. Let the others put his name where they pleased, on their own lists.

Ginny, of course, had been found guilty. Like Montalvo and Yanez, she was sentenced to die. There were many points at which his life could have taken a path away from theirs. Why did he take window washing when he really wanted yard work or hauling? Why did he seek out the Salvation Army instead of a mission? Why did he stay at Ginny's place after his stomach was full? To go back further, why did he get off at Colorado Springs when the driver who had picked him up was going as far as Pueblo? He should have gone on to Pueblo, even though he didn't like the name of the place.

Beef stood his time well. He did a favor for someone and landed a good job in the hot comfort of the prison bakery, plunging his hands pleasantly into the dough. He made no friends this time around and avoided involvements.

Like so many cons who had no interest in the news while on the outside, he became a newspaper addict on the inside. Unlike the others, he did not lust for the world from which he was removed. He scanned the papers only for news of Ginny's case and followed carefully the progress of the many appeals.

He wanted her and the boys to live. There was too much blood

239

on his hands already. He did not believe their deaths could make anyone feel better.

So much of what he read he was unable to understand. He read of the boys filing for appeal and of Ginny's deadline for appeal being extended two months and then another three weeks. Delaying tactics, he figured. He was fascinated to learn that Yanez's appeal ran to only nine pages while Montalvo's was one hundred twenty-one pages. Peculiar, he thought, since they were partners in crime. Beef sure admired anyone who could understand the law. There must be a good reason for why they made it so complicated, he thought, so that ordinary folks couldn't make head nor tail of it.

The DA filed a brief on their appeals, citing cases which supported the contention that the court did not err. Beef didn't know what that meant exactly, but he was impressed by the fifty-five cases. That's a lot of cases, just to support a contention.

Ginny's appeal was finally filed. Miss Ryan, her lawyer, claimed that some jurors were improperly kept on panel, and some jurors were improperly excused; extraneous and damaging issues about Ginny's past life were improperly permitted; the case should have been moved to another county because of the pre-trial publicity; Juan Barrajas should have been ruled an accomplice, making his testimony invalid.

Beef read about it carefully and it seemed to make sound sense to him. They *did* say a lot of unkind things about Ginny's past life. There *was* one hell of a lot of publicity before the trial. If Barrajas was *not* an accomplice, then who was? But a month later the DA answered the appeal, citing eighty references of law, ten legal statutes, and one constitutional provision in a ninety-two-page argument. Beef Buddusky was impressed all to hell. How could you lock horns with that? Imagine, eighty references of law.

Two weeks or so after the DA's argument, oral arguments from both sides were heard before the State Supreme Court. By this time it had become old stuff.

And all the while Beef Buddusky sat in his cell, not laughing at the dirty jokes from the bunk above him.

A death penalty abolition bill sponsored by the governor seemed to be gaining great favor but it was killed by the judiciary committee, and on the following day the State Supreme Court ruled unanimously that the trio, as they were often called, should die. The opinion on Ginny ran to thirty-seven pages, on Montalvo, eight pages. Goose Yanez got only three pages. It seemed to Beef to express a consistent pattern and to say something significant about the value of human life, though he couldn't say what.

When he looked at himself in the mirror, Beef saw daily a closer resemblance to his father, whose dark destination was foretold in his face, if one had the power to read it. The other convicts ignored him. After he began working in the prison bakery, no one even bothered to make any sexual overtures.

Beef was passed over for parole his first time up. Six months later he tried again. By this time the State Supreme Court had closed the door on Ginny Wynn. District Attorney Ferguson recommended that Beef be released. The three perpetrators would die for their crime; Buddusky had been punished sufficiently for his. The Department of Institutions concurred in the DA's recommendation and wrote in their evaluation of Beef for the Adult Parole Board:

He plans to attend night school. In his remaining spare time, will attend church, watch TV, attend spectator sports. He feels he can stay away from bars with little trouble and looks back and sees the line of reasoning he used when drinking. Since he knows that, he knows he can have a better time outside without drinking. Knows he was sick in the past, does not want to be sick again. Mind and body are better. He has become introspective. We have shown him the road, and he has not refused the help. His future will depend entirely on whether he can put into practice what he has learned here. If he can, his future looks good, and no troubles are anticipated. He should be able to cooperate with parole officer in an excellent manner.

He appeared before the Parole Board early in April and was asked what he hoped to do with his life. "I been giving it a lot of thought," he said. "I have met many strange people, and strange things have happened to me and I behaved in strange ways that I can't explain. What I'd like to do is study psychology. I'd like to know more about what makes folks do the things they do, because to tell you the truth I can't understand people worth a damn. I'm no brain, but seems to me if I work hard and not be in too much of a hurry I could come to figure it all out and maybe . . ." Beef was shy about saying it aloud, ". . . maybe, who knows, I could be a psychiatric social worker or something."

The Parole Board looked down upon him and smiled paternally.

"You show a mechanical aptitude, according to your test scores. Wouldn't you be happier in a service station?"

"No, sir, I think what I'd like to be is a psychiatric social worker."

They turned down his bid for parole without an explanation.

On April 20, executions were set for June 23. On the nineteenth of June there was a clemency hearing before the governor. Two days later a justice of the Supreme Court granted a stay of execution until July 1. Beef was relieved.

It went on like this, new execution dates followed by new stays of execution. In a way, they all waited together, Ginny at the women's section of Canon City, Rudy and Goose up on death row, and Beef in the prison bakery. They were fed the bread he baked.

After serving nineteen months and twenty-two days, he appeared before the Parole Board again. This time he promised to use his mechanical aptitude and forget about his notion of becoming a psychiatric social worker. He was paroled.

But he carried his prison on his back.

2

At first the consensus was that it would be unwise for Beef to try
to start a new life in Colorado Springs. There would be too many
unpleasant associations with the past. Beef explained that only by
immersing himself in these very associations did he hope to purge
himself and leave the old Buddusky behind. This immersion theory was something he had picked up in a psychology textbook out
of the prison library. Besides, he explained, he truly liked the
Springs, he felt secure there, and his ex-boss had agreed to put
him back to work shingling roofs. He wanted to get a foothold,
he told them, and to settle down finally to a decent everyday kind
of life. Marriage and kids, a feeling of pride and purpose, fried
chicken on Sunday nights.

You can do it, Harold, they told him, you can do it if you try.

His first day out, Beef shook hands with the boss, who threw
an arm around his shoulder and led him across the street for a
beer. Beef was so unaccustomed to little kindnesses that the offer
of a beer turned him softside out. He took a great long, cold
swallow, his first in so many months. He would have only one. He
was to stay out of honky tonks, a condition of his parole.

"Well, old buddy, it's nice you've come back to us," said the boss.

"Hell, you're the one's nice, hiring me back, after all that happened."

The boss lowered his head close to Beef's ear. "What the hell was really goin' on?"

"Aw, boss . . ."

"I'm only curious." He was actually leering.

"Everything I know I told on the stand."

"C'mon, buddy, nobody tells everything."

"*I* did. What do you expect me to say? Shit, thing is, I don't even want to talk about all that. I just want to make a living. And I don't want to be called Bomba anymore."

"No offense. I can understand, just gettin' out and all. But . . . what the fuck is the story?"

"I wish I knew, boss."

He bought a pair of faded coveralls at the thrift shop and started back to work. When he wasn't roofing, he mowed and trimmed and helped a trucker, anything to keep working and make a few extra honest dollars. Often he saw himself being pointed out to strangers as he loaded the truck. You know, the guy that was always with Ginny Mom Wynn, the one who posed as her son so she could bust up the marriage.

Beef told the boss to respect his privacy or he would have to go work for someone else.

"I feel bad enough, don't you think, for what I done. I don't want to have this thing hanging over me the rest of my life."

"Hell, Beef, sure it's gonna hang over you for the rest of your life."

Though Beef no longer drank, the general lousiness that surrounds a drinker remained. He lost interest in food and was losing weight. He smoked Kools until he gagged. He was always sleepy but unable to sleep, except to dream.

In dreams he would be back at Canon City, and upon waking would find himself of two minds: happy he was free, but homesick for the tight security and routine of captivity. Sometimes during the day he would hear a song on the radio that was popular in the joint, and he would stop what he was doing to remember hearing the song in Canon, as he kneaded dough or lay on his bunk, the earphones over his head.

At a hamburger joint, he ran into Ed, who used to tend bar at the Ponderosa Pines. He sat next to him at the counter.

"I heard you was back in town," said Ed.

"I called some time back. You were in jail."

"It was nothin'."

Beef ordered a cheeseburger and fries. "You back at the Ponderosa?" he asked.

"Naw, I'm at the Elbow Room now."

Ed finished his sandwich and wiped his mouth with a napkin. He took the last sip of coffee.

"You ever hear word of Mae?" Beef asked him.

He turned on his stool and looked at Beef for a moment. "She's dead, kid, I thought you knew."

Beef managed to ask how.

"She got some bad shit," said Ed.

"I hope she wasn't cold," said Beef, remembering how she hated the cold, how she pinned her blanket to her sheet.

Ed picked up his check. "Take care, kid. Drop in the place some night and have a beer." He paid the check and left.

Beef's food was placed before him. In the time it took him to eat one fry, the rest of the food went cold. Now two were lost who could have been saved.

He spent his evenings alone reading at the local library, mostly psychology. Though much of it made sense and Beef had no quarrel with what he read, it did not seem to go far in settling his own mind. He liked the part about defense mechanisms, because he felt he knew something about them. He knew any number of people, for instance, who couldn't get what they wanted so they convinced themselves they never really wanted it in the first place. Rationalization. And he didn't have to read the books to know that he had put his fist through so many windows and walls to keep from putting it through somebody's face. Now, however, he could call it displaced aggression, the proper name for it.

He found a bit of information on what they called a death wish, but not enough to satisfy him. He had the feeling the authors were avoiding facing it head on, as if their science had not come far enough to handle this concept. It seemed to Beef that anyone with a death wish could wrap it up neatly by stepping in front of a train, but no one with a death wish gets off that easily, he learned. They want to die but they're scared to death to believe it, so they drink and smoke and if they become impatient, they become Evel Knievel.

It frightened Beef. He was young, he wanted to live, he had not yet become the man he wanted to be. But he did not *like* living. The only joy he had out of it, since losing his childhood when he lost his father, was football, which in life is a very brief season.

Could he have a death wish? Did he want to die? Every decision he ever made was in the direction of unhappiness and destruction, and life held nothing for him, not now that both Maria and Mae were dead and Ginny was soon to follow. But could he kill himself? The very idea gave him pain beyond his own body. Then why did he open the door whenever darkness leaned against it?

One night, walking home from the library, a few books under his arm, he went out of his way, not quite deliberately, not quite by accident either, to the apartment where he had stood on the sidewalk and first seen her.

The apartment was apparently occupied.

Beef walked up to the manager's unit and rapped. When the landlady answered, he tried to smile. He said, "Your name is Mrs. Rogers, isn't it?" He remembered her. She had wanted to call the police, and he stopped her.

"Yes."

She checked the screen door to make sure the lock was in place.

"My name is Harold Buddusky," he said. He had planned to use an alias, but at the instant could not bring himself to lie. He hoped his name would ring no bells in her memory. He wanted no trouble. More than anything except a satisfied mind he wanted no trouble.

She looked at him curiously. Perhaps she recognized him.

"Yes?"

The trick was in telling no lies, because deceit is a slow but effective poison.

"I'm a student of psychology," he said, and showed her his books, "and I'm studying the Wynn murder case."

"Oh, my goodness," she said and ran her fingers over her lips.

"Now, you were Maria's landlady."

"She lived right up there in that apartment. She was the sweetest thing. An old-fashioned girl."

"Would you mind answering a few questions about the case?"

Beef thought she would ask him in but she kept the screen door between them. She had her hair wrapped in a bandana.

"Gee, I don't know. What's done is done."

"You testified at the trial . . ."

"Sure I did. I talked to the DA's men for hours."

". . . but they wouldn't let you say what Maria said to you."

"Hearsay."

"Right, but that's what I want to hear. Psychologically speaking."

"There was some funny psychological stuff going on, is my opinion."

"What kind of stuff?"

"And him supposed to be a newlywed."

"Who told you?"

"A blind man could see it."

"Did you know him at all?"

"Drank like a fish."

"How do you know? Did she tell you?"

"Well, I could see all the empty bottles in her garbage."

"Maybe she drank them."

"She wasn't that kind of girl."

"What kind of girl was she?"

"An old-fashioned girl. Many's the time I found her on her hands and knees scrubbing and waxing the kitchen floor, getting into every nook and cranny, on her knees with a brush and a rag."

Like my mom, thought Beef Buddusky.

"When I seen her like that, I said to her, 'Maria, Maria, you don't have to do like that. A mop, use, and some easy wax.' But no, she says to me, 'My mother showed me how to do floors and no cutting corners. She taught me to always do a good job and take joy in the job I was doing.'"

"Is that what she said?"

"Yeah."

Gee, thought Beef, she could have been a good wife for me. I would have stayed with her every minute and she would have kept the house neat and cooked good Mexican food and I would have made sure nobody ever hurt her.

"Could she cook?" asked Beef.

"Cook? Are you kidding? The smells that came out of that tiny apartment were from another world."

Mexico, thought Beef.

"Did he like her cooking?"

Except as a student of psychology, he would have taken the answer for granted.

"The only thing he ever liked was his own mother. Some cop."

"During the trial you testified about a time she came over here."

"Ginny Mom?"

"Yes. She came over, you said, and started a ruckus."

"She sure did. I should have called the police. If I'd called the police, poor Maria might be alive today."

Another accomplice, thought Beef sadly. "What happened after they left? What did she say?"

"What happened? Well, they left, and poor Maria came crying to me saying, 'Oh, Mrs. Rogers, what am I going to do? My husband goes home with his mother instead of staying with me, and my mother-in-law is always threatening to kill me.' "

"Well, do you figure she . . . *wanted* to be killed?"

"Huh?"

"Well, if she knew and didn't take steps . . . didn't try to protect herself better, wouldn't that say that deep down in the subconscious she wanted to die?"

"That's crazy."

"Sure, that's what the subconscious is all about."

"It's all Greek to me."

"Me too. Look, what did you do when she said that?"

"What do you think? I tried to comfort her and told her she and Gordon should put the old girl away in a loony home somewhere. She said they were going to."

"They were?"

"Sure. Maria said that Gordon agreed she was loony but said she was harmless, ha, ha, and it would hurt his reputation for people to know he had a mama in the loony house."

Beef, never having had much of a reputation one way or the other, could never understand the creepy things those who had them did to protect them.

"Did she ever say anything else about it? You know, hearsay stuff that you couldn't say in court."

"No, just like I told you."

He looked at the ground for a moment and said, "I wonder if she wanted to be killed."

"Say, what school do you go to?" asked the landlady, suspiciously.

"I'll be taking courses at Colorado College next term."

This too was not a lie.

3

A strange and sadly pointless research began with Beef's visit to
Maria's former landlady. He became hungry for hearsay. He trea-
sured knowing, for instance, that she did the floors on her hands
and knees, and he entered it onto new lists he was keeping.
Although each new thing made him know her better, he still
could not know how it all happened, and he hoped that quite by
accident someone would tell him some insignificant thing which
would allow him peace.

He read the newspaper accounts of the case on the library's
microfilm machine, furtively, spinning the film should anyone
pass behind him. The librarian taught him how to use the Read-
ers' Guide to Periodical Literature and he compared the *News-
week* account to that of *Time*.

On a map of the city he traced in red ink the route they took,
according to their confessions, after throwing Maria into the back
seat of their borrowed car. He taped the map to the dash of the
company pickup and after work followed the route himself. He
began by parking the truck in front of Maria's apartment house,
as her killers had parked their car, and walking into the inner
court. A dog barked, it sounded like a German shepherd. Why

couldn't it have been here the night of the murder, alerting the neighborhood to what was happening? He looked up at her apartment. The figure of a woman passed across the window. His eyes filled with tears of hopelessness.

He got into the truck and checked his watch. He wanted to time how long it took them, compensating for the difference in traffic due to the hour. (At a later date he borrowed the truck and covered the route at the same time of night as the killers. More than once.) He checked the speedometer reading. He drove up Hancock Avenue, turned left, and at Nevada turned left again. On a pad Beef marked a stroke for each stop sign and traffic light. He made a notation on the map: *40005.1*, the odometer reading at the first turn. Now toward Route 25. *40006.8* at the entrance.

Beef drove and in his mind heard them, anxious to find a place to drop her, worried that she took so long in dying.

At *025.7* miles they lost confidence in the car and a few miles later turned off at County Line Road. He checked his tally and saw that they had encountered six stop signs and four traffic signals. Did they stop for all of them, with a struggling girl in the back seat?

Beef Buddusky drove under the highway and along the narrow road that ran parallel to the railroad tracks. There was the trestle. He parked the car and got out. He tried but he could not walk across the field to the place they buried Maria Wynn. He could only stand at the side of the road, his hands in his pockets, and look, until dusk.

On his way home he passed a car parked at the side of the road. He imagined someone passing the killers' car that night, unaware that a young woman was just off the road, fighting for her life. He hit the brakes and put the truck in reverse. He had to be sure that no innocent victim was in need of a bold and inquisitive stranger. He backed up to the car and got out. The car was parked next to a shallow wash, and he grew light-headed when he saw below him two men. He no longer held sovereignty over his own imagination.

"Hey, you two!" he yelled down at them, not even knowing if they existed. He yelled in panic, his voice rising like a girl's. He was ready to throw himself down on top of them. They turned and looked at him. "What are you doing down there?" he cried in a high voice.

"Takin' a leak, okay?" one of them said.

They were teen-agers, probably full of beer, who had stopped to relieve themselves. Beef had to hold onto their car for support. He was breathing heavily.

Back in his rented room he spread the map of the city on the bed and perused his statistics and added them to his lists. He followed the red lines, checking his mileage and time notation. He was disturbed by what he saw. Professional killers, in a hurry to get their victim away from town, would have made the first left after driving away from Maria's apartment and then gone directly to the highway. They went out of their way, more than a mile. Careless? Beef looked at the map again and sweat formed on his palms and he felt a heavy drop of it running down from his armpit and over his ribs.

They had driven past Ginny's apartment.

What did this mean? What did this mean? They had five opportunities to turn left before turning down Ginny's street. Did they want to stop at her apartment? *Did* they stop? Did they want to honk the horn as they drove by? Maybe they had arranged a signal or something. They went out of their way and deliberately drove past Ginny's apartment. Did this mean anything? *Woi Yesus*, thought Beef, what if they were dropping off Gordon! What if he really was in the back seat, an accomplice to the murder? The street in front of Maria's apartment was well lit. She would have been able to see who was in the back seat. Besides, when Gordon was not in uniform he always dressed neatly. Yanez dressed like a bum. Wouldn't she know right away it wasn't her husband . . . unless it *was* her husband? Or was Beef just eager to find another accomplice, a partner in crime?

He pressed his temples between his hands until he thought he might crush his head.

The next day he called District Attorney Ferguson, a difficult call under the circumstances. He gave the secretary his name and in a moment Ferguson himself said hello.

"Hello, sir, do you remember who I am?"

"Yes."

Beef thought the DA's voice was guarded, as though expecting a threat of revenge.

"I'm a different person now, sir. I did my time and now I'm in the Springs on a job and makin' sure I'm flyin' right. You'll never see my ass in prison again. Excuse me, sir."

"Glad to hear you're behaving. What can I do for you?"

"Well, sir, I'm very troubled in my mind about all of this. See, deep down in the subconscious I knew it was gonna happen. Oh, subconscious shit, I *knew*. What's the use of kiddin' around, I *knew*."

"You were charged with perjury," said Ferguson. "Not murder. In the eyes of the law you are innocent, son."

"In the eyes of the law? Law's got her eyes covered, I seen the statue enough."

"That's justice, not law. Never confuse the two."

"Right. That's what I mean. When it comes to justice I'm guilty as the rest of them."

"This is something you'll have to work out for yourself."

"I know, sir, I am working on it. I swear I am. You know, yesterday I followed the route of Montalvo and Yanez. I found out they went past Ginny's apartment, went out of their way to go past it. Did you know that?"

There was a silence long enough to notice.

"No, I didn't," said Ferguson.

"They did, I can show you the map. I got it in my room all marked out. You want to see it?"

"Mr. Buddusky, the case is closed. They'll be executed soon."

"You don't think they'll beat it? People are sayin' they'll beat it."

"They'll die for murder, all three. I can assure you."

Beef gave a long and tired sigh.

"Thing is, sir, and the real reason I'm calling, do you think there's any chance it was really Gordon in the back seat and they dropped him off at the apartment on their way gettin' rid of Maria?"

The DA did not answer immediately, but when he did he said, "I do not."

"It would be a load off my mind if I could know for sure."

"Believe me, if I had the slightest doubt I'd pursue it. Bear in mind that the boys made full and complete confessions. There would be no reason for them to protect Gordon Wynn."

"Maybe because he's a cop . . ."

"That would be reason enough for them to try to involve him. No, Mr. Buddusky, Wynn has many failings, but he's not a killer. If I were you, I would put all this behind me."

The new load still lay as heavy as mud on his mind. The DA tried to end the conversation but Beef was reluctant to have him leave the line. It was a comfort to talk to someone about it, man to man.

"Mr. Buddusky, I'm afraid I have to get back to work," said Ferguson.

"Right, sir. I appreciate the hell out of it, the way you talked to me like this. Truth is, I don't believe I paid my debt to society. I gave it a little something on account but I got to find out myself how much I really owe."

"Well, we can talk again if you like."

"Can we? Could I come tomorrow?"

"Tomorrow?"

"Any time at all. I can move around my jobs."

"All right, come by at eight tomorrow morning. I'll be able to talk to you then."

"Good, sir. Thanks a lot."

Beef hung up feeling lifted by the prospect of talking to Ferguson. He went back to his map and tried to ascertain why they went out of their way to drive past Ginny's apartment.

4

The district attorney took a fatherly interest in Beef. Here was a criminal, perhaps, who might actually have been rehabilitated.

At first he was reluctant to give Beef the twenty-five volumes of transcript, so Beef read Ginny's trial for guilt, sixteen volumes, in the DA's office. It required several visits, even reading with the speed of *déjà vu.* Then Ferguson agreed to allow him to take the remaining volumes to his room, where he studied slowly and laboriously Ginny's trial for punishment.

The law in Colorado prescribed a bifurcated trial in capital cases, the first trial to determine guilt, the second to decide upon the penalty, a choice between life imprisonment or death in the gas chamber at Canon City. Both punishments were considered equally appropriate by the state for the crime of murder. The choice was entirely at the discretion of the same jury that heard the trial for guilt, using whatever evidence, criteria, or guidelines it pleased.

By the time Beef finished reading the transcript of Ginny's trial for punishment, he had lists and notes strewn about his floor like the work of some frenzied stockbroker. He reeled at the parade of witnesses, some whose experiences with Ginny went back to more than fifteen years before. He had to admit he loved her, in the groundless way one loves an unsavory relative, in the way his mother loved his father, in the way so many people love so many other people. The haunting question was why only Gordon and he were able to love her, a woman who would kill to have her way. Even Sally Ryan, in her argument for Ginny's life, said, "Here she is before you, a woman abandoned by all who know her, except for her son and a boy she helped send to prison."

Beef looked at the index of witnesses, sad-assed that no more would step forward to try to save her life. She had brothers and sisters somewhere. They would not show themselves and speak for her. Ferguson called thirteen witnesses whose experiences with Ginny Wynn were thought to argue well for her unnatural death, but no relatives (save her son), no priest, no landlord, no teacher, no respectable member of any community would say a word to try to keep her alive. In her years of living had she touched no one warmly enough for a public word on her behalf? Was Beef the only one? Why him and no one else? Until he knew himself better, it was a question he was incapable of answering.

The witnesses against her told stories that embarrassed Beef. Sam Leonard, the young man she had married, who later annulled the marriage, claimed that he married her for the promise of half of $100,000 that was due her upon her wedding day. "She slipped me a check for ten grand right after the ceremony," he said. "I couldn't cash the thing anywhere." On the drive back from Denver they decided to invest all their money in a cattle ranch. How Ginny wanted a ranch!

Beef, now a student of psychology, knew what to call it: delusions of grandeur. Maybe the key to Ginny. He had known many people with delusions of grandeur, though he did not know the proper term and at the time had assumed them to be simply full

259

of shit. He devised a plan for mass treatment of sufferers of the disease, for it was a disease. The government should sponsor an organization, the Knights and Dames of the Towering Great Iam, and tap into it only those who have been diagnosed as having delusions of grandeur. This should be done in a pompous public ceremony, with the Vice-President officiating. A pin could be worn on bodice or lapel, and it could carry some practical privilege, like reduced rates at the movies.

He wished he would have had a ranch to give her, to keep her from having to murder a woman he would have loved.

"When I saw I was taken," testified Sam Leonard, "I went my own way. It wasn't long before I got an order to show cause. She was claiming she was pregnant and I was failing to support her. I tried to laugh it off, because the whole idea was that she was supposed to support *me,* and I knew she wasn't pregnant, at least not by me. I thought she was beyond getting pregnant anyway. What I come to find out was that she had hired a pregnant girl to use her name and go to a doctor and get some certificate of pregnancy or something. I can tell you, I had to go through a lot of trouble to get that straightened out."

A real estate agent told of entering into a cattle ranch deal with Ginny, who negotiated the price down from $350,000 to $335,000. As a deposit she gave him a $50,000 personal check.

An assistant cashier from the First National Bank of Denver testified that at the time of this transaction Ginny had $32.08 in her account, and that the maximum balance for the entire life of the account had never exceeded $150. Delusions of grandeur.

A string of real estate agents testified, each one having once sold Ginny a ranch, for which he was given a deposit of a rubber check. The DA had arranged their appearances in descending order of the real estate value involved, from a $350,000 ranch to a four-acre rancho at $36,500. Finally he called a butcher who had sold Ginny a quarter steer, cut and wrapped for the freezer, and he still had the check, which had come back stamped INSUFFI-CIENT FUNDS.

Agents and collectors, landlords and tradesmen, ex-husbands and lovers, all testified to the failure of Ginny to give truth to her dreams.

What's it for, Ginny? asked Beef in his solitude. The emptiness seemed far from its end. With a gravity of half the world, he read on, each tale sadder than the preceding one.

And to urge them to let her live? Only Ginny herself, her son, and Harold Buddusky.

At first both Sally Ryan and Gordon were against having Beef back to testify for Ginny. The testimony of a convicted felon and perjurer could not endear her to the jury. But Ginny insisted they ask him, and Beef readily agreed.

Beef read in the transcript his own feeble words of praise for her: that she took him in when he was down and out, that she fed him and gave him money and found him a job, that she made him belong and for the few months he knew her he was not lonely, and the finest gift anyone ever gave another was to take away his loneliness. For this much humanity alone, she deserved to live, Beef in his stumbling way tried to tell the jury, but they looked at him as though his own loneliness was not an issue in the case.

As he was led away from the stand Ginny whispered, "Thanks, Bomba." She suddenly looked so much older.

He nodded to her and was quickly taken out of the courtroom and to prison. That was the last time he saw her, so different from the first.

In the falling dusk of his rented room he read Gordon's testimony. She was a good mother, he said. Granted she was over-possessive, granted she was jealous to a fault, she was still a good mother. She had had a hard and empty life, with grand desires and no achievements, except for one: her son, the only bright light in a frustrating life. "Can you put a mother to death for loving a son too much?" he asked the jury.

Beef floated in a bottomless melancholy, knowing that they would.

He could read no further. He went to bed. He must have been too loud, because the landlady rapped solidly on the door and said in her landlady's suspicious voice, "Who's in there? Who's in there?"

"A crying fool," answered Beef Buddusky.

5

With arrangements made by Ferguson, Beef was able to interview Martin Lowell, who said (after a promise from Beef that he would not repeat it to the DA) that he believed no one would ever go to the chamber for killing Maria, and Ronnie Fischer, who asked him, "Bomba, what's the big deal? Why are you bothering with all this?"

"Morbid curiosity, I guess."

"Well, it's your life."

"Not until I get this settled. Now, Goose said three or four times something about Maria was a witch. I remember Rudy saying the same thing. Do you?"

"I don't recall now."

"I read their confessions in the transcript. I'm sure they said witch. Do you know anything about Mex's? I mean, do they believe in witches?"

"I know a lot of them have some funny superstitions, but I don't know about witches."

"If they really do believe in witches, and if they thought they were taking a job to kill a witch, don't you think that makes it a whole other thing? I was always bothered by them killing another

Mexican. It never seemed right to me somehow. Now, if they thought she was a witch . . ."

"I'm not going to lose any sleep about it, Bomba."

"What I can't figure out is how they thought she was a witch. Ginny called Maria lots of names, but she never called her a witch."

"She used to call her a bitch," said Fischer.

"She did!" said Beef, rising out of his seat and pacing the office. "All the time! Hey, Fischer, when she and Mrs. Lister saw Barrajas that first time, Ginny probably said she wanted some help to kill a bitch. Barrajas has trouble with English. What if he told the boys the job was to get rid of a witch? Man, that's a whole other thing."

"You're only gonna give yourself grief, Bomba."

"There might be some of those extenuating circumstances or something here."

"It's crazy, pal, drop it."

Beef paced back and forth. He made some notations in his notebook and underlined them several times.

"I don't know," said Beef. "This Montalvo is supposed to be a very religious guy."

"There's nothing like murdering someone to bring you closer to Christ," said Fischer.

"But for all this time he's been talking about his conversion. He says he ain't afraid of the chamber."

"Good for him."

"You don't think he's sincere?"

"I've seen too many punks give their heart to Jesus. Once their ass is out of hot water they take it back again pretty quick."

"Do you think they'll really get the chamber?"

"The boys will. Ginny Mom will beat it."

"How do you figure?"

"You never get gas for murder. You get it for a lot of little things. These kids are dumb *pachucos*, conned into things all their lives. They're conned into buying cars they can't afford, they're conned into using drugs they can't handle, they're conned into committing crimes beyond their smarts. Mrs. Wynn conned them into murder, I conned them into confessions, their lawyers conned them into copping pleas. Society wants retribution against these kids, but not just because they murdered someone. They want retribution because of *how* they murdered someone. They don't like the premeditation, the brutality. They don't like the idea of Maria being buried alive carrying an unborn little girl. They don't like their motive for doing it and they'd like to see a lot more remorse from them. Most of all, what they're going to execute them for is their goddamn stupidity. They're so stupid they're dangerous."

"What about Ginny Mom?"

"Well, there are a lot of little things that people would like to see her die for. Maria was young and pretty and innocent, for one." Fischer started counting on his fingers. "Add to that her rejection of her unborn grandchild, her disregard for the sanctity of marriage, her not letting the young people live their own lives. It didn't help her either to smile when she was told that Maria's body was found."

"She smiled?"

"That's what I heard."

"Sounds bad," said Beef.

"Naw, she's just another old lady who believes she inherits the earth. Old ladies have this thing about believing they are entitled to incredible considerations and privileges. You don't execute an old lady, because . . . well, because she's an old lady."

"She ain't that old," said Beef.

"The culprits are the two boys. They should have been smart enough to say no. That's why they're gonna kill them. After all, every other little old lady on the block wants someone murdered. We all know that, we just don't listen to them. Ginny Mom will beat it."

Beef went back to the district attorney's office. He had to ask him about his witch concept.

"Mr. Ferguson, do you remember anywhere where the two boys said they thought they were killing a witch?"

"A witch?"

"Yeah."

"I really think you should relax."

"They both said they thought they were killing a witch. I figure somewhere along the line the word 'bitch' became 'witch.' Now, if they got some kind of superstition against witches, wouldn't that make it a whole other thing? Wouldn't that be extenuating circumstances?"

"Look, son, why don't you just forget the whole thing? Get it out of your mind and work on advancing yourself. This is going to make an old man out of you, the way you're going."

"Well, I don't mind, as long as it's worth it. I got to find out why they did it. I'm a psychology student."

"They did it for money, son."

"Not good enough. Folks think I was in on the annulment for money, but I wasn't."

Ferguson smiled at him. "Well, I suppose you have to do what you have to do."

"Tell me, sir, why weren't they all tried together? Why did they each have to go through a separate trial, since they were in it together?"

Ferguson actually chuckled. "I'll tell you a secret. If they *had* been tried together, they could have got away with murder, just by refusing to testify."

"I thought they never stood a chance."

"Without the testimonies of the two boys they could have made it scot-free."

"How?"

"I had a lot of circumstantial evidence. I was going to prosecute Barrajas as an accessory, but had to make a deal with him to get his testimony. The testimony of Mrs. Lister would have tolerated no cross-examination, and you were still at large. In short, I had a weak case or no case at all without the testimonies of Rudy and Yanez. I could use their confessions and their testimonies before the grand jury, which would have been admissible hearsay and potent evidence to convict *them,* but no jury would have convicted the killers if they had to let the driving force behind the conspiracy go free, and they would have had to let her go. The court probably would have instructed them to.

"I was being forced into making a deal with the boys, giving them life sentences in exchange for their testimonies, which I needed to convict Ginny Wynn. But no jury would sentence her to death if they knew the actual murderers were promised life sentences. It was a sticky situation for me. It looked as though the best I could get would be life sentences."

"But then why . . . ?"

"Montalvo had been building himself as a sincere convert to Christ. He figured he was young, good-looking . . . like everybody's paper boy. He was convinced that if he threw himself on the mercy of a jury he could draw a relatively light sentence. He didn't want to be judged alongside of his pal Yanez, who he knew would come off in an unsympathetic light. So he wanted a separate trial and of course Yanez had to go along with it. Their big mistake was in their resentment of Ginny. They wanted her to go to prison. They didn't mind serving some time themselves, but they wanted to make sure she served as much. So they made a deal for separate trials in exchange for guilty pleas and testimonies. That hung the three of them."

"You did that, knowing . . ."

"My job was to make sure they got the stiffest punishment possible."

"Well, how does that make you feel?"

"Fine."

"I mean, psychologically, doesn't it . . ."

Ferguson laughed. "It's been nice talking to you, Mr. Buddusky, but I really have things to do." He stopped Beef before he could leave the office and said, "You want to dabble in psychology?" He went to a file cabinet. He opened a drawer and took out a fat Manila envelope. "Read these. These are letters I got while the case had national publicity. They'll give you something to work on."

Beef took the envelope.

"You be sure to return this," said Ferguson. "Sometimes I like to remind myself of who's out there."

J.B.S. from Oregon sent the district attorney a scroll on which Psalm 1 was printed in Gothic letters. J.B.S. had written, "Give her the gas chamber for there is where she should go! Don't ever let her free to kill once again!"

Montgomery W. Douglas wrote on yellow legal paper from Jackson Heights, New York, to put his finger on the real cause of this murder. "What can you expect from one who was trained in the Roman Catholic Church?"

Mrs. Clapton, a student of criminal types, wrote from Newport News to say, "When the news of this dastardly crime was first known to the public and Gordie Wynn's picture first appeared in our paper, I studied it and I remarked to my family, 'I do not like his appearance and before this thing is over and done with, I believe he will be drawn into it in some way.' I watched him on TV and I was amazed at his manner and almost arrogant attitude. Not once did I detect any emotion of sadness in his manner or voice as he talked of the disappearance and death of his wife, the girl whom he said he loved. He was in on it, mark my words. Don't let him get away!" she pleaded.

From Haynesville, Louisiana, Betty Weldon wrote, "This is my first such letter, but this case is so close 'to home' with me. I had plenty just such to contend with, and was persecuted almost to death by a most jealous mother-in-law, and then to my face she was so sweet the sugar melted in her mouth.

"No, Gordie did not love his wife, for if he had then he would have told his mother where to head in. I had the same thing, and this man never told his mother what was what either. He yo-yoed back and forth for about forty years. I was a fool to put up with it like I did, and now that the mother is gone there are two old maid sisters who keep the yo-yo going. Isn't life a struggle?"

An old lady living on $85 a month Social Security wrote from Kansas City, "This is a lonely Sunday. I have spent so much for newspapers following the Wynn trial that I can't afford a bus ride, so I am writing to thank you for the outcome of the trial, and I hope no new trial is granted her. Everybody realizes what was going on between her and her son, even tho I'm sure it started when he was just a kid, still he could have put a stop to it when he got grown if he really wanted to. He should be sent to the gas chamber right along with his wicked mother and the two rats that done the actual killing and that crazy Bomba the Jungle Boy. Yours for a speedy execution, Angel Matteson."

Beef tugged hard at his chin.

Not all the mail came from proponents of capital punishment, however. A dissident from Los Angeles wrote, "Always before I've felt *some* compassion for criminals and murderers. Always I've hated capital punishment. My own worst enemies I leave to God, and I've some dillies, but Mrs. Wynn I can't take. There's something here worse than gore and wanton slaying. She can't be explained as almost every other criminal and human, nor excused. It isn't even that she appears in love with her son. Maybe it's evil, just plain evil, not as rare as we thought.

"Worse, or darn near it, is Gordie Wynn. The contempt I have for *this one* is overpowering. He acts like the most spineless, stupid, shallow and moronic creature ever born. That's my honest impression and I almost prefer him in the gas chamber. Any man so helpless and thoughtless to a girl as he, saying it kindly, should be a girl himself."

Beef read the last thought again and again, since this Solomon justice applied to him as well as to Gordon. He too had been so helpless and thoughtless to that girl, and to another girl. For it, he should be a girl himself.

The disconcerting thing was that no matter who was out there, no matter their spelling and grammar, their love of underlinings and quotation marks and exclamation points, no matter even their irrationality and the fact that you sometimes had to laugh at them, they were in you too. And none of them, thought Beef Buddusky, wanted to believe for a moment that Ginny Wynn was in them as well.

They're all over, thought Beef, out there, and there is a lot of Ginny Wynn in a few, and a little Ginny Wynn in all. Is that why he wanted her to live? Then why did they want her to die, those thousands of legal, moral, and psychological opinioners, steeped in TV, *Official Detective*, and *National Enquirer*, who ". . . had a husband like that," who ". . . have a mother-in-law like that," who gasp in the solitude of their parlors and shake in their kimonos, who take up a stubby and chewed pencil and root through their kitchen drawers until they find a postcard, to cram onto it the benefit of their experience for a district attorney they imagine will be grateful:

Dear Sir,

Gordon Wynn, flatfoot, is a pronounced case of a male? with Oepipus Complex. The kinsey report overlooked this angle. My years of observation and close experience with this type of psychastenians possessed with the desire of sex consummation with closest blood relative—is more prevalent than is publicized; such as a mothers? desire for her son's frigging, or a desire for a father? to sleep with his daughter, or a brothers unnatural love for his sister and vice versa. There will be a dearth of numskull reports by psychiatrist, psychoanalysts, psychologists, etc. in this case—but the simple fact is Mrs. Wynn's obsessed desire for her son's sexual love—period.

Another student of psychology, like Beef Buddusky. He probably had as many lists as Beef himself.

Beef read every letter, flinching when someone mentioned him and his share of the guilt. By the time he finished and rose from his table, his mouth was full of canker sores, sending shocks of pain to his ears and his throat.

6

Beef continued to roof houses, mechanically. He now worked only enough to pay for his few needs. He was humorless and his body stayed pale. The truth of his life existed in the commission of a single criminal act, to which he was losing himself entirely. A chance remark about Mexico would send him there, trying to see her as a child, a student, and eventually the images would lead to Maria as a decomposed corpse. He overheard some weekend gardener say, "The ground is very hard," and he was with her killers taking turns at clawing the ground like dogs, strangling her as they rested.

He wrote letters to both Montalvo and Yanez, exploring his theory that they might have thought they were executing a witch. They did not reply. He wrote their lawyers. He did not hear from them either. He took to hanging around Mexican bars, in violation of his parole, asking individual patrons about their fear of or belief in witches.

"Tell me there, ace, you a superstitious sort?"

The wetback ranch hand he was talking to smiled and slapped his shoulder and shook his hand, anything to avoid admitting he didn't understand a single word of English.

Beef turned to another, determined to be more direct. "Say, ace, do you think witches are for real?"

More explanation was required. "Witches," said Beef, "witches," and he pantomimed a witch, to the broomstick and cackle.

They laughed and applauded and someone shouted *"¡Olé!"*

One man approached him to tell him about the morning his baby boy saw the Virgin of Guadalupe floating on the ceiling.

Sometimes Beef saw Gordon curled up in the back seat of the murder car, other times it was Yanez, until it hardly seemed to matter. Always it was Montalvo walking up the steps, his hand on the gun, in the dark, quiet night. "I got your husband in my car. He's really drunk. He told me to take him here."

He had written Gordon's Denver number on the edge of his figuring table, next to the text on psychopathology, and had called him a few times. Gordon would not speak to him or return his calls. Beef wanted assurance from him that he was not the one in the back seat of that murder car.

One night Beef had a dream from which he awoke screaming so loudly that his landlady told him he would have to move. In his dream he saw himself curled up in the back seat of the murder car, waiting for Montalvo to lead down Maria.

His reason for living was locked within that night Montalvo led her to the car, and nature, man's or the universe's, was attempting to obliterate too many traces of the crime. It was not enough that Ginny Mom and the two boys would be gone in two weeks, twelve days exactly. Physical evidence useful to his bizarre investigation was being destroyed or altered, and the cast of characters scattered.

He could find Mrs. Lister nowhere, though a careful scanning of the obituaries from the time of his imprisonment indicated she might be still alive.

When he went to look at Ginny's apartment, he found the whole structure had been leveled and a small shopping center was in its place. The Purple Cow Drive-In was now the Mountain View restaurant. The hot rods and hang-abouts had disappeared and its new booths were filled with businessmen having the luncheon special. The Panama Club was now a secondhand store. Beef walked inside. Where the jukebox had been, now a card table loaded with used coffee percolators, this one missing a top, the other missing a wire, all missing something. Where the bottles had been arranged against the wall, now row upon row of used books, brittle, yellow, and smelly, ten cents apiece. Old items, dust catchers at home, now festooned the ceiling and walls like wisteria at an outdoor confectionery—walls that earlier heard a plot of murder—waiting to catch the eye and imagination of a secondhand-shop scavenger.

A woman asked if she could help him. Like a fool he answered that no one could.

Juan Barrajas died in prison, where he had been sent for receiving stolen property; Joyce Shaw, the manager of the apartment from which Maria was kidnapped, had moved to New Jersey.

Only Beef, of all the accomplices, kept returning to the scene of the crime, doggedly.

"Nobody's taking responsibility for this," he told the street below the window of his room. "Somebody's got to take the responsibility."

The case was like a blown dandelion, but in spite of its fragmentation, Beef Buddusky was able to uncover tiny gems of information, which he dutifully added to his growing number of lists.

At Howard's, where Ginny Mom and Mrs. Lister had often had lunch, the waitress told Beef that she nicknamed Ginny "the Duchess," because she would always leave a penny tip next to her plate but hide a dollar bill under the plate. Beef had the feeling she was confusing Ginny with someone else. He added it to the embarrassingly brief list of Ginny's redeeming qualities anyway, where he had recorded the fact that when Gordon skinned his knee as a little boy Ginny would paint a Mercurochrome funny face on the wound.

From Lupe Martinez he learned that Rudy had once sung to her with the voice of an angel, but once only. He was ashamed of having a singing voice. Beef could not get over it. A singer of songs, and yet he would kill so cold-bloodedly.

From Goose Yanez's brother-in-law Beef learned that when Goose went for his Army physical and was told to bend over and spread his cheeks, Goose bent over and spread the cheeks of his face.

With the help of Martin Lowell, Beef finally located Mrs. Lister in a state-supported rest home. She was bedridden and old beyond estimation and would die soon, but she recognized him and took his proffered hand with a surprisingly firm grip.

"Bomba," she said in a dry and cracking voice, like the edges of a badly fried egg. "Bomba."

"It's me, Mrs. Lister, hyuh."

"Bomba."

He sat down and twisted his forefinger to keep from crying. Lately he found himself crying for everyone. After his conversations with Ferguson he cried for Maria or her killers, and then wound up crying for the district attorney. He feared he might be slipping away from himself.

"I'm outa prison," he told Mrs. Lister.

"Good fellow."

"Trying to live a decent life."

"You'll make it, Bomba. My blessings."

"Thanks," he said. He had questions on his mind and had brought his pad and pencil to record her answers, but now he felt reluctant to tax her. He knew, however, that they would not talk again in this life.

"How're you feeling?" he asked.

"I don't feel nothing."

Beef nodded, his hands on his knees. "Mrs. Lister . . ."

"Call me Alma."

"Alma, then, do you remember the night they killed Maria Wynn?"

She shut her eyes and her lower lip trembled.

"No, now, Alma," he said, pressing a hand over hers, "there's only me and you here."

She nodded and said, "I remember."

Her hand felt like dried chicken bones.

"Were you with Ginny that night, in her apartment?"

"Yes."

"Now, here's the important thing. Was Gordon with you that night?"

"He came in later."

"You sure? How later?"

"It seems so long ago, Bomba, did it ever really happen?"

"You bet, missus. I'd cut off both my arms."

"Gordie was not a very good husband to Maria," said Mrs. Lister.

"For treating a girl like that, to put it kindly, he should become a girl himself," said Beef.

"She was such a beautiful girl. No one could ever deny that."

Beef blew his nose. "Sometimes the cruelty of life seems pretty deliberate," he said.

She nodded.

"Alma," said Beef, and it was a long moment before he spoke again. "Alma, what did Ginny Mom have on you?"

She actually chuckled. "Bomba, what did she have on you?"

He shook his head, equally unable to answer.

She was drifting off to sleep. "Mrs. Lister? Mrs. Lister?" He put his hand on her shoulder.

"Alma," she said.

"Alma, I sure wasn't gonna ask, but I gotta. There's nobody here but you and me. Now, if anyone knows, you do."

"What?" she asked, hardly able to keep her eyes open.

He shook her shoulder gently. "Alma, Alma?" She opened her eyes and looked at him and said, "Bomba, would you call me Mother?"

"Mother, Mom. Do you have to go to sleep, Mother?" he said, holding her bony little hand between both of his.

She was already softly snoring.

7

Students of such things were excited to learn, and Beef Buddusky also thought it profoundly significant, that Ginny Wynn, alone among the nation's sensationally publicized murderers, received no proposals of marriage through the U.S. mail.

Neither was there a public drive to save her. Of 575 messages on her case reaching the governor, 505 urged that she and her two hired killers be executed. Of the remaining 70, 3 came from Beef Buddusky, awkwardly typed on the library's coin-operated typewriter.

The governor, a nationally known opponent of capital punishment, was technically able to grant clemency in spite of public opinion. Those close to him believed him to be leaning that way. No woman had ever been executed in Colorado. This was Yanez's first conviction. Montalvo, though a prior felon, was very young, a repentant, now known as Rudy Sincere.

A group of eight Quakers gathered at the outer gate of Canon City with their sleeping bags slung over their shoulders. They silently milled about, beginning their customary nightlong vigil. They carried no signs.

The prison duty of spending the last night with the condemned is called "sitting the deathwatch." Two matrons volunteered to sit with Ginny in her cell at the Women's Institute, four miles away from the chamber. One was Ginny's age, the other was young.

The younger one seemed weary even at the outset. "Don't fret," Ginny said to her, "I suspect Gordie and Miss Ryan will get me off first thing in the morning."

Danny Yanez and Rudy Montalvo, harnessed and shackled, were taken downstairs to the holding cells. They walked down the corridor of death row and called farewell to the condemned still waiting, those still with hope.

"Gettin' short," said Yanez.

"Walk right under the door," said one of the condemned.

"See you tomorrow, boys," said Montalvo.

"Better not. There's enough spooks here already."

"Good luck, it's been fun."

"It's been a gas," said Yanez, laughing the coldness out of the prison bars.

The others laughed too, until Rudy and Goose were gone from death row. No one would bet even money on their coming back again.

Great public interest surrounds the practice of the last meal. What was ordered and, more importantly, how much of it was eaten? The public thinks that the condemned invariably either cannot eat what he orders or throws it up after he has eaten it.

The public also believes in the tradition that the condemned may have whatever he desires for his last meal. Such is not the case.

The order is always taken three days before the execution and it breaks the monotony for the men on the row.

"Give the kids a couple a bowls a *frijoles* and a *tortilla*. Make 'em feel at home."

"Make sure to give 'em a Bromo. They might get gas."

"You can have anything you want, within reason," said the guard taking the order from Montalvo and Yanez.

"What do you mean, within reason?" asked Montalvo.

"Well, for instance, you can't have broiled yak. Broiled yak ain't within reason."

"Yak?" said one of the other men. "They yakked too much already. That's why they're here in the first place!"

Montalvo began to order. "I'll have filet mignon . . ."

"Me too," said Goose Yanez.

". . . and lobster thermidor and crepes suzette . . ."

"That for me too," said Yanez with very little idea of what he was ordering.

"Would you like the same as me, Goose?"

"Yeah, Rudy, like you."

"All right, give us with that some French fries, guacamole salad, spareribs . . ."

"Ah, nigger hard shells," said one of the other men.

". . . corn on the cob, coffee and milk, banana cream pie, and ice cream . . . I guess that's about it."

"Yeah, that's about it for me too," said Yanez.

The press reported what the condemned men ordered. What they got was steak, French fries, peas, green salad, banana cream pie, coffee and milk.

They ate all of it with gusto and counted it among the best meals of their lives.

In her cell, Ginny Wynn ordered and received steak, peas,

mashed potatoes, and coffee. She couldn't finish the potatoes. They were a bit lumpy.

The two holding cells form a right angle so that the partners in crime may enjoy their own society.

The men were now wearing new blue denim trousers and chambray shirts. On their feet they wore cloth slippers. This too was part of the ritual.

The two guards who were sitting the deathwatch volunteered to play four-handed cards with them, but Yanez knew no card games and Montalvo could find no reason to try to win.

They had a phonograph and a selection of records. One of the guards held the records up and flipped through them slowly in front of Montalvo so that he could read the labels. The condemned are never allowed to handle the records themselves because they can be broken and used on the wrists or throat to cheat the state.

Yanez said, "Rudy, do you think you did the right thing?"

"What thing?" asked Rudy, still reading the record labels.

"Givin' your body to science like that."

"Look, at the eye bank some poor blind person can get my eyes and see again."

"Yeah, but what good's that to you?"

"It's just nice, I guess. The rest of the body will be good practice for the medical students."

"Hey, Rudy Sincere's goin' to college tomorrow! He's gonna be a matriculator. Hey, Joe College!"

"Oh, shit, try to explain something to you."

Rudy stopped the guard and read the record label closely. "Bluebird of Happiness," sung by Jan Peerce.

"Play that one," he said, suddenly excited.

The guard put it on the phonograph and played it.

They all listened quietly and when it was over, Rudy said, "Play it again. It's beautiful."

The guard played it again and Rudy asked for another replay.

Yanez was soon fast asleep. Rudy had the guards play the record over and over throughout the long night, and he sat, almost transfixed, listening to it. In a short time, the guards hated the song more than they thought they could possibly hate any innocent musical composition. They had to take breaks from it and nap for a while. Rudy insisted that the song be played repeatedly, and of course, they could not deny him the pleasure.

Yanez awoke at six and the first thing he heard was "Bluebird of Happiness." Rudy sat on the floor, holding the bars and listening intently, as though it held a secret for him. He was humming along now. "Gets a little rep'titious, don't it?" said Yanez. Rudy did not answer.

Ginny went to sleep at three o'clock and awoke at seven-thirty. The matrons wished her good morning but she did not speak to them until she was served bacon and eggs and coffee. She flattened the yolk of a fried egg with her tablespoon, the only utensil allowed, and said, "Why do they call them eggs?"

The two matrons looked at each other, smiled, and shrugged. The older one said, "I don't know. Because they *are* eggs."

"No, no, no," said Ginny impatiently. "The cyanide eggs."

"Bluebird of Happiness" played unceasingly in the holding cells. At ten minutes before ten, the guards gave them fresh sets of blues to wear.

Montalvo began to tremble. Yanez looked at him and said, "You gonna shit?"

"My asshole is twitching!" cried Rudy. "Jesus, it's gonna turn me inside out!"

Montalvo slid to the floor. Yanez knelt down at the bars of his own cell and coaxed him back to his feet. "Don't be a pussy, baby. There'll be people watchin' out there," he said.

"I can't help it, my asshole is twitching," whined Rudy Montalvo.

The guards rolled a green carpet from the holding cells to the chamber, so that Rudy and Goose would not slip on the slick floor. Because Yanez had had a better record in life, he was led first to the chamber and strapped into seat "A." There are two seats in the chamber, and the condemned sits with his back to the witnesses, so that they do not have to look at each other. Yanez turned to find the four friends he had invited. His fifth guest was to be District Attorney Ferguson, who declined.

"Look in on my kids," he said to one of his friends.

When he saw Montalvo being brought through the door of the ready room, pale and trembling and needing the support of the two guards, Yanez yelled, "Well, look who's here. Have a seat."

The guards helped Montalvo into seat "B" and strapped him there.

Although the official time of a morning execution is 10:00, the warden never gives the signal to lower the eggs until 10:03. This is to compensate for any malfunction of the timepiece, no matter how slight. Also, if the governor is going to call he will certainly call before 10:03, because he knows it is futile to call after that.

In the maddening silence before the warden's signal, a melody was heard. It unnerved the staff and witnesses. Rudy was humming the strains of "Bluebird of Happiness."

The guards having strapped them securely, each in turn patted their shoulders.

"Good-bye."

"Good luck."

Yanez smiled and called out, "Hey, Warden, helluva way to make a livin', ain't it?"

Rudy smiled, shut his eyes, and sang two lines of the song in his beautiful voice.

At 10:03 the warden gave the signal and the cyanide eggs were lowered into the acid.

Rudy stopped singing when he heard them sizzle. He yelled, "It's down!"

Then Goose Yanez, the mental retard, contributed to science original information on the study of lethal gas when he yelled, "I can smell it! It don't smell good! It smells like rotten eggs!"

It had always been believed that the gas was odorless.

He turned his head to the spectators and said, "I'm going out nice . . . I'm going out nice . . ."

Two newsmen fainted and were carried outside.

8

There are two entrances to the ready room. One connects directly to death row; the other is by way of the preparation room and the witness area, which of course is in full view of the chamber itself. It was this second entrance that Ginny had to use to reach the ready room. One of the administrators wanted to save her the experience of coming face to face with the chamber before the appointed time, so they draped off that area with an old gray curtain.

At 11 A.M. she and her two matrons were driven from the Women's Institute to the chamber. She took several steps from the sedan to the massive metal door with her head back, face to the sky. She was drinking in the natural light.

Once past the preparation room, the business side of which was also draped to save her the sight of the deep sinks and the valves, she was led into the ready room and locked into one of the two holding cells. She and the matrons looked around the room like three girlfriends moving into a cheap apartment in the wrong end of town. The cells were too tiny, the mattress on the floor was soiled. There was not even a seat on the stupid john. The folding metal table attached to the bars of the cell represented the entire furnishings.

Fortunately, the radio and phonograph worked and there was a supply of records. In a little alcove was a coffeepot and the makings.

All three shrugged and sighed when they were finally left alone, resigning themselves to the inadequacies of their temporary quarters.

"If they had the sense to give us some cleaning gear," said Ginny, "we'd have it spic 'n' span in no time, right, girls?"

They smiled and the older one said, "Why don't you just rest your feet, Ginny?"

"Might as well," she said, easing herself to the mattress. "Can't dance."

At noon she had a BLT on toast with a small green salad. She wiped her mouth and hands with the napkin and said, "Girls, has anyone heard from Gordie?"

"Not yet, Ginny," said the older one.

"He's working for Miss Ryan now, in Denver. He's the best investigator they ever had. Right now they're trying to get another judge to intercede. Don't worry, this thing isn't over yet. Not with Gordie on the job."

"You must be very proud of him," the younger one said.

She nodded distractedly. "I wish he hadn't quit school. That's the one thing that bothers me. Tell him to go back to school, do me that favor."

The younger one was embarrassed. The older one asked, "Can I turn on some music for you, Ginny?"

"Turn on the news," she answered.

At fifteen minutes before one, the chaplain came into the holding cell area.

"Good morning, Virginia."

"Good morning, Father."

"How's the food?"

"All right."

"Anything you care to talk about?"

"Like God?"

"That too," said the chaplain. "Anything you like."

"Have you heard from my son?"

"No, I haven't, Virginia."

She looked at the clock. "Well, it's still not too late."

"Virginia, it is the destiny of every man and every woman. Have you any letters or messages I can convey?"

Somehow she had expected to see Gordie, and there was no one else to write to.

"Did you hear that Mrs. Lister died yesterday?" asked the chaplain.

"Who?"

"Mrs. Lister, your friend."

"Oh, yes. Well, she was due."

At ten minutes before one she heard a clanging sound and jumped. She waited a moment and heard it again. She asked, "What's that?"

The chaplain tucked his chin against his shoulder like a bird and mumbled, "They're testing the door."

"What door?"

"The door, my dear."

Somehow it seemed all right, however, to forgo certain other elements of the ritual, since a woman was involved. For example, she was allowed to wear her black pumps, street clothes, and underwear.

The staff psychiatrist entered the holding cell area and said, as an official question, "Virginia Ann Wynn?"

"Yes," she answered.

"How do you feel?"

"Has Gordie called?"

"Could you evaluate your current attitude?"

"Pardon?"

"Can you make an assessment of your state of mind, in relation to your deeds and your punishment?"

"Is this part of the routine, or what?"

"You don't have to answer my question, of course."

"Then I think maybe I won't."

"Naturally I'd appreciate your cooperation."

"Oh, don't worry about that, son."

The warden entered, wished her good afternoon, and said, "Mrs. Wynn, there are members of the press present. They always ask if there are last words."

She thought for a moment and said, "No, I don't think so."

"In the past, others have chosen this time to confess their crimes," said the warden.

"Have they?" said Ginny, but she would say no more.

He shook her hand, said good-bye, and he and the psychiatrist left. Immediately, the doctor came into the area with two guards, who turned their backs as he went into the holding cell to tape a stethoscope detector to her heart.

He took her pulse and said, "Normal, Mrs. Wynn."

She was pleased to hear it.

The doctor opened a small plastic bag and said, "Better drop your dentures in here, Mrs. Wynn."

"Do I have to?"

"It's better that you do."

"But what's the difference, for goodness' sake?"

"They might fly out, Mrs. Wynn, if you struggle. You wouldn't want that to happen, would you?"

"I'm not going to struggle."

"Yes, but one loses control over his body. The body acts on its own."

Ginny could picture it. "Oh," she said. She removed her teeth and dropped them into the bag.

The doctor turned to leave, but she stopped him. "Doctor," she said, awkwardly without teeth, "what do you think would be the effect of someone taking ten to twelve Seconals a night, grain and a half, for about ten years or so?"

"That's a lot of medication."

"Do you think it could cause brain damage?"

"I wouldn't be at all surprised."

When the doctor left, three inches of tubing extended from Ginny's bodice like a dart.

At one o'clock the warden signaled the guards. They opened the cell and walked on either side of Ginny, ready to support her should she need it. She did not. She was poised and dignified and, as the reporters who jammed the witness area would write, proud.

Inside the chamber itself, she looked through the glass at the roomful of spectators and said, "Where's Gordie?"

Gordon at that minute was getting into his car with Sally Ryan at a parking lot in Denver. They had just lost their last-minute appeal to another federal judge. He looked at the time stamped on the back of his parking ticket. 1:01. His mother, he knew, was in her moment of death.

The guards helped Ginny into the seat marked "B," since this one required less hose to hook up the stethoscope. The metal seat was cool to her skin, like a freshly made bed. Her feet dangled just above the floor. As they strapped fast her waist, chest, legs, and forearms, she had a second's amazement and sorrow that all those people she had confided in had told on her. Mrs. Lister, Bomba the Jungle Boy, Barrajas. Everyone. Not one of them would lie to save her life. They would stand by and allow it to happen. They were all accomplices in her execution.

One guard attached the length of rubber tubing through which the doctor would ascertain the exact moment of death to the detector already taped to her chest. He whispered to her, "Breathe deep as soon as you hear it, Ginny Mom. Good-bye."

She heard the phone ring! No one was rushing to answer it. "The phone," she moaned. "Gordie's on the phone. We'll be together again."

The guard patted her shoulder twice and said, "Easy, Ginny Mom, take it easy."

She no longer heard the ringing.

Before the warden gave the signal Ginny turned her head to the witnesses and said, "I loved a son."

The witnesses did not know if this was the long-awaited confession of crimes or a listing of virtues.

She did not fight it. With her first breath of gas, her head rolled to her right shoulder and then forward. Her mouth opened, her face grew pale, and her arms fluttered violently. She gasped for air and her body shook and jerked against the straps. Her head went back. Her eyes, half closed, flared wide open in a death stare at the ceiling. The executed always drools.

9

For two months after his mother's execution Gordon Wynn continued to work for Miss Ryan, who grew to resent his presence in her offices. It seemed no one in the country wanted to pay for his story, and she had lost a fortune defending his mother. Even the publicity did her no good. For several weeks after the trial and again as the date of execution approached, clients were drawn to the firm, but most of them were sight-seeing phonies.

A few secretaries quit, claiming that Gordon Wynn got on their nerves. The other lawyers and investigators felt peculiar around him and felt guilty for feeling peculiar. Miss Ryan eventually had to fire him, releasing him from his debt.

Beef tried to get in touch with him. He had disappeared. He would probably change his name, Beef thought, and move to a distant city. Good luck, Gordie.

Beef got a job at St. Francis, where Maria's path first crossed Ginny's, and became their best orderly. The duties of an orderly can in time make a man coarse and unfeeling, but he accepted every assignment cheerfully. He often worked overtime and never refused to take the duty for some other orderly who had a date or something better to do. The hospital staff respected and admired him, the patients adored him. He made a game of sweeping up an old bedridden man or woman in his arms and walking the patient through the wards, just for the ride.

When Maria's old apartment on Hancock Avenue, Number 9, became vacant, he moved in. He touched all the walls and doors and cabinets with his fingertips, as though looking for a pulse. He sat with a cup of coffee at the kitchen counter scraping her stolen barrette across it, scratching rhythmically for hours at the stillness of her apartment which would not yield. He put the barrette in his hair.

Mornings, he goes from bed to bathroom and empties his stomach of a kind of morning sickness.

Nights, lying and waiting for the pilfered Demerol to catch hold, he hears the footfalls of Montalvo, coming up the stairs.

About the Author

DARRYL PONICSAN was born in the coal-mining town of Shenandoah, Pennsylvania, in 1938. He has had varying experience in the Navy, as a teacher, and as a social worker, and is now a full-time writer. He lives in Ojai, California, with his wife and young son.

75 10 9 8 7 6 5 4 3 2 1